They Don't Play Fair

Clifford "Spud" Johnson

www.urbanbooks.net

Urban Books, LLC
300 Farmingdale Road, NY-Route 109
Farmingdale, NY 11735

They Don't Play Fair

ISBN 13: 978-1-60162-127-6
ISBN 10: 1-60162-127-2

First Trade Paperback Printing April 2019
Printed in the United States of America

10 9 8 7 6 5 4 3 2 1

Distributed by Kensington Publishing Corp.
Submit Orders to:
Customer Service
400 Hahn Road
Westminster, MD 21157-4627
Phone: 1-800-733-3000
Fax: 1-800-659-2436

They Don't Play Fair

Dedication

This book is dedicated to the Real Special Ms. Tezlyn Figaro. You've been so special to me in so many ways!

Chapter One

Special checked to make sure that her son, Li'l Papio, or Li'l Pee as she affectionately called him, was properly secured in his car seat before turning toward Poppa Blue and Bernadine. She smiled at him, kissed him, and said, "Are you ready to go on a trip with Mommy? We're about to go spend some time with your other grandma." Li'l Pee gave her a sweet smile and waved toward Bernadine.

Bernadine waved back to the toddler that she had been taking care of since his birth fifteen months ago. She knew the day would come when Special would decide to start playing a larger role in her son's life. She understood; yet, she regretted it because it felt as if she were losing her own child. She sighed as she gave Special Li'l Pee's diaper bag along with some stern instructions.

"He's started to teeth, so I made sure to put in a couple of extra bottles of Tylenol liquid for him. You'll know when it's bothering him because he'll whine and put his hands on his cheeks."

"Okay, I'll be sure to look for that and let Mama Mia know as well. All right, let me get on the road. I'll give you a call to let you know we made it once we get there."

"So, you're going to let him stay with Mama Mia while you're out in Texas?" asked Poppa Blue.

Special shrugged and said, "That depends on how they get along. If it looks like it's all good, yeah, I'll let her keep him for a few days and tell her that you and Bernadine will come and get him in a week or so."

Bernadine smiled and said, "That's fine, Special. I'm sure they'll get along great. No need to rush. Go on and let my baby boy enjoy his other grandmother."

Special hugged Bernadine and said, "Thank you. Thank you so much. I know this is hard for you, and believe me, no matter what, you'll never be removed from our lives. You raised my child ever since he was born. He is your grandchild, Bernadine. If anything happens to me, you and Poppa Blue will have full authority to make the decisions for Li'l Pee's life. Everything has been taken care of legally, so don't worry about anything, okay?"

With tears in her eyes, Bernadine nodded and smiled as she waved at Li'l Pee who was staring at her from the backseat of Special's BMW. "Now, you go on and get my baby to his grandmother. We'll talk to you guys later."

Poppa Blue smiled and said, "Give me a call when you hit Dallas. Jimmy Ross will be waiting for your call, so you make sure you get at him when you touch."

"Be safe."

She grinned and said, "Always." As she got inside of her car, she waved before starting the car and pulling out of the driveway.

Poppa Blue and Bernadine watched until they were out of sight and then turned and went back inside of their home, both caught up in their own thoughts. Bernadine was wondering if there was anything she had forgotten to tell Special about Li'l Pee, and Poppa Blue was wondering how all of this mess was going to play out. He hoped and prayed that Papio did right by Special because if he didn't, he knew that he would have to kill that young man with his own hands. Special was more than just a business associate. She was like his own child, and he loved her as such.

Special and her son enjoyed the ride out to Riverside laughing and singing as she drove on the freeway. She couldn't believe how much fun she was having with him. Li'l Pee was so alert and smart; he had the same intense light brown eyes as his father and was just as handsome. Though Bernadine had taken care of him since he was born, Special made sure that she saw him as much as possible, so there weren't any problems with them knowing each other. Li'l Pee knew she was his "momma," and she loved that more than anything. Never in a million years did she think she would have any kids, but when she found out that she was pregnant three months after the shooting in Dallas, she knew she could never have an abortion. She knew without a doubt that the child growing inside of her belly was Papio's.

She went and had a sit-down with Poppa Blue and Bernadine and told them everything. When Bernadine offered to take care of the baby, Special instantly knew that would be the right thing to do because she was too heavy in the streets to be taking time out to raise a child alone. So everything was arranged. After the birth of her child, she would give him to Bernadine and Poppa Blue to raise until she felt it was time for her to slow down and take care of him herself. It may have seemed cruel to those looking in from the outside, but it made perfect sense to Special, and that's all that mattered.

Here it was, almost a year and a half later, and everything was good. Papio seemed to be back in her life, and shit was going to be straight with the Cubans, thanks to the device and Papio. Now, all she had to do was drop the bomb on him and hope that he wouldn't be too salty at her for keeping this from him for so long.

When she informed Mama Mia about Li'l Pee, Mama Mia was so excited she practically jumped her. She couldn't wait for this meeting, and now that it was about to happen, Special realized she was just as excited as Mama Mia was. Li'l Pee was about to meet some of his family, his blood-related family. This meant a lot to her because she was the only child and didn't have any living relatives to her knowledge. She lost her mother when she was young to her female lover, and since then, the only family she knew was Poppa Blue and Bernadine. To be able to give her son some real blood-related family members meant the world to her. It was important to her that he has as much a normal life as possible.

No fucked-up life for my child, she thought. *I'm going to make sure he has everything and wants for nothing. I know once Papio sees him, he's going to fall in love with his seed.* Li'l Pee had the same bronze-colored complexion as his father, as well as his long, silky hair. Li'l Pee's wasn't past his shoulders yet, but it was well on its way. Bernadine had wanted to cut his hair when he turned one, but Special told her no way. She wanted him to grow his hair long like his father's. Right now, it was just a bunch of tangled, jet-black curls and made her child look absolutely adorable.

When Special pulled into the driveway of Papio's home in Riverside, Mama Mia was standing in the doorway smiling brightly. As soon as the car stopped, she ran outside to greet them. Paying no attention to Special, Mama Mia went directly to the backseat of the car and opened the door with tears in her eyes as she smiled lovingly at her grandchild. One look at Li'l Pee and she knew without a doubt that Special had told her the truth. He was her son's twin!

"Oh, thank you, Virgin Mother! Thank you for my little *mijo!*" she screamed as she undid the car seat and smiled as she planted wet kisses all over Li'l Pee's face. Li'l Pee giggled and smiled from all of the affection he was receiving from his grandmother. Mama Mia turned and carried him inside of the house, holding him tightly against her chest.

Special followed them inside with the child's diaper bag, smiling as she watched Mama Mia interact with her son. This was truly a special day for both of them. "Mama Mia, here is his diaper bag. I know he's wet, so we better change him."

"Sí, Special. You go; let me take care of my little mijo. We will be just fine. Go make calls or do something. We will be just fine!"

Special started laughing as she sat down and watched the two of them. *Everything just may be all right,* she thought with a goofy grin on her face.

Papio had a smile on his face when he heard the garage door to his home in Oklahoma City begin to open. He arrived home a few hours before Brandy, and he knew she would be surprised and excited to see him. Though he was excited to see her, he was still having some serious doubts because he couldn't seem to get Special off his mind. A part of him wanted to hurt her, and a part of him wanted to love her, and that was eating at him constantly. *She cannot be trusted; she cannot be trusted,* was what he kept telling himself. But then he could close his eyes and see that small gap between her teeth when she smiled, and his heart began to skip beats. He knew he was still in love with her, and that was so fucked up. Or was it?

He shook his head and smiled. "Fuck it, I'll deal with that shit later," he said aloud as he went to go greet Brandy. He planned on enjoying her for a few days before he went to Dallas to relax and get things ready for the move that Quentin was looking for him. Until then, he would put Special on the back burner, and Brandy's sexy ass would have his full attention.

When Brandy walked into the kitchen from the garage and saw Papio standing next to the stove with that cocky grin on his face, she dropped her purse, ran, and jumped into his arms. "Daddy!" She planted a firm kiss on his lips and gave him some deep tongue action. After she pulled back for some air, she smiled at him and asked, "When did you get in town? Why didn't you call me so I could have come and picked you up from the airport? Is everything okay? Nothing has happened, has it?"

"Whoa, mami, hold up. Everything is good. I'm home for a few days before I go to Texas to make some moves. What, I can't come back and spend some time with my baby? You do know I've been missing you, right?"

"Humph, you better have been missing me, especially after you made me come back home so fast."

"Stop that. You know how it is when it comes to the business. Later for that, though. I'm home now, so let's kick it. What you wanna do? Go out and get something to eat or stay here and chill?"

She smiled seductively, stepped away from him, and began to undo the slacks of her pantsuit. By the time she had pulled off her blouse and was down to nothing but her thong and matching lacy bra, she said, "I think we better stay here and chill, daddy, because I need me some of that dick. I need it bad. Come fuck me for a couple of hours, and then I'll make you something to eat."

"Come fuck you? Damn, mami, what's gotten into you with all of this aggression?"

"It's been a few weeks since this kitty has been touched, daddy. I'm hotter than a six-shooter right now, and only you can cool me off. Dead all that talkin'. Get naked and come upstairs and give me what I need!"

He smiled as he pulled off his Ed Hardy tee and said, "Hotter than a six-shooter, huh? That's some straight country shit right there, mami. Don't trip, though; I got your fine ass. You'll be begging me to pull this dick outta ya ass in a few hours! Now get up them stairs 'cause it's on!" he said as he slapped her hard on her firm ass cheeks.

After several hours of taking pictures, playing, and eating, the day finally came to an end. Mama Mia bathed Li'l Pee and put him to bed in her bedroom. She was not letting that gorgeous child out of her sight for anything in the world. Special was resting downstairs in the media room watching television when Mama Mia came down and joined her.

"Tell me, *mija,* how are we going to do this? I want my grandson to be able to spend as much time with me as possible. I understand what you say about Poppa Blue and his wife, Bernadine. God bless them both. But I want to be able to see my little mijo as much as I can."

"I give you my word, Mama Mia, you will always be a major part of your grandson's life. I'm so sorry for keeping him away from you this long. It looks like me and Papio may make a go of being together, so that makes everything that much better. If we don't make something good out of this relationship, I'll make sure Li'l Pee gets to spend plenty of time with you," Special said sincerely.

"Thank you, mija, thank you for blessing me with such a beautiful grandbaby. I love him so much! He's so wonderful! You have to tell Papio soon, mija. He needs to meet his son. Maybe, just maybe, this child will take him from the things he do. Please, mija, tell my mijo about his son soon, sí?"

Special nodded and said, "I plan on telling him as soon as I make it to Dallas in a couple of days. I want him to know his son and hopefully love him as much as we do, Madre. I just hope he won't be angry at me for keeping Li'l Pee from him this long."

"Bah, he may be a little mad, but once he sees his son, all of that will vanish quickly, you will see."

"I hope you're right." Before Special could continue, her cell phone rang. She checked the caller ID and saw that it was an 805 area code number. She smiled because she knew it was from Keli who was chilling with Twirl in Hawaii. She answered her phone. "What's good with you, tropical girl?"

Keli laughed and said, "Girl, if you thought it was fly out there in Aruba, you must come out this way. It's totally awesome! What you been doing?"

"Not much really, other than relaxing and introducing Li'l Pee to his grandmother."

"What? Get the fuck outta here! How did she react? Was she mad?"

"Nope. She's madly in love with her grandson."

"Who wouldn't? That little boy is fine and is going to break plenty of hearts when he grows up. So, I assume you're going to tell his father about him soon, huh?"

"Yep. I'm bouncing to Dallas in a couple of days, and then we'll have that talk."

"Good. I won't front. I wasn't feeling that nigga, but after meeting him and watching his swag, I have to admit he is on some real shit. After hearing the way Twirl speaks about him makes me feel even more comfortable with him. He loves you too. I can see it in his eyes, girl."

Special smiled into the receiver and said, "I know. That's the same thing his mother told me."

"It's going to work out, and everything will be good."

"I hope so."

"Know this; if that nigga does decide to do the goofy, he will be dealt with, serious talk."

"You are in no position to be that way, K. I'd never ask you to get all in my B.I. like that and ruin the happiness you've found with Twirl."

"You sound really stupid right now. I love my baby, and I do plan on being with him for the rest of my days. But if that nigga crosses you in any way or harms you in any way, it's off with his fucking head, straight up and down. And as much as it pains me to say this, if my baby gets in the way, he will get it too."

"That's the love, girl. I appreciate that. Hopefully, it won't go that route, and everything can be everything. Look, I'm about to get some rest. It's been a long day out here. Me and Mama Mia have been busy wrestling with Li'l Pee. It's time for me to take a long, hot bath and crash. I'll hit you up in a few days once I make it to Texas."

"Okay, that's what's up. Twirl wanted me to ask you if you have spoken to Papio. He's hit him a few times and got his voicemail every time."

"I spoke with him a couple of times when we first made it back from Colorado. He's good, though, because he sent me a text the other day when he first made it out there. He's probably busy checking on things out that way. Y'all just make sure you're on point so when everything is ready to go down, we can make it do what it do."

"We're on some chill shit right now, but when y'all call, we'll be there, you better believe that shit. We're always ready to get that fucking money!"

"I know that's right. All right, then, girl, I'll give you a holla when I make it to Texas."

"Bye, girl," Keli said and hung up the phone.

Mama Mia went upstairs to go to bed while Special was talking to Keli so after she ended that call, she decided to give Papio a call. When his phone went straight to voicemail, she wondered if he was okay while she left him a message.

"Hey, Clyde, it's me. Just checking on you. Keli and Twirl were wondering if you were good out there; me too. Hope everything is everything, baby. I've been thinking about you. Get at me when you get this message to let me know you're straight out there. I'll give you a call tomorrow to let you know when I'll be that way. I love you, Clyde, I really do. Some straight corny shit, I know, but it is what it is, Clyde. I'm your Bonnie; never forget that. Bye."

After she hung up the phone, she went into Papio's bedroom and found one of his T-shirts and took it into the guest room where she would be sleeping for the night. After taking a long, hot bath, she slipped on Papio's T-shirt and climbed into bed and fell asleep thinking about her son and his father. Could they be one happy family was the question running through her mind as she slowly drifted off to sleep.

Chapter Two

Papio left Oklahoma City after spending two days with Brandy. They enjoyed the two days spent together having incredible sex, eating at the finest restaurants Oklahoma City had to offer, and shopping at the best malls in the city. The two days went by way too fast for Brandy, but she knew better than to complain. She was used to how Papio moved, so when he told her he had to leave to take care of some business in Texas, she accepted it without complaining. She wished him well and went back to her normal routine of working at the Federal Correction Institution in El Reno, Oklahoma. She missed him as soon as he left and prayed for his safe return to her. Life with Papio was unpredictable, so there was nothing left for her to do but work and wait for her man to return, and that drove her nuts. *Ugh!*

Papio made it to his home in Dallas and went straight to work. He opened all of the windows and let some fresh air enter the house as he began dusting and getting the place back in order. When he went into the bedroom, he couldn't help but think about the last time he had been there bleeding from the two gunshot wounds from Special's gun. How Twirl had to fly out to Texas and help him get rid of the two dead bodies of the Indians that came to take his life. The same Indians that Special helped for $4 million.

Damn, here I am waiting for the same bitch that was about to leave me for dead in this very house. What the fuck am I doing? That bitch can't be trusted. If I help her get out of that shit with Mr. Suarez, all she's going to do is cross me out later in the game. I gots to smash this bitch. But what if she is loving me like she said on that damn message she left me the other day? I could be fucking off the one woman that I have ever really loved. Damn, this is some fucked-up shit, he thought as he continued to clean up the house.

He left and went to the grocery store and picked up some steaks and other foods to stock up for the time they would be spending in Texas. When he made it back and put the groceries away, he called Quentin to see if he had any news for him.

When Quentin answered the phone, he said, "What's up, white boy? What you got for ya boy?"

"Something super sweet, dude. Still got some checking out to do, but right now, it looks like the one we've been waiting for, dude. Big. No, fucking humongous! I'm talking figures around ninety fucking million, dude," Quentin said, extremely excited.

"Ninety million fucking dollars? Yeah, that would put me way over the top," Papio said to himself. "Where are we now on my ends?"

"Slightly over forty-five mill. This goes the way we want it to, you should clear at least twenty mill, dude."

Papio did the math quickly in his head and said, "More like sixteen-plus after the splits and the 10 percent to you and the others. It's all good, though. Tell me what and where has that much loochie on deck."

"Another credit union. This time, one of the biggest in Texas. The ninety mill is a rough estimate because it may be more. Let me finish getting everything in order as far as the dates and time when the most will be available, and I'll get back with you."

"Do I need to get my people out here now?"

"Not yet, but you do need to start getting everything in place as far as the tool needed, vehicles, and your game plan in order. I'll be in contact with you if I think it's going to go down any sooner."

"Holla at me, then, white boy," Papio said with a smile on his face as he thought about that fucking money.

"Oh, you know I will! Later, dude!" Quentin hung up the phone laughing.

Just as Papio ended the call, his phone started to ring. When he saw that it was Special, he smiled and answered. "What's good, Bonnie?"

"I just got in town. I'm about to get a rental, and I should be there within the hour."

"Why get a rental? Catch a cab here. I got my Range out here, so we're good with transportation."

"Not really. Remember, Twirl and Keli will be out here soon. Plus, you never know when I may have to make a move while you're doing you. Don't trip; it's all good. I'll see you in a little bit."

"All right, just hurry your ass up."

She started laughing and said, "Mmm, sounds like somebody is missing this bomb-ass pussy!"

Laughing as well, he said, "You got that right! Hurry up!"

Special hung up the phone smiling as she headed for the rental car counter. After renting a new Sonata, she quickly left the airport and headed toward the city of Garland. She called Poppa Blue to let him know that she was on her way to meet his man, Jimmy Ross.

"Remember what I said. When Jimmy sees you, he is definitely gonna have his hormones on his mind," Poppa Blue said, laughing.

"Well, he'd be shit out of luck. My hormones are kicking right about now, but not for no old nigga's dick. I'm about to spend the next few weeks with a *real* Pussy

Monster, and believe me, he knows how to handle this pussy just right."

"TMI, Special."

"You started it!" She began laughing and said, "Let me go. I'm almost in Garland. I'm about to give that old fart a call."

"Be safe," Poppa Blue said and hung up the phone.

Special called Jimmy Ross's cell phone, and he answered on the first ring. "Speak it," he said in a serious tone.

"My name is Special. I'm Poppa Blue's people."

"Where are you?"

"I'm on 635 East getting ready to come up on Northwest Highway."

"Good. Get off on Northwest Highway and take that to Jupiter, and you'll see a Walmart. Park in the rear of the parking lot and hit me when you get there."

"All right."

Jimmy Ross hung up the phone, and Special followed his instructions. Ten minutes later, she pulled into the parking lot of the Walmart and called him back. "I'm here."

"What are you driving?"

"A black Sonata."

"Get out of the car and walk into the store and go to the pay phones that are right by the refreshment area. Make sure you leave the car doors unlocked," Jimmy Ross said and hung up the phone.

She did as she was told and grabbed her purse; then she strolled toward the store looking around to see if she would be able to see this Jimmy Ross character. She didn't see anyone that she thought might be him as she entered the store. As soon as she stopped at the pay phones, she saw an older man dressed too damn clean to be inside of a damn Walmart walking toward her. He stood around five foot eight and was dressed in a tailor-made suit that looked very expensive to Special as she watched him approach her. The expensive fedora he had on his head was tilted at the brim, and the dark shades he had on hid his eyes she noticed once he was in front of her.

She smiled and said, "You must be Jimmy Ross?"

The well-dressed man said, "You must be the lovely Special. And special you are, I see," he said as he pulled off his expensive Versace shades.

"Thank you. You do know you're looking too damn fly to be in here, right?"

Jimmy Ross laughed and said, "Darlin', I'm the flyest man in Dallas, Texas. This is daily garb, dear heart. Believe me, this is just a quick put together. You should see me when I *really* want to clean up."

"I bet. Okay, Mr. Jimmy Ross, how are we gonna proceed? I'm kinda pressed for time here."

"The business has already been handled, dear. What you requested has already been put inside your vehicle. Plus a few extra items I thought you might need. All we have to do now is discuss how and when we're going to hook up and spend some time getting better acquainted."

"What about the fee?"

"No fee, darlin'. Poppa Blue and I go way back to my days spent in California. I could never charge that man. He's family."

"That's cool. I'm going to have to take a rain check on the getting better acquainted part, Jimmy Ross, but believe me, when the time is right, I will definitely give you a holla. I'm going to be out here in your state for a few weeks, so after my business has been taken care of, I will holla. Cool?"

Jimmy Ross smiled at her flirtatiously and said, "If that's the best I can get, then, yes, that's cool. Please don't disappoint Jimmy Ross because it would crush me as well as my spirit."

She laughed and said, "Never that, handsome." She kissed him on his cheek and whispered in his ear, "I never let a mature man who knows how to dress get away from me. Top-of-the-line garments on a man have a way of getting my pussy real wet." She licked his earlobe sensually and said, "Bye for now, Jimmy Ross." She turned and strolled out of the store with his eyes locked on her nice, firm ass.

Jimmy Ross watched her leave, mesmerized by all of that ass she was packing and shook his head as he pulled out his cell and called Poppa Blue out in California. When Poppa Blue answered the phone, Jimmy Ross said, "You old fucker, why didn't you tell me she was that damn bad?"

Laughing, Poppa Blue said, "She's young enough to be your child, Jimmy Ross."

"So is my daughter's man, you old fool! You know I don't give a damn about no age. As long as she's legal, she's old enough for Jimmy Ross!"

"Has the business been handled yet, you old pervert?"

"Yes, she's strapped and ready for war."

"Good. Bye, Jimmy Ross!" Poppa Blue said and hung up the phone laughing.

Special got inside of her car and eased out of the parking lot, then headed back toward the highway. As she drove, she grabbed the medium-sized gym bag that was on the passenger's seat and opened it. She smiled when she saw three pistols with four extra clips for each weapon. A 9 mm, a small .389-caliber pistol, and even a smaller .25 automatic. *Good,* she thought as she grabbed the smallest gun and slid the clip inside of it and put it inside of her purse. She then looked inside of the bag again and smiled when she saw what looked like some Kevlar bulletproof vest. She zipped the bag closed satisfied with its contents.

"Always stay ready, and you won't have to get ready," she said to herself as she drove toward Plano, Texas, where Papio's home was located.

Twenty minutes later, Special pulled the car into the driveway of Papio's home. By the time she got out of the car, Papio was standing in the doorway. He came and helped her with her bags. She kissed him and followed him inside the house.

Once they were inside, he set her bags down and said, "Welcome back."

She stepped into his arms and gave him a hug and a kiss. Then she pulled from his embrace and said, "Don't let the past linger, Papio. I was wrong for that shit. I knew what I was feeling, but I fought it because of the money. My heart is yours, Clyde, believe me because I am not bullshitting you."

"Check it; for real, it's going to take me some time to have some solid trust in this. I won't fight it, though. I know how I feel about you, and I know it's real. It's always been real. Because of that, I'm going to go with the flow but don't cross me again, Special."

She stared into his light brown eyes and said, "I won't. Come on and feed me now. I'm starving!"

"Good thing I went shopping earlier, huh?"

"Shopping? As in grocery shopping? I'm too damn hungry to be waiting for something to be cooked. Let's go pick up something and come back so we can do the damn thang. You do know I am in dire need of my Pussy Monster, right?"

He started laughing and said, "In that case, fuck going out; let's order some pizza and get this shit started while we wait!"

Special started taking off her clothes and said, "Now, that's the best damn thing you've said since I've been here. Get naked, nigga! Let's get this party started!"

Chapter Three

Special and Papio spent the next few days enjoying each other's company in Dallas. They tore up several malls as well as some very exclusive shopping boutiques Papio knew of around the Dallas area. They even went to Six Flags amusement park and had a wonderful time riding the many different rides and eating junk food all day.

Papio was amazed at how much he enjoyed himself with Special. He kept comparing the time he was spending with her with the time spent with Brandy when he was in Oklahoma City. Though they did similar things, it was totally different to him. With Brandy, everything seemed more cultured and mature. While with Special, everything was more laid-back and natural. Brandy was his mature, older mami, and Special was the one he clicked with on every level. She was winning, and that scared the shit out of him because the trust factor was still a major concern. *Damn,* he thought as he carried the last of their bags inside of the house from their day of shopping at the Grapevine outlet mall outside of Dallas/ Ft. Worth.

Special was sitting down on the expensive leather sofa in the living room of Papio's 4,550-square-foot Florida-styled home. She kicked her feet up onto the marble coffee table and thought about how comfortable she was in his home. Two fireplaces, five bedrooms, four and a half baths, a gourmet kitchen, with an office overlooking a perfectly landscaped yard, front and back. The heated in-ground swimming pool was an added bonus, she thought as she suddenly jumped to her feet and began to take off her sundress.

Papio stared at her as if she was crazy and asked, "What the hell are you doing?"

"I'm hot, and I want to go swimming. Come on, let's go take a dip in your pool," she said as she turned and left the living room completely naked, headed toward the backyard.

Papio shook his head as he began to shed his clothing and followed her outside. Thirty-five minutes later, they were resting in the shallow end of the pool trying to catch their breaths from the thirty-five-minute fuck session they had while playing around in the pool. Special had her head on his chest as he softly rubbed her smooth arms.

"Damn, girl, you got a nigga right back gone like I was last year."

"You act like something wrong with that shit, Clyde. It's right now. It's how it's supposed to be. I got my Rude Boy, and I'm not letting you get away from me again. I fucked up and almost lost you; I can't afford to let that happen again. We need you too much for that shit."

"We? What are you talking about, Bonnie?"

She sighed and said, "Tell me something. How do you feel about kids, Clyde? You want some?"

"I never thought about that shit before, for real. I've been so caught up trying to get this money that that's all that has been on my mind. I mean, at one point before I went to the Feds, this broad Mani I was fucking with got pregnant, but she miscarried after two months. After that, I was on some strap-it-up shit and watching how I got down. Not because I didn't want any shorties, but because I wasn't knowing if she was the one I wanted to have my seeds with, you know what I'm saying?"

"Yeah, I feel you. What about me, Clyde? Would you feel comfortable having a child by me? I mean, it's not like you've been on your strap-it-up game with me. Shit, I can only think of maybe two times that we ever used protection. So, what's up?" she asked as she turned and faced him to look into his eyes when he answered her.

He stared at her for a few seconds and then started grinning. "Don't tell me you done went and gotten pregnant, Special?"

With a smile on her face, she slapped him lightly on his shoulder and said, "Don't be silly, nigga. We just hooked back up a few fucking weeks ago. Ain't no way in hell I would know if I was pregnant that damn fast. Now answer the question, Clyde."

"As long as we were good, yeah, I could see me having some kids with you. For some reason, me and you are always on the same page. It's like an instant connect. I can't explain this shit, but it's like it was when we were in Miami that time. I knew then that I wanted to be with you for the long haul. It feels right. Like right now, even though I have reservations about you and your get down, it still feels right to me. On some real shit, though, that bothers me, Special. It bothers me because I cannot say that you are 100 percent real with me. I don't like being like this, and I know if I'm going to give us a fair shot, I gots to rid myself of these feelings. Your slick ass has me with my guard up. I can't help it, Bonnie. I know that may sound fucked up, but it is what it is," he stated honestly.

"I respect that, and I ain't even mad at you for feeling that way. If the shit were the other way around, I'd be feeling the same way. I guess it's time for me to sho' you that you can totally trust me as well as love me without any doubts whatsoever. I'm the one for you, and you're the one for me, Clyde. I love you. I'm in love with you. I've been in love with you ever since we hooked up in

Miami for that wonderful seven days. I fought it because like you, money consumed my every thought. But it doesn't any longer, baby. I have a new passion, Clyde."

"What's that?"

She smiled at him and stood to get out of the pool. "Sit back and relax. I'll be right back. I want to show you something," she said as she stepped out of the pool and ran naked back inside the house. Three minutes later, she returned to the pool with her cell phone in her hand. After getting back comfortable, she sighed and said, "What I'm about to tell you will either solidify us totally or destroy us. It's all your call, Clyde. Remember, no matter what you say, I love you."

Papio became nervous because he didn't know what to expect, so the first thought that came to his mind was that she was up to something again, and he was spooked big time. "Talk to me, Bonnie. Just keep it real with me."

She was a nervous wreck, but it was time to tell him about his son. This was it, she thought as she gave him her phone and said, "It can't get any more real than this. Go into my pictures and tell me what you think."

Papio accepted the phone from her and began punching the necessary keys on her cell phone to bring up the pictures she had saved. He started laughing and said, "Damn, girl, when did your freaky ass go back to Miami? This is that badass broad Inga we met when we were out there last year."

Special took a look at the picture he was looking at and smiled. "Yeah, I did go back out there a few months ago when I was getting at some of my people trying to get a feel for those Cubans. I got a man out there trying to find a weakness in their get down just in case I had to look at those mothafuckers."

Papio frowned at her and said, "Did you really think you could get at the Suarez operation like that? You gots to be stupid. The security around him is crazy tight. He has no weaknesses, Bonnie."

She rolled her eyes and said, "Every man has a weakness, Clyde. Later for that; go on to the next flicks, nigga."

Papio did as she told him and was silent for several minutes as he stared at a bunch of different pictures of a cute little boy who looked vaguely familiar. When he turned to the next picture, his eyes grew as large as an owl's when he saw his mother, Mama Mia, holding that same gorgeous little boy. He could tell that they were in his home back in Riverside, and all of a sudden, his heart rate increased as he stared at the picture again. He felt as if he'd lost his breath as he focused on the picture and then at Special, who was holding her breath as she waited for him to say something. After a few more minutes of silence, he finally spoke.

"What's his name, Special?"

A single tear slid slowly down her face as she smiled and said, "Preston Ortiz Jr. We call him Li'l Pee, short for Li'l Papio. Your son, Clyde. Your son."

Papio was staring again at the picture of his son repeating over and over, "My son. My son. Damn." After a few more minutes, he seemed to snap out of his trancelike state and asked, "Who takes care of him while you're doing you?"

"Poppa Blue and his wife Bernadine have taken care of him for the most part. I go spend time with him when I can, but I've been kind of distant, not wanting to reveal too much about my life just in case shit went left, like it did. I was prepared to take him and move to the islands somewhere and live the rest of my life tucked away nice and safe. But I didn't want to take my child and force a life on him that he didn't deserve. He deserves to have the choice of what life is best for him. See, that's why I was going to try to go all out against the Cubans, Clyde. I'd do anything for my child. Anything."

"What if you would have gotten smoked in the process?"

"Then Li'l Pee would be raised by Bernadine and Poppa Blue. He would be with a loving family, and financially, he would be good. I made all of the necessary arrangements for him to be taken care of in every way. I also left word for you and Mama Mia to be notified about him so you would be a part of his life. None of that matters now that you can get the Cubans off my ass. I can lie low and raise my child and stay out the way. I'm good with ends now, and with the moves we're making with that device, I'll be really good, and I'll fall off the radar after you put the move down with those fools in Miami. Seems everything has happened for a reason, Clyde. You're all I want and need in this life, baby. You're my baby's daddy," she said with a smile.

Without saying a word, he stood and pulled her to her feet and scooped her into his arms, then carried her inside of the house. When they made it to the bedroom, he made love to her so passionately that she felt as if she was in a wonderful dream. His every touch was soft as a feather and made her whole body tingle. By the time they finished, their bodies were drenched in sweat. Papio rolled off of her and said, "I love you, Special. I love you."

She grinned and said, "I love you too, Papio. With all my heart and soul, baby."

Chapter Four

Special was relaxing while soaking in the sauna in Papio's backyard listening to an old-school slow jam mixed CD. Every song that came on seemed to make her think about Papio and how good it felt to be in love with him. "We've Only Just Begun" by Freddie Jackson came on, and she smiled.

"That's right; we've only just begun," she said to herself. For the next thirty minutes, she listened to the old-school jams like R. Kelly's *12 Play* and "Sex Me," "I Miss You" by Harold Melvin and The Bluenotes. "Something in My Heart" by Michel'le to "I Just Wanna Be Close to You" by Maxi Priest.

She was so caught up with the music she was listening to and the soothing heat from the sauna that she didn't realize that her right hand had slipped under the water and began to run circles over her very hard clitoris slowly. She started to moan as she felt a nice orgasm mounting. She was right at that point when someone kissed her on the cheek. She opened her eyes and smiled dreamily when she saw Keli standing over her smiling.

Keli shook her head and said, "Now you know I know that look on your face, girl. Don't stop, go on and finish what you started. I'll stand right here and enjoy it along with you."

Without saying a word, Special did just that and finished bringing herself to a very satisfying orgasm. After the last little tingles subsided, she sighed, opened her eyes, and smiled at her lover/friend. "Welcome to Texas!"

"I wish I could get in that bitch and lick you real good right about now. But I don't think our dudes would understand that part of our relationship yet."

"Yeah, I know. We'll have to spring that on them later on in the game. Speaking of the boys, where are they?"

"Bringing in our bags. You know I did some crazy shopping in Hawaii, girl. I tore that mall up and some other cool little spots I stumbled onto while Twirl's ass was riding around the island in a fucking helicopter."

"Helicopter?"

"Long story. Anyway, I was like, yes, when he got the call from Papio telling him that we had to hurry up and get our asses out here for this next move. Is it true it's going to be more than $90 million, girl?"

Special shrugged and said, "That's what Papio's man told him. For the last few days, Papio has been getting up early in the morning going out and checking out shit and getting everything ready for the move. When that fool's mind is on the business, he ain't no joke with it. His preparation skills are on point."

"That's what's up. You ready?"

"I'm always ready to get paper; you know that."

"What about that business with the Cubans?"

"Papio's going to handle that after we make this move. He's going to make everything good, so I'm good, K."

"You trust him like that, huh?"

Grinning, Special answered honestly. "Yeah, girl, I do. I love that fine-ass nigga. Now that he knows about Li'l Pee, everything is even better with us. All he's been talking about is meeting his son for the first time. If it weren't for the business out here, we'd be in L.A. right now chilling with Li'l Pee and Mama Mia, then pick up Li'l Pee and fly out here for a few days. I'm telling you, K., this is exactly how I dreamed it would be."

"I guess that means there's no more nightmares, huh?"

"That's right. No more nightmares, only pleasant dreams. I haven't slept this good in I don't know how long."

Keli started laughing and said, "You do know that you're sitting there sounding like a complete square bitch, right?"

"It is what it is, girl. Pass me that towel so I can get out of this tub." As Keli gave her a towel, Special asked, "So, it's still all good with you and Twirl, I see."

"That's right. I love that nigga, Special. It feels so damn right. He's no punk, and at the same time, he has a soft spot for me that makes me feel all funny inside. I've never felt like this for any nigga before. I want these feelings to last forever."

After wrapping herself in the large terry cloth towel, Special smiled and said, "Come on, girl, let's get inside and see what them niggas are up to. We're being way too *All My Children*–like right now." They started laughing as they turned and went into the house.

Papio was sitting next to Twirl on the sofa telling him about the plans he made for the upcoming robbery of the credit union in Dallas. "The spot couldn't be better because it's right off the corner of the main street, and the highway is right there. So after everything is everything, we'll slide right onto the highway to the switch spot two miles away and then be clear all the way back to the house. The town should be on fire, so we'll lie low and play house for a few days before we box up the ends and mail it west."

"I'm feeling that shit. How much do you think it's going to be in that bitch, dog?" asked Twirl.

"Q. said it should be close to ninety million; so most likely, it will be that or a little more. You know that white boy remains on point with the intel."

"Damn, my nigga—ninety fucking million dollars. That's like what, damn near twenty million apiece?"

"Something like that. After we take care of the 10 percent drop-offs to Poppa Blue, Fay, and Q., then we'll be good, for sure. Any way you look at it, we'll be right; no doubt about that," Papio said just as Special and Keli entered the house. Before he could say a word, his cell phone started ringing. He grabbed the phone and listened as the federal operator finished telling him that he was receiving a call from a federal inmate. He pushed the number five key on his phone and accepted Kingo's call.

"What it do, Old Dread?" he asked after the connection was made.

"Everyting criss, mon. What do out there?"

"Shit, just getting ready to make it happen out here in Texas. What's up with you?"

"Mi waiting for mi transfer to go through. I should be out of here within a month or so."

"A low, huh? Looks like they're getting ready to ease your ass back into the world, my nigga."

"You can say that. I wish mi could do a camp, but they won't let a shotta like Kingo get that low of a security level. No problem, mon. Mi happy as long as I stay with the weights for the last few years I have left. But listen, I need you to make that happen for me again so I can be good for a long time before I leave."

"I got you; don't trip. I'll get at my people after we get off the phone."

"Thanks, mon. I hear everything has been good for you, and I hope that you are still being cautious while doing you."

"All the time. My moves are right, and my crew is tight. I'm winning, Dread, I'm winning for real. On top of that, guess what?"

"What?"

"I have a son, Dread."

"A wah?"

"You heard me. I said I have a son."

"By who?"

"Special."

"Special? As the-one-who-did-you-harm-Special?"

Papio started laughing and said, "It's a long story, but, yeah, *that* Special. We're together again, and this time, everything is right."

"Are you sure, mon?" Kingo asked, concerned.

Papio was staring directly at Special when he told his close friend and confidant, "I've never been more sure of anything in my entire life, Kingo. I love her."

"I'm happy for you, mon, you know I am. But I don't understand some things, so mi radar is gone wicked right now. I want you to listen to mi good right now and pay close attention because this is important to me, mon."

"Holla at me."

"Your best moves have always been by yourself. That's what I have always admired about you, mon. You play the game your way and never move with a crowd for too long a time. You just say to me that your crew is tight. Mi not feeling that one at all. I trust your judgment, but when mi radar goes off, I have to pay attention to it and speak wah mi thinking, you know?"

"I got you. Keep talking."

"Dead covers all angles, mon. Watch yourself because it will come at you from a place you least expect it. I understand this love you have for Special, and if you have the love feeling right inside your heart, it is true, and it will last. I'm no worried about her because I trust you. This 'crew' thing just no sit right with me, mon. Be careful."

Papio felt his friend's words and warnings as he thought back to when he was almost killed during a move back in

Oklahoma City with a shiesty-ass beautician that helped him set up and rob a young hustler from Dallas. Kingo's warnings got him to thinking about all sorts of things.

Stay on point at all times, Papio, he said to himself. To Kingo, he said, "It too late in the game for any slipping, Dread. No matter what, I will remain on point."

"I hope so, mon; mi really hope so. Let mi go now. Make sure you make that happen for Kingo soon. Mi time is short before I go to the low."

"I'm making the call as soon as we end this call. You make sure that you get right at me as soon as you get to the new spot."

"No problem, mon. Be safe and take heed to mi warnings, Papio. It's serious, mon."

"I got you. Later, Dread," Papio said and ended the call.

After he got off the phone, Special asked him, "Was that your man Kingo?"

"Yeah, he's about to get transferred to another spot." Changing the subject he said, "Everything seems good, so you should go on and make that move to get the device. As soon as you get back, we'll make it happen."

"All right. Let me get at Poppa Blue and see if old girl has gotten back at him yet." Special turned and went into the bedroom and returned a few minutes later with her cell in her hand. She sat down on the love seat and called Poppa Blue while Papio sat across from her on the sofa speaking with Brandy, letting her know that she needed to take Kingo a substantial amount of weed before he was transferred.

Special got Poppa Blue on the line and said, "What's good, old man?"

"Chilling, waiting on the Lakers game to start."

"Oh, snap, I forgot game two of the finals is tonight. We got to take this game. We get this one, and we'll be in a good position to win it all for real."

"That's correct, young lady. But I'm kind of worried about that shit Pau Gasol said about Kevin Garnett the other day after the game 1 win. That fool may have woken up a sleeping giant."

"Fuck K.G. It's a wrap for his ass. Pau told the truth. He does seem more like a jump shooter instead of a beast in the low post like he once was. His knee injury last year is still fucking with him to me. But whatever, because it's all about Kobe and ring number five!"

"We'll see. So, what do you want? I know you ain't call me just to spit Lakers talk."

"We're ready to make you some more money."

"Let me make a call, and I'll call you right back," Poppa Blue said and hung up the phone.

Special set her phone on her lap and repeated what Poppa Blue told her. Poppa Blue called her back before she finished her sentence. "What's up?"

"When can you be here?"

"Tomorrow, I guess."

"I'll see you then."

"Cool."

"Tell me, how did your man friend feel about finding out he's a dad? You never told me the outcome on that issue."

"He's good, and everything is good. I'll see you tomorrow afternoon," she said, laughing as she ended the call.

Turning to Papio, she said, "Everything is straight. I'll fly out in the morning and be back the day after tomorrow. Most likely, I'll catch that red-eye back and be back here before noon."

"That will give me enough time to get the vehicles ready and make sure everything is ready for Wednesday, then. This is going to be a real nice one, y'all, so we got to make sure we're on point. We can't take anything for granted. Just because we got the device, we still have to play it as

if we're just going in hard and making it do what it do.
Be on point at all times and watch each other's back 100
percent."

"I know that's right," said Keli.

"Not one mistake allowed," said Twirl.

"Mo' money! Mo' money!" screamed Special, and they
all started laughing.

Chapter Five

The next morning while Special was getting ready to go to the airport for her flight to Los Angeles, Papio was on the phone speaking to a friend of his in Oklahoma City. Since everything was going smoothly, he felt it was time to start preparing for the move he was going to make for Special to free her from the hit that was put on her by Mr. Suarez.

"Check it, Cheese; I need for you to get at Myron and tell his square ass I need him to take care of some photos for me and to get at me like ASAP."

"All right, big homie, I got you. What's up? You got some major shit popping or something?"

Papio laughed and said, "I *always* got major moves in motion, fool. You know how I do. This is something personal, though, and I'm going to need Myron's help big time. Make sure you break him off nice for me, so he won't waste time getting at me. I'll get back at you when I hit the city."

"Don't insult me like that, big homie. If it wasn't for your ass putting me on money, I wouldn't be holding this bitch down and eating so good. I got you. If I don't got nobody else, I got you, dog."

Papio smiled as he thought about how he blessed Cheese when he robbed that guy from Dallas and put him back in the game by hooking him up with Q. and his X-pill game.

"All right, that's a good look. Now, hurry up and get at Myron for me and have him call me as soon as he can. Later," Papio said and hung up the phone. He turned and faced Special and said, "Come here, baby; I need you to do something for me."

Special stepped over to him and asked, "What's good, Clyde?"

"Take off your shirt."

She smiled and checked her gold and diamond wristwatch and said, "Come on with that horny shit, Clyde. I got a flight to catch."

He shook his head and said, "Stop playing. I'm serious. Take your shirt off real quick. I need to snap a few pictures of you. I'm about to get everything ready for Mr. Suarez, and I'm going to have my man out in Oklahoma City Photoshop some real messy flicks of your dead body. All I need is a few different head shots for him along with some body shots, and he'll do the rest by working his computer magic."

"That's smart. But what, you're going to send the Cubans some stills of me like that? I thought you would send them from your phone?"

"I am. But first, I'm going to let my man Myron tweak some shit for me. Then he'll blast the pictures to my line, and I'll then send them to Mr. Suarez and the chief. It's all good, now come on, so we can get this out of the way."

Special took off her blouse, and Papio pointed his phone at her and took several different head and body shots of her. Some from the front and some from both sides. After he finished, he said, "All right, that should do it. I'm going to roll up to Oklahoma City after my mans gets at me and give him these flicks and pick up some more heat for this move."

She frowned and said, "Make sure that's all ya ass do while you're up there. Don't stop by and give any of my dick to that old bitch of yours, Papio."

He smiled and said, "So now you're on some jealous shit, huh?"

"I've never done the exclusive shit, but now that that's the lane I'm in, I don't do no damn sharing."

He kissed her and said, "I'm going to have to deal with Brandy and let her know the business. Right now, it's time for our business only; later for the soap opera shit. I'm going to hit the city and bounce right back. As a matter of fact, I'll take Twirl and Keli with me, cool?"

After rebuttoning her blouse, she smiled and said, "I love you, Clyde. I want to keep this family we've started right. I've never had a real family before. You know what I'm saying?"

"Yeah, I feel you. Now get your ass out of here. Call me when everything is everything."

"I will," she said as she turned and left the bedroom with a smile on her face.

Five hours later, Special was standing in front of Poppa Blue waiting for him to wrap up talking to someone on the phone. When he finished, he sat back in his seat behind his desk and said, "Talk to me."

Special took a seat across from him and said, "We got a nice lick at this credit union out in Dallas. Papio's man says it should produce ninety-plus."

"That is nice. Fay was about to head east and make a move with her people out that way, but they ran into a few setbacks. So she's gonna need the device back before the end of the week."

"No problem. We're moving Wednesday; we'll lie low for a day or so, then fly out, say, Saturday, and bring it back to you along with a shitload of ends."

That put a smile on his face as he thought about the 10 percent he would receive from their move. If they did get ninety million, that would be a cool nine million for him and Fay. *Damn, this is serious,* Poppa Blue thought.

"I'm going to get at Fay and have a serious talk with her. After she and her peeps are through out east, I think we should fall back and let things cool off. I mean, your guts are about to make a major move, and then she's going to do whatever they're going to put down. Shit, the heat is going to be super crazy. Sooner or later, the Feds are going to get hip to lucky. Either way, if we fall back for a minute, we can make this shit last."

"I'm good with that. I'll get at Papio and let him know what's up when I get back."

Poppa Blue smiled and said, "So, looks like you're a team now, huh?"

She smiled and said, "Yeah, you could say that. That nigga is on top of his game, Poppa Blue. You know how I get down. Together, we can't lose. Neither of us plays this game to lose, and we damn sure don't play fair, so the only outcome should be a W, feel me?"

"That's what all of this is about, Special . . . winning. No matter what, we have to win."

"You got that right," she said and smiled at her mentor and longtime friend.

By the time Papio, Twirl, and Keli made it back from Oklahoma City, they were real tired. Papio stopped at the KFC and picked them up a few buckets of chicken so they could have something to eat and just chill for the rest of the evening. Once they were back at his house, they all ate and relaxed.

Papio said good night and left them downstairs in the media room to chill and watch television. He went up to his bedroom and took a long shower. While showering, all he could think about was what Kingo had told him the other day on the phone. His luck had been holding up pretty good since he got back into the swing of things, and no way was he trying to get twisted this late in the game.

I have to make sure that everything is good all the way around, he thought as he got out of the shower and began to dry himself off.

When he finished, he threw on a pair of shorts and a wife beater and went downstairs to the garage and brought the big duffel bag full of weapons upstairs to the bedroom. He then began to methodically clean and check all of the artillery they had brought back from Oklahoma City. After checking each weapon and each silencer, he then began to go over the plan in his head until he was positive that he touched every single base. An hour or so later, he fell asleep, comfortable that everything would be all right when it was time for them to make the move on the credit union. He smiled as he drifted off to a peaceful sleep thinking about Special and his son.

Special returned from Los Angeles and made a beeline from the airport straight to Papio's house. She sighed with relief when she walked inside the house to see everyone chilling in the living room. She was bone-tired, and all she wanted to do was take a long, hot bath and sleep for the rest of the day.

She set her purse on the coffee table and said, "Let's have a quick chat before I lay it down for the entire day." Everyone turned and faced her so they could pay close attention. She grabbed her carry-all bag and pulled out the device and tossed it to Papio.

"Poppa Blue feels that we should fall back after we make this major hit. Fay is going to make a move in the east when we're through out here, and the heat from the lick we're going to put down, accompanied by the moves that have already been made, combined with whatever Fay puts down, is going to make shit extraordinarily hot. He feels that we should fall back before the Feds gets lucky or get onto us or somehow figure out we're winning with the device."

"How can that happen when the only people who know about this are in our circle?" asked Keli.

"Anything is possible, baby, and for real, I think Poppa Blue is speaking some real talk. After this lick, we'll be good for a minute anyway, so why push it? If we put it down right, this device will be around for us to make moves whenever we feel like it," Twirl said seriously.

Papio gave a nod of his head in agreement with his mans and said, "Check it, I was thinking the same shit for real. Plus, I want to take some time off to spend with my son anyway. So, it's agreed after this hit, we'll fall back and go have some nice relaxation time."

"Agreed," said Special.

"For sure," said Keli.

"There's nothing better than spending some easy-earned money and chilling in the process," Twirl said with a smile on his face.

"It is what it is, then. Check it; I'm going to make sure everything is a go for the a.m. We're going to make our move out of here at 10:00 a.m. We should make it to the credit union no later than 10:45. By 11:30, we should be back here counting a whole lot of loochie. So get some rest and relax. It's on tomorrow," Papio said seriously.

Special yawned loudly and said, "You ain't saying shit, baby. I didn't sleep at all on that long-ass, red-eye flight. I'm about to go shower and hit the bed. Later, guys," she said as she grabbed her bag and purse and went upstairs to the bedroom, followed by Papio.

Once they were inside the bedroom, Papio closed the door and smiled at her. "I got something for you, Bonnie." He went to the dresser drawer, opened it, and pulled out a yellow 8x11 envelope and pulled out five glossy photographs of Special. A very *dead-looking* Special.

When she saw the pictures, she gasped and put her hands over her mouth. She couldn't believe how real the photos looked. Each one was taken from a different angle, but there was no mistake about it. It was Special in those pictures, at least, it was her face on them. She took the pictures from Papio and examined them more closely. Each one showed her to have a bullet hole in the side of her neck and one bullet hole in her chest. The authenticity of the pictures gave her goose bumps all over her arms.

"Damn, Clyde, your man is really good. I mean, *really* fucking good."

"Yeah, he's one of the best computer geeks in the business. It's all good now, Bonnie. Once he gets at me with the shots for my phone, I'm going to blast them to Mr. Suarez, and then everything will be a wrap with them. Then we can move forward with trying to make some sense out of our crazy lives."

She put the pictures back inside the envelope and gave him a hug and a kiss. "Shit is finally starting to make sense for the first time in my life, Papio. Everything happens for a reason, and I know now that you came into my life to be mines, baby; all mines."

He smiled and kissed her again. "I love you, Special, and I want to be able to raise our son with you. This is the most important thing in this world to me, baby. Please know this. But you have to understand this because I don't ever want you to get it twisted. If you ever, and I mean *ever*, even make me *think* you're crossing me, I will not hesitate to take you. I'm not threatening you, mami, I'm keeping it all the way real with you. When you shot me, you hurt me in so many ways that I damn near wish you would have gone on and let those Indians kill me. I cannot stand ever to be hurt like that again, Bonnie. I mean that."

She was nodding her head as she listened to him. When he finished, she began to cry softly. A few minutes later, she got herself together and said, "I love you too, Papio. I swear I do. I know I tripped the fuck out about that paper, but never, and I do mean *never,* will I ever put anyone or any money before you and Li'l Pee. You two are my world, and I'll die before I ever cross you again." She then smiled, wiped the last of her tears, and added, "But don't *you* get it twisted, nigga. If I ever think you're on some bullshit time, I will blast ya ass! You got me, Clyde?" she asked and smiled.

He returned her smile and said, "Yeah, I got you, Bonnie. Now, get some rest. I'll get you up later on when it's time to get some grub. Tomorrow this time, we'll be having one hell of a celebration going on in this place."

She laughed and said, "You got that right!"

Chapter Six

Papio woke up at 8:00 a.m. on the dot and took his shower and started to get dressed. By the time he was putting his clothes on, Special had woke up and went and took her shower. When she finished, she came back into the bedroom and watched as Papio was putting on his black army fatigues over his sweats.

She stopped him and said, "Hold up, Clyde." She then went and got the gym bag that Jimmy Ross had given her and pulled out two Kevlar bulletproof vests and gave him one. "I wish I had more of these for Keli and Twirl. Since I don't, we might as well have that added protection."

"I know that's right. I should have been thinking like that. I could have gotten some of these from my mans and had us all straight."

"You can't be perfect with shit all the time, baby. Make up for it next time. This time, I got your ass."

"That's right. Now hurry up and get dressed so we can go over everything one last time before we make this move."

"Roger that!" she shouted as she turned and began to get dressed while he went downstairs to see what Twirl and Keli were doing.

Twirl and Keli were sitting in the kitchen sipping some orange juice when Papio entered. He saw that they were already dressed in their black army fatigues and ready for business. *Good,* he thought as he went to the refrigerator and poured himself a glass of grape juice. He checked the time and saw that it was closing on 9:00 a.m.

"All right, y'all, let's get miked up and make sure all of that shit is ready before we go over everything one last time."

They gave him a nod and followed him into the living room where Special was sitting, tying up her black combat boots. Papio sat down next to her and began to pass the wireless ear mikes to each member of the crew. Once everyone had an ear mike inside of their ears, they ran a mike check.

"Papio, mike check one-two."

Special went to the far side of the living room and whispered, "Special, mike check one-two."

Keli stood and went to the kitchen and said, "Keli, mike check one-two."

Twirl stepped up the stairs out of sight of everyone and said, "Twirl, mike check one-two."

When Twirl came back downstairs, everyone agreed that everyone's ear mikes were operating properly. Papio sighed and said, "This is it. We're about to be precise with our moves and on point the entire way. Same as before, Keli and I will rush the counters while Special holds everyone down inside with Twirl at the door watching Special's back and the street, as well as our ride out of that bitch. If anything looks remotely left, you make sure no one goes near our ride."

"Got you, dog."

"The only difference this time is when we're on our way out. As soon as I bring up the rear with the bags, I want you to hit the truck first, Twirl. These bags may be too heavy for the ladies, so I'm going to carry the heaviest ones. If shit looks like it will be too heavy for y'all, then fuck it; we'll make two trips. We'll have time as long as everything goes right. Remember, Special, if anyone looks as if they're mumbling or any shit like that, get right on they ass because they might be on a Bluetooth or some shit. You watch everyone with eagle eyes at all times."

"I ain't missing a thang, Clyde; believe that shit."

He smiled and said, "That's what's up, Bonnie. Keli, you hit the counters first and fill up your bag and then join me at the vault to help me fill up the rest of the bags. Once they're maxed, we're out of there. Our goal is to clean out that bitch totally. I'm not trying to leave one bill in that place, feel me?"

"Fucking right!"

Papio checked his watch again and saw that it was now five minutes to ten and said, "Let's load up."

Everyone got to their feet and, one by one, went into the garage and got inside of the stolen GMC Denali that Papio stole a few days ago from the Valley View Mall. Papio tossed Twirl the bag with their weapons inside and told him to make sure that each weapon was loaded and ready once they were inside the truck. As they eased out of the garage, Twirl was passing each member of the crew a loaded 9 mm equipped with a silencer. After each person had two pistols apiece, they were each handed extra clips for their weapons. The truck was silent as Papio drove toward the Callin Credit Union and Loan, the biggest credit union in the city of Dallas. It was time for the business, and each member of the crew was ready to get the job done. Special took a quick look at each one of them and smiled.

"Let's get this fucking money, y'all!" That broke the tension, and everyone inside of the SUV seemed to relax some and smiled. It was on.

Papio pulled in front of the credit union at 10:45 a.m., pulled out the device, and turned it on. He gave it to Special who was sitting on the passenger's side, aiming the device toward the front door of the credit union. While she waited for the red light on the device to turn green, Papio, Twirl, and Keli were letting their eyes roam all over both sides of the streets looking for police cruisers or anything out of the ordinary.

When Special saw the light on the device turn green, she said, "It's a go!"

Papio took one last look around outside of the truck and then said, "Let's hit it!"

They jumped out of the truck with their pistols held down by their sides and quickly entered the credit union. Papio moved with determined and precise movements as he entered the credit union and took complete control within one minute of entering. Special was yelling at everyone and making sure that they kept their hands held high where she could see them, while Papio and Keli went over the counters. Twirl was on point at the front door, watching the streets and their SUV. Keli was emptying each drawer at the counter while the tellers sat there with their hands in the air.

Papio was inside of the vault, filling each of the four duffel bags he brought inside of the credit union. By the time Keli joined him inside of the vault, he had two bags filled and was working on the third. She wasted no time and began filling up the fourth bag. She couldn't believe how much money they were taking as she was steadily stuffing the money inside of the bag. After the fourth bag was filled, there was still a very large amount of money left inside of the vault. She whispered into her ear mike that she had an idea and quickly left the vault with the bag she had just filled. She dragged the bag over to where Special was standing and left it with her as she returned to the vault. On her way back to the vault, she stopped and grabbed two small waste baskets that were next to two desks.

Papio smiled when he saw Keli reenter the vault carrying the two small trash cans. *Fuck it, whatever works,* he thought as he quickly began to dump the money inside of the two trash cans. Once they were filled, he grabbed the three duffel bags while Keli grabbed the trash cans, and they quickly left the vault.

Special smiled as she watched Keli run by her toward the truck. She then pulled the duffel bag toward the door and watched Papio's back as he went right by her and scooped the heavy duffel bag up as if it only weighed a few pounds.

After everyone was inside of the SUV, Special took one last look at everyone inside of the credit union and started laughing as she stepped outside and got inside of the truck. Twirl eased away from the curb and into the morning traffic. Three minutes later, they were on Interstate 635 headed toward the switch location. They made it to their backup vehicle and quickly switched SUVs. Once they were all inside of Papio's Range Rover, there was a collective sigh of relief from everyone.

Within ten minutes after switching vehicles, they pulled into Papio's garage. Papio cut off the truck and checked the time on his watch and saw that it had taken them a total of forty-seven minutes to get to the credit union, rob it, and make it back to his home. He started laughing as they all climbed out of the truck and went inside of the house, each carrying a duffel bag full of money. Keli was carrying the small trash cans, and that seemed to make Papio laugh even harder as he sat down in the living room.

"We did that shit! We did that shit!" Twirl said as he sat down next to Keli and kissed her. "Damn, did y'all see how cool my baby was as she came out and grabbed them fucking trash cans? She was on point for real!"

"That's right. Way to use your head, Keli," Papio said seriously.

She shrugged as if it was nothing and said, "You said we wasn't leaving a bill in that bitch, so I damn sure tried to stick to the game plan."

"I know that's right! Now, fuck all this chatter. Let's count this fucking money!" Special said as she grabbed one of the duffel bags and emptied it in the middle of the floor. Everyone started laughing as they grabbed a bag and began emptying them.

Once all the money was piled in front of them on the floor, they began counting the $10,000 stacks of money. Two and a half hours later, they had all the money sorted and stacked in $5 million piles. Papio counted each pile and couldn't believe what the total was. He looked at Special, and as if reading his mind, she shrugged and said, "Yep, one hundred and twenty-five million, Clyde."

All Papio could say was, "Damn." *So this is what a hundred million looks like,* he said to himself as he continued to stare at all of their ill-gotten gain.

Twirl did the math real quick in his head and said, "Okay, that means after giving Poppa Blue, Fay, and Q. their 10 percent, we're clearing $22 million for less than an hour of our time."

"I swear I love this shit!" screamed Keli.

Papio sat down next to Special and thought about the forty-plus million he already had and knew that he was almost at his goal of a hundred million. He realized that with Special's cut, they were close enough to that goal, so why risk it any further? Time to fall back for good and raise their child and maybe have some more shorties, he thought as he stared at her.

Once again, it was as if she could read his mind because she said, "Yeah, Clyde, we might as well wrap this shit up and lay it down. Game over?"

He gave her a nod and said, "Yeah, Bonnie, game done."

They were so caught up in their emotions and what they were thinking that neither of them paid any attention to Twirl and Keli who had stood and taken a few steps away from them with their weapons pulled out and aimed directly at both Papio and Special.

"You got that shit right. The game is definitely over—over for you two, that is," Keli said in a deadly tone.

Special couldn't believe what she was seeing as she jumped to her feet quickly and yelled, "Aww, hell nah! Fuck you doing, K.? I know you ain't going to do us dirty like this shit! After all we've been through, *this* is how you gon' get down? Come on, girl, put that fucking gun down! Don't do this to me, K.!"

Keli smiled and said, "Special, do the math, bitch. There's $125 million right there. What the fuck sense does it make to give three mothafuckas 10 percent of that shit, and they didn't do shit to help take it? Better yet, why the fuck should we split it when we can take all of that shit and split it two ways instead of four? Come on, mami, that math don't lie. Fuck twenty-two million when I can have sixty-two and a half mill."

Papio calmly stood and asked, "So it's like that, Twirl?"

Twirl stared at his mans and said, "Yeah, my nigga, it's like that. My baby makes perfect sense with what she's spitting. We planned this move when we were in Hawaii, dog. It is what it is. I don't want to do you dirty all the way and lay you down, but I know if I don't, you'll hunt me down and try to take me. So you gots to go. There's no other way."

Not with the crying-and-begging-for-his-life-type of shit, Papio smiled and said, "Why not take the ends and let us make it? You know I'm still good. I give you my word I won't come after you, my nigga. I got a shorty now. Shit's changed with me, Twirl. I want to raise my son, dog. Let me make it because of that."

Keli saw Twirl was starting to fall weak, and she wasn't going to let him go out like that. "Fuck that shit, baby. We made a plan, and we're sticking to it!" she screamed as she aimed her gun at Papio and shot him three times in his chest. Papio fell to the floor and didn't move.

Special screamed but didn't move as she stared at Papio's motionless body. "You dirty, trifling bitch!"

Keli smiled an evil smile and told Twirl, "Your turn, baby. Smoke this bitch so we can clean up this mess and get the fuck out of Texas with our money and that device," she said as she lowered her pistol.

Big mistake, Keli—fucking humongous and fatal mistake.

When Twirl turned and was raising his gun toward Special, he didn't see Papio as he turned and pulled out his gun and quickly shot Twirl right between his eyes. Twirl's dead body hit the floor with a loud thump. Before Keli realized what happened, Special had pulled out her gun from the small of her back and shot Keli once in her forehead. Keli's body fell right next to Twirl's, and the couple that had tried to cross Special and Papio were now a dead couple.

Special dropped her gun and quickly went to Papio. She helped him get to his feet and eased him onto the sofa. He was grimacing from the pain of the three bullets that had embedded in the Kevlar bulletproof vest that Special had given him when they were getting dressed earlier.

God bless you, Jimmy Ross, she thought as she helped her man out of his clothes. When she had his clothes off, she saw that he had three deep bruises on his chest where the bullets struck the vest.

"Damn, Clyde, talking about some lucky shit. I knew you were playing possum, but I was sure wondering when the hell you were going to make your move. You took long enough, don't ya think?" she asked with a grin on her pretty face.

He shook his head and tried to laugh, but it hurt too much. "Had to wait for the right time. No way in hell was I letting them take us out and get away with all of that fucking money. I'd rather be dead for real."

"I know that's right. Now look what they done went and did. We both just came up an extra twenty-two million bucks. We're definitely out the game now, right, Clyde?"

He smiled weakly and said, "Definitely, Bonnie."

She returned her man's smile and said, "That's right, baby. Tell me, how in the hell are we going to get rid of these two scandalous, dead mothafuckas?"

With a smirk on his face, he said, "Thanks to your ass, I have some expertise at the 'disposal game' out here in Texas."

She rolled her eyes. "Are you *ever* going to let that shit go, Clyde?"

"Probably not. You fucking shot me, Special! Look at it this way; we're even now. You saved my life in this house last year, and this time, I returned the favor by saving your ass. We're even on all accounts."

Laughing, she said, "You do know that this house is janky as fuck, right? I think we should sell it."

"No-fucking-way! This house is the best thing that has ever happened to me. I've survived two different attempts on my life in this spot. Ain't no way in hell I'll ever get rid of this place," he said seriously.

"Since you put it that way, you're right. But, baby, I don't want to live in Texas. It's too damn hot our here," she whined.

He stared at her pretty face and sighed. "We can live wherever you want to live, Special. I don't care where we live as long as I'm with you and my son." She grinned, and that smile of hers that he loves so much melted his heart.

"Promise?"

"I promise, Special."

Chapter Seven

Brandy hated when she had to be the duty officer of the week at work. That meant she had to work the weekends, and though she didn't do much on the weekends, she still hated having to drive all the way out to the city of El Reno to work. It seemed that was all she ever did was work. Granted, she loved her job. It was just that she felt like she was trapped in a life that was soooo boring.

Never in her life did she think she would have another boring day after she met and fell in love with Papio. But for the last two months without hearing from him, she felt as if she was losing her mind with not only her boredom but her jealous feelings as well. She knew he was with other women wherever he was. That was his way, and she accepted that from the very beginning. What was crazy was the fact that him being with other women didn't bother her one bit. It was the thought of him being with Special that drove her nuts. She was the one woman that she felt could steal Papio from her forever. The thought of not having him even for a little while scared her to death. She had never met a more exciting, sexy, generous man in her life until she met Papio Ortiz. Damn, she missed him.

After finishing her weekly unit inspection to see what unit would get to eat first for the upcoming week, Brandy stopped by one of the TV rooms located in the unit and listened to a reporter on CNN speak of a rash of credit union and bank robberies all over the U.S. She shook her head as she again let her thoughts go back to Papio. She wouldn't be surprised one bit if he had something to do with what the news reporter on CNN was saying.

"The FBI and other law officials seem to be totally baffled at how easy these robberies across both the East and West Coast seem to go down without a hitch. Almost as if there was some kind of inside job involved. But surely that cannot be at so many different locations across the country. When asked this question, the spokesperson for the FBI again admitted that the top cops across the United States are totally at a loss at what has been taking place over the last ninety days. But he did vow that the FBI, along with every other law enforcement agency across the U.S., will continue to work together diligently to bring this rash of robberies to an abrupt halt. This is Susan Hawkins reporting for CNN."

Brandy left the TV room and marched toward her office. After hearing that news report, she had to talk to Papio. His number one rule was never to call him unless it was a serious situation, and, dammit, this was a serious situation. She missed her daddy! She entered her office and sat down behind her desk and quickly dialed his number before she lost the nerve to do it.

When he answered the phone, she sighed and stuttered, "Hi, Da-Daddy. How have you been?" She held her breath, praying he wouldn't be too upset with her.

Papio smiled into the receiver of his smartphone and said, "I'm good, baby. What's up with you? Everything straight out there?" he asked, instantly concerned for her well-being.

"Yes, everything is good. Just missing you like crazy and really needing to see you, Daddy. It's been two long months."

"Yeah, I know, but thangs have been real hectic for me. I know I need to make a trip out there and touch them guts before you give my good pussy away," he said and started laughing.

"Ugh. You know better than that, Daddy. I would never give what's yours away to anyone. This pussy belongs to you and you only. I'm 46 years old, and I have never cheated on anyone in my life, even when some of the jerks I've been with totally deserved it. Cheating isn't in me, Daddy."

Her words touched him and made him feel extra guilty for not getting at her. He knew it was way past time to let Brandy go. With him and Special being as serious as they were, it wasn't right to do this to her. But he couldn't tell her this over the phone. He prided himself on being a man and keeping it real at all times. So, he knew it was time for a trip to Oklahoma City so he could let Brandy go.

"Check it; I'll fly out there Friday so we can have a cool weekend and have a serious talk about some things."

"Is everything all right with you, Daddy?" she asked now with concern in her voice.

"Everything is perfect, baby. My money is right, and all is good."

"How's your mom?"

"She's great, just enjoying my so—, I mean me to the fullest. I'll tell her you asked about her."

"Okay. Do you need me to pick you up from the airport?"

"Nah, that's cool. I'll catch a cab. I'll text you and let you know what time my flight arrives."

Smiling, she said, "That's fantastic, Daddy. I cannot wait to see you! I have a doctor's appointment Friday, so I'll be taking off work earlier. By the time you get home, I'll be all dolled up and pretty for my daddy."

Laughing, he said, "Yeah, I bet your horny ass can't wait for this good dick."

"You better say it! You have made me wait for two months, Daddy! That's cruel," she said and pouted. "You could have at least called me and given me some freaky Skype sex."

"Now, you know damn well I don't get down like that. If it ain't the real, then Papio don't want none of that. Wait a minute, what are you going to the doctor for, Brandy? Are you okay?"

"I'm fine. Just time for my yearly examination. You know, female stuff. Mammogram and all the normal stuff my gynecologist does for me yearly. You do know it's going to be really real when you come Friday."

"And you know I am going to come!"

"You are so silly."

"And you love it. Okay, let me go, I'll hit you in a day or so and let you know what time I'll make it to the city."

"Thank you, Daddy. Thank you for not being mad at me for calling."

"It's all good, but don't your ass break protocol again, Brandy. You call me only for emergencies. You never know what I got going on," he said in a stern voice.

"I understand, Daddy. I won't do that again, promise."

"Good. Love you, Brandy."

"I love you more, Daddy. Bye," she said and hung up the phone, smiling and content.

After Papio hung up the phone, he sat back on the bed and thought about what he had just said to Brandy. He did love her. In his own mixed-up way, his love for her was genuine. The only thing was he wasn't *in love* with her. Special owned his heart. And even though they still had trust issues because of how she did him, he still felt in his heart that they were meant to be together. He shook his head and smiled. Thinking about her and Li'l Pee made him feel as if everything he'd encounter in his life was worth it. Next to Mama Mia, they were his everything. His world and there wasn't anything in this world that he wouldn't do for those three very important people in his life. As if she knew what he was thinking, his mother entered his bedroom with a smile on her face.

"I heard you talking, mijo, so I knew you were awake. When are you going to get my grandson and bring him home to me? I miss him, mijo," Mama Mia said as she sat at the end of the bed.

"Special is bringing him out here today, Mama Mia. You know she's trying to slowly get Li'l Pee used to not being around Bernadine and Poppa Blue. This is a delicate situation and has to be dealt with right."

"Sí, I understand all that. It's not as if we are taking my li'l mijo from them; we are sharing his love. We all love that adorable baby."

"I know, Mama, I know."

"Tell me, mijo, when are you and Special marrying? Don't you think it's time for you to settle down so you can take care of your family properly?"

"I do. It's way past time, Mama, but I have to make sure that everything is how it needs to be. I'm in love with Special, and I feel in my heart she is in love with me."

"But?"

"But I have to make sure I can trust her 100 percent," he said as he pulled the covers off of him and pointed to the two bullet holes, one on each of his thighs, and continued. "She hurt me, Mama Mia. She hurt me, and I have to make sure that I can trust her before I can ask her to become my wife."

"Bah! If you didn't trust her, you wouldn't have ever brought her back here to live with you. Stop avoiding the obvious, mijo. She is the one for you. You know this just as well as I do. Everyone knows you two are perfect for each other. Señor Blue, his wife, Quentin, as well as myself. We all notice how less tense you are around her.

How happy you both are with each other. Don't waste time. Do what's right and follow your heart, mijo."

He smiled lovingly at his mother and nodded but didn't speak as he let her words sink in. She was right, and once he handled everything with Brandy, he was going to step to the plate and hit a grand slam and ask Special for her hand in marriage.

Damn, I cannot believe a cold-ass nigga like me is ready to do the family thang and live a normal life. My money is super good now. I made it outta the game with only a few scars. I got a down ride-or-die woman by my side and a beautiful son who owns my heart. Yeah, it's time to square up and live a good, normal life, he thought and smiled.

Mama Mia smiled at her only son, slapped him on his bare thigh, and said, "Now get dressed and come downstairs and have breakfast with me. The food will be ready by the time you finished showering, mijo."

"Mmmm, you do know how I love how you spoil me, Mama."

"Bah! Spoil me some and marry Special!" she said and left the room with a smile on her face.

Twenty minutes later after Papio had finished showering and getting dressed, he went downstairs to the dining room to the aroma of one of his mother's better meals. His stomach began to growl as he sat down and poured himself a glass of orange juice as he waited for his mother to bring him his food. Soon, his phone rang. He frowned because he didn't recognize the number showing on the caller ID. He started to let the call go to voicemail, but something told him to answer it . . . Something he would soon regret doing.

"Hello?"

"Papio, my friend, how are you doing out there in sunny California?" asked Kango, the younger brother of his close friend and confidant, Kingo.

Papio made a silent prayer hoping everything was good with Kingo, but in his gut, he knew something was amiss. "I'm good, Kango. You and the crew straight?"

"Me, I'm just fine. The crew, not so good. That's why I'm calling. I need you, my friend. Can you come to see me?"

"In New York?"

"No, I'm in Boston."

Boston? That's why I didn't recognize that 617 area code, he thought. "Okay, I am not about to ask you why you're way out there. What's up, though? Am I needed for business or pleasure?"

"Business *is* pleasure with us, Papio."

"If you say so."

"Macho and Brad are out of commission, and I need you along with your lovely sidekick."

Even though his money was more than good, he saw dollar signs instantly, a habit that he really had to work on. "What's up with Brad and Macho? They all right?"

"Yes, they are fine. But they're currently in Jamaica taking care of some very serious family matters, and as I stated, out of commission for the next few weeks."

"I take it I'm needed because you don't have a few weeks to wait for them."

"Exactly."

"What about Foxy Fay?"

Kango started laughing and said, "Now, you know my cousin is in no way able to assist me with matters such as this."

Nodding into the receiver, Papio said, "Yeah, I know."

"I'm currently taking care of what needs to be taken care of with Steven. If you and Special can take a few days' trip out here with me, I'll make sure that it's more than worth both of your time."

"Oh, I know that already. The thing is when we are needed. I have something that needs to be taken care of this weekend."

"That's fine because I won't need you until the weekend after this one."

"Let me hit Special and hit you right back. Is this number good?"

"Yes."

"Gimme five," Papio said and ended the call and quickly dialed Special's number. As soon as she answered the phone, he wasted no time with a greeting and said, "Just got a call from the East Coast, and our assistance is needed. You with it?"

Laughing, she said, "I thought we'd retired, Clyde?"

With a smile on his face, he asked her the question again. "You with it, Bonnie?"

"Yep."

"I'll hit you with the details later. When are you and Li'l Pee heading out this way?"

"Within the hour."

"See you then," he said and hung up the call and called Kango back. When Kango answered the phone, Papio told him. "We'll see you next week. Wednesday or Thursday good?"

"Either will suffice."

"See you then," Papio said and ended the call and thought about what he had just locked in on.

More money. More money for the family. This shit has to stop, but, damn, I'm so greedy! he thought as he looked up and saw his mother walking toward him with a plate full of breakfast food.

Chapter Eight

Papio couldn't believe how happy he was with a son in his life. Every time he saw his son, he felt like a totally different man. Li'l Pee gave new meaning to his life. It wasn't about him and the money any longer. It was about making sure that his son had everything in life that he didn't. Though he was a greedy man, his greed had an entirely new meaning. Li'l Pee was his world, and when he stared into his brown eyes, eyes exactly as his, his heart beat faster, and the love he felt was something he never previously felt. Before Li'l Pee, the only person he felt he would give his life for was Mama Mia. Without a doubt, he would die for this adorable child that God blessed him with. And to think he owed it all to Special.

Damn, I've got something I've never had before. A family. A complete family. A beautiful down-ass, ride-or-die woman, a loving mother, and a healthy 20-month-old son. I have it all, now, yet, here I am about to go on another moneymaking move. What the fuck is wrong with me? Papio thought as he held onto his son and smiled.

Special was sitting across from the two men next to Poppa Blue who she loved most in the world. Watching Papio interact with Li'l Pee made her feel as if all were right in this crazy world. And, really, it was.

Now, I just have to bide my time and show Papio that he can trust me never to cross him again. She knew he knew her love was real, but what she did to him was something that only time could heal. With him making the Cubans think she was no longer breathing gave her the opportunity and all the time she needed to show him that she was his and his only and never would she betray him again. *I'm in love, and it feels so right. Thank you, God, for blessing me. Thank you so much,* she prayed silently.

Mama Mia came into the living room where they were seated and started fussing over Li'l Pee, taking him from Papio with a smile on her face. "Come to Mama Mia, my li'l mijo. Let's go play while your mama and daddy do something with themselves, sí, baby?"

Li'l Pee smiled happily at his grandmother and playfully put his hands on her face and giggled. "Ma-ma Mi-a!"

Mama Mia laughed and said, "See, he loves his Mama Mia! Now you two go. Don't you have something to do?"

Shaking his head, Papio smiled at his mother and said, "Sí, Mama Mia, we do have something to discuss. We'll bid you two adieu for a while. If you need us, we'll be upstairs in my room."

Without paying any attention to her son, Mama Mia left the room speaking childish gibberish to her grandson as she carried him in her arms.

Special followed her man upstairs to his bedroom, amazed at how much he turned her on. After almost two years, she still was head over heels for Papio. As soon as they were inside the bedroom, she began to undress. Papio sat on the end of the bed and said, "Damn, someone seems to be kinda horny, huh?"

"I'm always horny when I'm around your pretty ass, Clyde."

He frowned.

"Stop tripping about me calling your fine ass pretty, nigga. You are what you are, and that is one handsome man. *My* man! Now come give me some of that good dick, Pussy Monster."

Thirty minutes later after some pretty intense sex, they were lying next to each other sweaty and spent. Papio sighed and said, "Damn, I don't think I'll ever get tired of this good pussy."

She slapped him playfully on his chest and said, "You better not. If you do, then we *will* have problems, Clyde. Now, tell me about the business on the East Coast you were talking about."

"I got a call from Kango. He's out in Boston, and he needs some help to put something down. Two of his people are out the way for a minute, so he needs us."

"For what exactly?"

"Knowing Kango, a big-ass money lick; most likely a bank."

"Shit, you obviously haven't been watching the news, huh? All they been talking about on CNN is the rash of bank robberies poppin' off around the U.S. It's way too hot for that shit, Clyde. Kango needs to stand down for a while. We might be pushing our luck with that fucking device."

"You right. I haven't been watching the news, but so what? Making moves with that device is foolproof. It's not like they know when and where the next bank will be hit. Let's bounce out there and get at him. We check it out. If we're with it, we hit the lick with him and then tell him it's time to slow this thang down for a minute."

"And if we don't like it?"

"We don't like the setup, we get the fuck back to the West Coast and do what we been doing for the last two months."

She smiled and said, "Sex and shop and spend time with our child?"

He returned her smile. "Exactly."

"When do we leave?"

"Next week. I'm flying out to Oklahoma to take care of some things Friday. I shouldn't be out there no longer than a couple of days. When I get back, we'll fly out to Boston on Wednesday or Thursday."

"Oklahoma, huh? What, your old bitch calling?"

Never one to lie, Papio answered her honestly. "Yeah. She misses a nigga and wants to see me. It's time I went out and put that situation in its proper place."

"Humph. Don't think you're going out there to give her a goodbye fuck, Clyde. Your ass is mine now, and that sharing shit is something Special doesn't do."

"I'm going to let her know the business and end it, Special, that's it, and that's all. But for real, I am not trying to get into all that soap opera shit with Brandy. She deserves to be let go, and I can't keep stringing her along."

"I feel all that, and I got mad respect for you for handling this with her, but like I said, nigga, no one for the road shit, Clyde. I mean that."

"Whatever, Special."

"Ugh! You are! You are going to fuck her! I can see it in your eyes, nigga! That's some fucked-up shit. You ain't even trying to deny it! You a cold-ass nigga, Clyde!" Though she was screaming at him, she was smiling.

"You tripping the fuck out and smiling. What's wrong with your crazy ass?"

"I'm smiling, but I'm still salty with you, nigga. But I respect that, and I love how your gangsta ass puts it down. Even though the mere thought of you with her makes me feel sick, I know how you get down, and if you're going out there to tell her it's a wrap, and that you belong to me, then I'm good. I guess I'll do the same thing out this way and give a couple of goodbye fucks to some of my strays as well. I mean, all fair in this shit, right?"

He frowned and said, "Since when have you ever known me to play fair, Special? And if you think you can go have some goodbye fucks—plural—then you are definitely out of your fucking mind!"

"Aaah, is my Clyde a little jealous?"

"I've never had the jealous gene, baby. I'm built more solid than that. You forgetting that I know your ass. You threw that at me to get a rise out of me. You forgot, though; you told me that the only man you've been with other than me in the last two years was that fool you paid in Aruba with Keli," he said with a smile.

"Ugh! Whatever, nigga. I got an idea. Why don't I fly out there with you, and we toss Brandy together and make her last time with you one she will never forget? You know, do her like we did that badass Dominican in Miami?"

Shaking his head, he said, "Nah, she wouldn't be with any shit like that."

"How do you know? You'd be surprised how my get down is with women. A bitch like me has been known to turn a square, straight bitch out easily. Don't underestimate my skills, Clyde."

"Trust me, one thing I have definitely learned about your ass the past two years is never to underestimate you. Let me do this solo, though, baby. Then I'll come back, and we'll go get some more bread to add to that kitty."

She smiled and said, "A fat-ass kitty at that!"

"You better say it, and it's about to get even fatter."

"Will this be the last lick for us, Clyde?"

He shrugged and said, "I never say never, Bonnie. We in it to win it at all times."

"That's right, and as long as we play this game together, we ain't playing fair."

"Exactly. Now give me some more of that great sex since Mama Mia is holding our son hostage from us."

"Mmmmm, you read my mind, baby," she said as she slid down to his crotch and inserted his dick inside of her mouth and moaned.

Lance loved his life of luxury. Living in Hawaii doing whatever he wanted, having any woman on the island of Oahu was a dream come true. And it was all because of his invention. Creating the alarm-disarming device was the best thing he'd ever done in his life. With $10 million in an overseas account after all of the expensive spending he'd done over the last past six months, he had absolutely no worries, and it felt real good, he thought as he relaxed and let the young, beautiful Hawaiian woman continue to give him a full-body massage.

He moaned as she began to massage his temples and rub all over his smooth, bald head. He stopped her abruptly and sat up and focused on the flat-screen television mounted on the wall of the Hawaiian masseuse's massage parlor. He frowned as he listened to a news reporter give a report about all of the credit union and bank robberies happening all over the U.S. What really held his attention was when the news reporter said that in the last six months, well over $400 million had been stolen from the credit unions and banks on both coasts.

Four hundred million fucking dollars! Over four hundred million fucking dollars! he thought as he hopped off of the massage table and grabbed his robe and asked the masseuse for a little privacy while he made a call. After she left the room, he grabbed his cell and quickly called Poppa Blue in Los Angeles. When Poppa Blue answered the phone, Lance's tirade began furiously.

"How in the fuck could you do that shit to me, Poppa Blue? Ten million! A measly *ten million bucks,* and you guys are coming off like some of the biggest bank robbers since Jesse James and Bonnie and Clyde times fucking one thousand! That is some cold shit, and you know what? I want fucking in! If you think I'm going to sit back and stand for that shit, you are out of your fucking mind!" screamed Lance.

Poppa Blue listened and patiently waited until Lance was finished and then calmly stated, "You fucking jerk! How fucking dare you call me and talk on this phone about some shit you know nothing about. You have obviously been watching too much TV. On top of that, you should know better than to speak to me about anything on the fucking telephone. Now, you got what you asked for. You. Gave. Me. That. Number. Think back to the conversation, and your dumb ass will remember that you said *ten million and not a penny less.* Now you hear some stupid shit, and you want what, more? Get the fuck out of here 'cause you know damn well that ain't happening. You are outta your fucking mind for calling me being stupid, Lance. You're too damn smart for that shit. Now, if you want to get at me about anything, and I do mean *anything,* you bring your ass to me, and we'll sit down and talk about things face-to-face. But don't you fucking ever call me with no shit like this again. You know the business, and you know what comes with the business. Goodbye, Lance," Poppa Blue said and hung up the phone with a deep sigh.

"Shit, I should have known this shit would get fucked up sooner or later," he said to himself as he quickly dialed a number from memory. When the phone was answered, Poppa Blue said, "What's good, Fay? We need to talk."

"What the wrong problem, mon?" asked the Jamaican.

"There's a big one. Your boy Lance is acting stupid."

Fay sighed and said, "Mi should have known that bloodclaat would get stupid sooner or later. Mi come your way in a day or so, and we talk, mon, good?"

"Yeah, good. This needs to be addressed as soon as possible."

"Mi understand. Day after tomorrow we talk," Fay said and hung up the phone.

"Damn, Lance, why couldn't you just enjoy the ten fucking million you got? Now you got to die, you dumb sonofabitch," Poppa Blue said as he set his phone down.

Chapter Nine

"Oh my God! I wait until I turn 41 years old to get pregnant! Papio is going to go nuts," Brandy said to herself as she sat in her car in the parking lot of her gynecologist's office. She had a silly grin on her face as she replayed in her mind what her gynecologist told her a few minutes ago.

"You're a healthy woman in her early forties. There's no danger whatsoever for you to have this baby. Women in their forties are having babies all over the world."

"I'm healthy, and it must be meant to be. I can only pray that Papio won't go ballistic on me when I tell him this evening when he arrives," Brandy said as she started her car and pulled out of the parking lot. As she drove, all of a sudden, she felt queasy. "Great, Brandy, just great. You wait until you're two and a half months pregnant to get some form of morning sickness finally. Jeez," she said aloud as she drove on.

Her destination was clear. First, she was going to get something to eat. After that, she was going shopping to find the sexiest outfit she could find. She wanted to look extra good for Papio tonight because after they go out to eat and enjoy a nice evening with each other, she intended on wearing the skimpiest and sexiest nightie she could find so she can sex him like she'd never sexed him before. Then afterward, when he was worn out completely, she was going to drop the bomb on him and pray real hard with her fingers crossed that he wouldn't be upset about becoming the father of her child. Jeez!

Papio's flight from Los Angeles to Oklahoma City's Will Rogers World Airport arrived right on schedule. It was ten minutes after six p.m. when he deplaned and stepped quickly toward the escalator so he could hurry and get his luggage and catch a cab to his place. He smiled as he thought about Brandy. He knew he was going to have to give her the best fucking of her life because when he dropped the bomb on her that he had a son and was in a serious relationship with Special, she was going to lose it.

He wasn't looking forward to all of the extra emotional shit she was going to lay on him. That was some soap opera shit that he wasn't with at all. That's why he refused to lie to females, to avoid the drama. Even though he always kept it real with Brandy, he knew she loved him; shit, she loved him so strongly that he had to question if he was making the right decision with Special. Brandy was a good woman, a woman that any man in his right mind would love to settle down with so she could love him and take the best care of him. But, Special, damn, Special was perfect for him in so many different ways. He couldn't even put it in words, he thought, as he grabbed his one piece of luggage and stepped out of the airport and quickly hopped into the first cab he saw available.

After giving the cab driver the address to his home in Oklahoma City, he sat back in his seat and sighed. Special was the one, but yet, here he was about to have some incredible sex with one badass, older woman, an older woman that loved him like crazy. An older woman that he seriously and truly loved. He was just not in love with her, and that's what the difference was between her and Special. "I'm in love with Special; I love Brandy. I trust

Brandy. Brandy will never cross me or ever hurt me in any way. Special has crossed me and hurt me; yet, I'm still in love with her? What the fuck is wrong with me?" Papio asked out loud.

The cab driver looked through the rearview mirror of the cab and said, "Sounds to me like you're battling within, young man. No need to battle within where love is concerned. Just follow your heart. Trust your heart because your heart won't betray you. Trust your heart, son."

Papio nodded his head at the cab driver and said, "I feel you. But sometimes, this heart makes me make the wrong decisions."

Shaking his head, the cab driver said, "No way, son. That's not your heart that has made you make the wrong decision; that's your partner between your legs. He will lead you astray every time. Trust your heart—not your partner down there!"

Laughing, Papio said, "You may be right, old man; you may just be right. Thanks."

"No problem, son; no problem at all," said the cab driver as he continued to drive with a smile on his face thinking back to when he was a young, handsome man with love issues in his life. *You live, and you learn, that is, if you're lucky enough,* he thought.

Twenty-five minutes later, the cab pulled into the driveway of Papio's home. Papio jumped out of the cab and gave the cab driver a hundred-dollar bill, shook his hand, and said, "You keep that change, old man. Thank again for serving me that real talk."

"You just make sure you take that real talk I gave you seriously and follow your heart, ya hear?"

"Yeah, I hear you. And I will. Take it easy, old man," Papio said as he picked up his suitcase and stepped quickly toward the front door. By the time he made it to the door, Brandy had opened the door with a smile on her gorgeous face looking stunning in a form-fitting black dress that hugged every curve on her slim body.

"Damn, baby, is it me or are you looking even finer than you did the last time we saw each other?" he asked as he stood there staring at her in awe.

Brandy reached out her hand and grabbed his hand without saying a word and pulled him inside the house. She closed the door behind them, turned, and stepped into his arms, and gave him a tender kiss that turned passionate instantly. A full minute later, she pulled from his embrace, smiled, and said, "Welcome home, Daddy."

Laughing, he said, "Now that's a hell of a way to welcome Daddy back home for real!"

"That's nothing. Wait until you see what else I have in store for you. First, you need to go upstairs. I have a hot bath ready for you. After that, I want you to get dressed in the outfit I've laid out on your bed. We have a little over an hour before our reservation for dinner at Kevin Durant's restaurant."

"Thought you were going to cook me something to eat here so we could relax and chill?"

"No. Tonight is going to be a night to remember, and I wanted for us to enjoy it all."

"That's cool. Dinner, then what?" he asked with a devilish smile on his face.

"The freakiest, the longest, the most intense sex you've ever had, Daddy, is what's on the menu after dinner. You concur?"

Staring at her dress with the split damn near all the way up to her crotch, he moaned as he felt himself start to get rock hard and said, "You damn right I concur!"

"Don't you think it's time to fall back some and let the heat cool down, Special? I mean, damn, those fucking dreads are getting it in on the East Coast something serious. That, combined with the moves you and your man made, shit is hot," said Poppa Blue as he stuck the half-chewed cigar back in his mouth and lit it.

"True. It's hot, but, fuck, the device makes shit fool-proof, Poppa Blue. As long as we watch how we move, when we move, shit is all good. Papio wants to fall back, though, so we will, sooner or later. We're going to hit Boston and look at it. If it don't look right, then, we not fucking with it, and we're going to tell Kango we pass. But knowing Papio and how he trusts Kango's get down odds, we're going to hit the lick and then fall back after that."

"You know, I'm not one to ever trip about getting no money. Shit, I love it when y'all get down that 10 percent of the shit you guys bring in. It's serious money. But we cannot let greed lead us, or it will lead us all right into a fucking train wreck."

"I feel you."

"You should, 'cause there has already been some shaky shit going down that you don't even know about."

"What's up?"

"That weak fucker Lance wants more ends."

"Stop playing! What the fuck does he think he owns? We gave that nigga ten tickets! He got to be out of his fucking mind!"

"Calm down; everything is being taking care of. I got with Fay the other day, and she's agreed to handle things for us."

"Handle things?"

Poppa Blue stared at his protégé, his friend, the young woman he loved like a daughter and repeated his words. "Yes, *handle* things."

"Since when did you get this gangsta with it, Poppa Blue?"

He shook his head and said, "What, you think because I'm an old man sitting behind this desk making shit happen, I ain't got that gangsta gene? You better recognize who I am. Never think differently. When it comes to my freedom, my family's well-being, and my fucking money, there ain't much that I won't do."

With a nod of understanding, Special stared at Poppa Blue with nothing but the utmost respect in her eyes for him. "I feel you."

"Like I was saying, Fay is going to take care of everything concerning that prick, so that's one less worry for us."

"Does she even know where Lance is? I thought he took his money and shook the spot."

"He did. The dumb fuck called from his phone, and I was able to track him down."

"Where is he?"

"Oahu."

"Hawaii? He gets ten mill and moves to Hawaii? That wasn't all that creative. You'd think a nigga who could invent a device that has changed the game in bank robberies would be smarter than that."

"You would, huh? That's what I thought too. But then, I never thought the prick would be stupid enough to try to bounce back at me for more ends because he saw on the fucking news how much money has been taken. You can be super smart and still be dumb as fuck, Special. You're a smart young lady. Street smart, savvy, and gangsta. Your intelligence is respectable, but your decision making remains in question. I say that because I don't want your emotions ever to override your intellect. Your love for Papio seems to have made you take a step back and let him lead. That's not you. What's up with that?"

She sighed and smiled at her mentor. "I love him. It's that simple, Poppa Blue. That man does something to me that no man ever has or ever will again. He's my soul, Poppa Blue. The father of my son and the owner of my heart. He could lead me straight to hell, and I'd gladly follow him. I betrayed him when I shot him, and that hurt him way more than the scars on his thighs where the bullets hit him. I have to earn his trust in order for us to continue this journey. So, yeah, for the first time in my life, I'm letting someone else lead. And you know what?"

"What?"

"It feels good. It feels right, and I love the fact that I have a real man, a take-charge type of nigga that does shit the gangsta way and don't play fair at all. A man that I can respect, admire, and ride or die for. I trust him with my life, not because I love him, though, but because he has already shown me that he would put his life on the line for mine."

"By faking out the Cubans with your mock death?"

"Yep."

"You do know that that could one day come back and bite both of you in the ass, right?"

She shrugged and said, "I doubt it. If it does, we'll deal with it together, side by side."

Poppa Blue stared at Special and inhaled some of his cigar and smiled.

"That's right! Ride that dick, baby, ride that dick!" Papio screamed as Brandy was on top of him in a reverse cowgirl position riding him hard. He held onto her firm ass cheeks tightly as he watched as his dick slid in and out of her super wet pussy. *My God, this woman has lost her mind!* he thought as he continued to enjoy the sex they were having. When she came, she began to tremble and shake, and all of a sudden, he watched as his dick was heavily coated with the thick, white, creamy juices of her come. She went from bouncing on the dick nice and hard to a speed that was damn near blinding.

"You love this pussy, Daddy?" she panted. "Tell me you love this pussy! Please, Daddy! Please! Tell me you love this pussy!" she screamed as her orgasm took over her and had her feeling as if she were flying high on love and bliss.

"You know I do, baby. You know I love this pussy! It's all mines, baby! It's all mine!" he screamed as he let her orgasm ignite his own, and he came long and hard. When he came back down from one of God's most special highs, he lay his head back on the pillow and sighed.

Brandy crawled off of him, turned around, and cuddled next to him, and in a sweet voice, asked, "Are you okay, Daddy? Did I make you feel good?"

He wiped her hair from her sweaty forehead and kissed her and said, "I'm fine, Brandy. You always make me feel good whenever we're together. Don't you ever forget that, okay?"

"Okay, Daddy. I want you to know that no matter what happens, I will never stop loving you, and I will always be here for you. Whatever you need from me, I will do. Whatever you tell me to do, I will follow your instructions without question. I'm yours for as long as you want me, Daddy."

Her words made him feel like a complete jerk. Here he was way out here in Oklahoma City getting ready to dump this fine-ass woman, and she's declaring all of this love and devotion to him. *Fuck!*

"I know, Brandy. I know you're all mine, baby, but don't you think it's time you got more out of life than sitting out here waiting on me? I mean, I feel like, damn, I'm doing you wrong, and I don't like feeling like that at all."

She sat up in the bed and stared at him for a moment and then sighed. "I think about you all the time, Daddy. I wonder what you're up to, and if you're okay doing whatever it is you be doing out there to get your money. A part of me has questioned what the hell I am doing. But a larger part of me," she pointed toward her heart and continued, "tells me that I belong to you. So I don't care how long I have to wait for you to come to me and give me some QT. I accepted your ways from the beginning, so I cannot change up now. I know what I signed up for when I hooked up with you, Daddy. You have given me nothing but the best of everything since we've been together. A home of my dreams, money, cars, and the best dick a woman could ever have. True, I want more, much more. But I have to wait until you're ready to give me more, so wait I will. As long I have some of you, I'm content. That's how I have always felt, and those feelings keep me good while you're away from me."

Papio was speechless. He didn't know how to respond to her words, and he damn sure didn't feel now was the time to tell her about his feelings for Special or that he had a son who he loved with all of his heart.

Maybe in the morning, but definitely not right now, he thought.

Brandy kissed him on the lips and said, "I have even more incentive now to be patient with you, Daddy."

"More incentive? What's that?"

She stared at him lovingly and took a deep breath, bent forward, and gave him a tender kiss. She pulled away from his face and stared directly into those sexy eyes of his and spoke softly. "I'm pregnant, Daddy. I'm two and a half months pregnant with your child."

Papio smiled. He couldn't believe what he had just heard. This was a fucking dream! Or was it a fucking nightmare? He was uncertain at that moment. Once again, he was speechless as he stared at Brandy who had a scared look on her face. She was terrified of his reaction, and that look on her face melted his heart. He reached out to her and said, "So, you about to be my baby mama, huh?"

Brandy lay her head on his chest and sighed. "Yes, Daddy. I'm about to be your baby's mama." She then started to cry softly. Not from sadness but joy.

Chapter Ten

For four days, Papio felt like a total jerk because of the negative thoughts he was having about the news that Brandy was pregnant with his child. Was it really his? No doubt. She wasn't the type of woman that would lie about something like that. Should he make her get an abortion? No way. His Catholic upbringing wouldn't allow him to do something like that. Though he felt he was a bad Catholic, he was still a Catholic, and abortion was a no-no. What to do? These were the questions he asked himself over and over for the last four days.

When he made it back to the house Monday evening, his last night in Oklahoma City, he made up his mind, and he knew Brandy would be happy about his decision, but, boy, was Special going to be pissed. He was having another baby. One thing for certain was he was not leaving Oklahoma without telling Brandy about Li'l Pee. She had to know, because he couldn't take it every time she said something like, "I'm giving you your first child, Daddy!" He cringed every time she made a statement like that. So he made up his mind just as soon as Brandy came home, they were going to have the major sit-down and get everything out in the open.

Now, here it was ten minutes after five p.m., and Brandy should be pulling up any second, he thought as he went to his bar and poured himself a stiff drink. And just like he thought, Brandy was pulling into the garage just as he'd downed his drink and quickly poured another. She came into the media room and smiled at him, looking absolutely gorgeous. She deserved this happiness in her life.

"No way I can deny her that," he said to himself as he downed his second drink, grimaced from the liquor, and said, "Hey, baby, how was your day at the federal joint?"

She set her purse down, shrugged, and said, "The usual, Daddy. Nothing out of the ordinary." She stepped to him and kissed him. "How was your day?"

"It was straight. Didn't do too much but ran around town getting at a few people. My business out here is done, so it was chill for real."

"Well, at least you were able to chill for these last few days instead of doing your normal running around, scheming, and planning some dangerous move. I like it when you are in chill mode, Daddy. You seem more relaxed."

"Yeah, you right. It does feel less stressful," he admitted. "Check it, Brandy, we got to talk about some things kind of important. No, some things that are *very* important."

She stared at him for a moment and then sat down on the couch, patted the spot next to her, and said, "Sit and talk to me, Daddy. Your tone has me nervous here."

After he was seated next to her, he inhaled and said, "I want you to know that I am truly happy that you are pregnant, and I cannot wait for you to have our child. Life is a precious gift from God, and even though I never had any plans for children, I am grateful for this gift."

"That's so sweet, Daddy."

He held up his hand to stop her and said, "Hold up, baby, there's a whole bunch that you need to know. You know how I get down. I don't play games, nor do I do the lying shit. I have to keep it one hundred with you all the way."

"That's one of the things I respect most about you, Daddy. You are the only man I have ever been with who doesn't play any games or pull any punches."

He nodded. "You may respect what I'm about to tell you, but I highly doubt if you're going to like it."

She sighed and said, "Special. It's something to do with Special, isn't it, Daddy?"

"Yes. But there's more to it than her. She's the mother of my son, Brandy. While she was hiding from me all that time, she was pregnant with my child and gave birth to a beautiful baby boy. My son, Preston Ortiz Junior. We call him Li'l Pee," he said as he pulled out his phone and brought up his pictures and gave the smartphone to Brandy and waited for her to go snap off on him.

Brandy accepted the phone and stared at the gorgeous little boy and tried to process the information she had just been given. After a few minutes of staring at Li'l Pee, she sighed, then smiled.

"I'm happy for you, Daddy. Your son looks just like you; there's no denying that. Look at all of that hair! Long and silky, just like his handsome father."

Papio stuck out his chest a little at her compliment and said, "Thanks, baby. That boy is my heart and soul right there. I never thought I was built to be a father, but let me tell you, there's nothing in this world I wouldn't do for that boy."

"That's the real man inside of you. You are a good man behind all of that gangster persona you display on a daily, Daddy. That's one of the reasons why I'm so excited to be having this baby. *Our* baby."

He smiled. "Yeah, our baby."

Brandy frowned and then said, "Okay, now give me the rest about Special."

He shrugged and said, "I love her, Bandy. I still have some serious trust issues with her, but I love her. Just like you said that time when I was ranting and raving about killing her ass, I really love that woman. What's so damn crazy is I love you too."

"Just not as much as you love her?"

He thought about her question, and though he felt he was in love with Special and did love her more than he loved Brandy, he didn't feel that would be appropriate to say. He didn't lie, but he didn't have to answer that question either.

"You are about to be the woman who brings another one of my seeds into this world. There's no comparison to something like that, Brandy. That child growing inside of you keeps us linked to each other for the rest of our lives. The love I have for you is just as strong as the love I have for Special."

Okay, that *was a lie. Fuck!* he said to himself.

"So, what do we do from this point on, Daddy?"

"We do what we been doing. The difference now is I will be here much more because I want to be here for your pregnancy. I missed that process with Special, but I refuse to miss it with you."

That put a smile on her face. "I'm sure that's going to piss Special off."

"So what? That's my decision, and it is what it is," he stated firmly.

"What about your business, Daddy?"

"I still got some moves to make but not too much more. Things have been real good for me these last few months, Brandy; real good. I have some things I need to take care of in the next few days. After that, I'm going to have a lot of free time to come out here and be with you. I won't lie and say I'll be here for long stretches early, but by the time you're in your last few months, I'll be on deck twenty-four and some more. My word."

"Thank you for that, Daddy. That means a lot to me. That shows me that though you're in love with Special and not me, you still have enough respect for me and our child to be here for us. That's all I ask of you, Daddy."

"Now where did you get that I'm-in-love-with-Special-and-not-you shit from? I didn't say that shit."

"Some things don't have to be said, Daddy. I always knew you were in love with her. I hate that. I hate it with a passion that it can't be me that you're in love with, but as you like to say, it is what it is. I'm a forty-six-year-old woman. I've seen a lot in my days, and I'm mature enough to recognize the obvious, Daddy. I never disillusioned myself of being able to hold onto such a fine-ass man as yourself. I feel lucky enough to have held onto you as long as I have. No woman likes to be number two, but I guess I have no choice. You are Daddy. My daddy, and I won't ever stop loving you. Promise me that you will never stop loving me. That's all I need to hear, and I'm good."

He smiled as he grabbed her and pulled her into his arms for a tight hug. He then kissed her tenderly and said, "I will love you until the day I breathe no more, Brandy. You my baby mama!" they both started laughing and shared another kiss.

"Come, let your baby mama put some more of this good pussy on you before you leave me in the morning," she said as she stood and pulled him to his feet and led him to the bedroom.

Papio stepped off the plane and quickly went down to the baggage claim area to get his luggage so he could hurry up and get with Special because they would be flying right out the next day to Boston. He had reserved a suite at his favorite hotel, The Westin, so he wouldn't have to drive out to Riverside. Special would be bringing him some clothes, so everything was all set. He was dreading the conversation he would have with her because he knew there was no way in hell it would go as smooth as it did with Brandy—no-fucking-way. *Damn*, he thought as he left the airport and went to the parking area where he parked his car.

Twenty minutes later, he was sitting in his suite waiting on Special. He was about to take a shower when he received a call from his main man Kingo from federal prison.

"What you do, mon? You good out tere?" Kingo said after Papio pressed the number five on his phone to accept the call.

"You know I'm good, Dread. What about you? You straight at that low facility?"

"Yeah, mon, me real good. Staying out the way, you know, and working out good. Missing tat bad!"

Laughing, Papio said, "Your ass should have denied the transfer, then, and got an incident report so you could have stayed put."

"Nah, it was time for change, mon. Change is good when you've done as much time as me have."

"I feel you."

"So, how you do? How is that baby boy you got?"

"Man, it's all good. Li'l Pee is great and getting bigger every day."

"Everyting criss, mon. Me proud of you with that there."

"That's what's up because you're about to be even prouder." He then went on and told Kingo about Brandy's pregnancy.

"Shit, mon! You not playing out there!" Kingo said and started laughing. "How Special feels about tat?"

"She doesn't know yet. I just got back from Oklahoma, and I haven't told her yet."

"You in trouble, mon."

"Don't I know it."

"That Brandy is a champ, though, mon. Respect to her for how she handled that."

"Yeah, I know. I am praying Special don't act too fucking stupid."

"Sorry, mon, that prayer won't be answered. You are in big trouble."

"Thanks for the support."

Laughing, Kingo said, "You know Kingo keeps it real at all times, mon. But you be all right. You always comes out on top. Proud of you, mon." Turning serious, Kingo said, "I been watching the TV, mon, and it looks crazy, real crazy out there in tat world. It may be time for you to go spend that pregnant season with Brandy and relax some, you know?"

"That's the plan. But your brother needs me for something real important. After that, then that's what I'm going to do."

"Aah, yes, me heard about the situation with Brad and Macho, mon. You taking Special wit' you?"

"Yep."

"When you leaving?"

"In the morning."

"And you say you haven't told her about the bun in Brandy, mon?"

"Nope, not yet."

"You wait, then, mon. Don't you tell tat woman before you go wit' me brother. You wait until you come back and everyting criss, you understand Kingo?"

Papio thought about what Kingo said and agreed. He didn't need Special out there tripping out on some other shit and not be focused on the business. "Yeah, I got you, Dread. Makes sense."

"Perfect sense, mon. Okay, mon, almost me time, so let me go. Tings are going to get good real soon for Kingo. It's almost my time, you know."

Papio smiled and said, "What? When? Don't tell me you got some action on your time?"

Kingo smiled into the receiver and said, "Soon, Papio. Soon you see Kingo, top-rankin' Kingo at his best!"

"Come on, Dread! Don't do me that! When?" But the phone disconnected, ending their fifteen-minute phone call. As soon as Papio set his phone down, there was a soft knock at the door. He smiled 'cause he knew it was Special. When he opened the door, she was standing there looking good as always, dressed in a pair of expensive jeans and her shoulder-length hair freshly done with a tight-fitting blouse on, always looking sexy, he thought as he stared at his woman.

"Stop staring and get naked, pretty nigga. I need me some dick."

Papio shook his head, and though he hated when she called him pretty, he couldn't help but start laughing. He was still laughing as he began to do as he was told and started taking off his clothes. Special had that effect on him.

Chapter Eleven

Miami's Cuban drug lord, Mr. Suarez, sat behind his huge cherry wood desk in his office with tears in his eyes. Normally, that kind of emotion was never seen by anyone. Today was an exception only because his right-hand man, Castro, was the person who had brought him some very heartbreaking news. His longtime friend and business associate, Chief Hightower, was found dead in his bedroom. The chief died peacefully in his sleep. Though he was sad of the loss of his longtime friend, he was satisfied that at least he had been able to give him some peace by knowing that the woman who had set up his sons had been taken care of. That thought put a smile on Mr. Suarez's face. He wiped his eyes and took a deep breath and then exhaled.

Life must go on, he thought sadly.

"Castro, get Papio on the line for me."

"Sí, sir," Castro said as he pulled out his phone and dialed Papio's number from memory. When he received the voicemail, he left a message for Papio. "Hey, you prick, this is Castro. Give Mr. Suarez a call back at this number, the sooner, the better."

With a frown on his face, Mr. Suarez said, "Must you always be so disrespectful to Papio, Castro? The man has served us well over the years. He came through for the chief, and for that, I will forever be grateful to Papio. Show him respect; he's earned that."

"Sí, sir. It's just that I don't like that arrogant fuck."

"You don't necessarily have to like a man to show respect. Now, I need to rest. Make the arrangements for our travel to New York for Chief Hightower's funeral."

With a shocked expression on his face, Castro asked, "We're going to the funeral, sir?"

"Sí."

"I cannot remember the last time you left this estate. Are you sure?"

"Sí, I'm positive. It would be a blatant show of disrespect if I weren't present at the chief's funeral service. Make sure that security is tight, and all will be well. No one would ever expect me to show up there because, as you said, I don't leave this estate often. This is my fortress, and I know no one would ever try to make an aggressive move toward me here. But this is a time where I must leave my security blanket."

"You never know who may be watching us, sir. We have plenty of enemies that may be patiently waiting for an opportunity such as this."

Nodding his head in agreement, the drug lord shrugged and said, "I agree. But this is a chance I am willing to take. As I said, that would be disrespectful if I didn't pay my proper respects to the chief. So to New York, we go. I trust you will ensure my safety, Castro."

"Always, sir," Castro said as he quickly left the office so he could go do as his boss ordered.

When the door closed behind Castro, Mr. Suarez shook his head sadly and sat back in his seat. "Life is full of surprises. Rest in peace, my friend; rest in peace."

It was a rainy day in Hawaii, and the bad weather fit Lance's mood perfectly. He was frustrated and angry. How in the fuck could Poppa Blue think he would just sit back and watch as he made hundreds of millions of dollars without doing something about it? That shit wasn't right, and he knew it. The hundred million-dollar question was, what in the hell was he going to do about it?

It's not like I have the power to get at Poppa Blue, Lance thought as he stood in front of the picture window in his living room staring at the heavy downpour of rain. The more he thought about it, the more upset he became. *Fuck it. If I can't get at Poppa Blue with some muscle, I'll do the next best thing. I'll give the FBI one hell of a tip that can hopefully lead them to the arrest of the crew that Poppa Blue has doing his dirty work for him.*

Lance suddenly smiled as he realized that his idea was perfect. He would drop a dime on Poppa Blue, and when his crew got knocked, he would get the $10-million reward that the Feds were offering. It may not be hundreds of millions, but it sure in fuck would double his money, he thought as he turned and went to grab his phone. He picked up his cell and was about to dial 411 to get the number to the FBI's office, then stopped.

"What am I going to tell them without implicating myself in this mess? Ugh!" he said to himself as he sat down on the couch and tried to come up with something that would help him put his plan in motion because there was no way he was going to let Poppa Blue get away with beating him out of what he felt he deserved. He snapped his fingers and smiled. "I'll tell them that I was forced to create the device by Poppa Blue and paid $10 million for it and sworn to secrecy or he would take my life. They'll deal with me for sure, but I will make sure I get immunity for my assistance, plus my reward for helping them. Yeah, they'll go for that for certain," Lance said out loud as he picked his phone back up.

"Put that phone down, you stupid man, you," a cold voice said behind Lance.

Lance damn near peed in his pants as he jumped up, turned, and saw a dark-skinned woman standing there with a gun aimed directly at him. "Wh- who the fuck are you? And how in the hell did you get in my home?" Lance screamed, trying to act as if he wasn't terrified.

"Shut up and sit the fuck down, weakling," the woman said as she pointed toward the couch with her weapon. A weapon that Lance noticed had a silencer on it.

After he was seated again, the woman stepped to him and said, "You couldn't leave well enough alone, so your greed has cost you your life." She then shot him three times in his chest. Lance fell back on the couch gasping for breath. The woman stepped a tad closer to him, then shot him once right between his eyes. She then put her gun inside of her Birkin bag and went back to the kitchen and left the same way she had entered Lance's home, through the back door.

Once she was inside her rental car, she pulled out her phone and dialed. When the other line was answered, she said, "It's done."

"Any issues, mon?"

"None. Good thing you made this move when you did. He was just about to make a call that would have made things very hard for you, Mother."

Fay smiled into the receiver and said, "Mi instincts told me to move fast, mon. You did good, daughter of mine. Come home, and we shall celebrate with a nice shopping spree."

Fay's daughter smiled and said, "My flight will arrive late tonight."

"I'll see you when you arrive," Fay said and ended the call.

She then called Poppa Blue and said, "No worry, mon. Everything has been handled in the land of pineapples."

Poppa Blue smiled and said, "Good. You do know it's time to chill, right?"

"I'll be talking to mi cousin soon to ensure that that happens, mon. Be good," Fay said and ended the call.

Papio and Special arrived at Boston's Logan International Airport Wednesday morning and caught a cab to the Hyatt Hotel since it was one of the two hotels closest to the airport. Special chose the Hyatt over the Hilton because she didn't care for Paris Hilton. Papio thought that was ridiculous but knew better than to argue with her. Once they were settled in their room, he called Kango to let him know they arrived and where they were staying. Kango informed him that he was making some adjustments for their upcoming robbery and would be by to pick them up within the hour.

After Papio hung up with Kango, he checked his messages and saw that he had three, one from his man Q. in L.A., one from Brandy in Oklahoma, and the last one which caught his attention was from Castro in Miami. He wondered what Mr. Suarez wanted, so he called Miami first. When Castro answered the phone, Papio hit him with his normal, sarcastic insult for Mr. Suarez's number one man.

"What's good, flunky number uno? You rang?"

"Yeah, you stupid prick. Mr. Suarez wants to speak with you."

"Well, hurry along and put him on the phone, fat boy. It's not like I want to be on the phone with your ass any longer than I have to."

"I continue to pray that the day will come that I will be given the go-ahead to take your life, you scumbag piece of shit."

Laughing, Papio said, "If I was you, I'd beg the Father to please give you the strength necessary to deal with a beast such as me. Because if you're given the green light to get at me, you're going to need not only the help from God but your entire army, bitch, because I'm nothing easy. So like I said, hurry along, you flunky piece of shit. I'm a busy man."

"One day, Papio . . . one day," Castro said as he went into Mr. Suarez's office and gave him the phone.

"Papio, how are you doing, señor? Good, I hope."

"I'm lovely, Mr. Suarez. How about yourself?"

"Healthy and blessed. But my spirits are down at this time, and I need you to do me a favor."

"You already know if I can I will, sir. Holla at me."

"I just received news that my longtime friend Chief Hightower has passed on to the afterlife, and I intend to attend his funeral. It would mean a lot to me if you accompanied me to pay my last respects to my friend. You did him a great service, and I know for a fact that he died a happy man, and that happiness was because of how you handled that 'situation' for him. It would mean a lot to me if you joined me in New York to say farewell to my dear friend."

Papio knew this was not a favor he was asking of him. It was an order, an order that he couldn't disobey. Fuck! "I'm currently caught up with something rather important, sir. I don't know how long I'll be before I'm able to move."

"The funeral isn't until next Tuesday. I'm sure you can have your business taken care of in the next six days, sí? I mean, this is very important to me, Papio."

"I understand. Sí, I think I'll be finished up with what I have going on. As a matter of fact, I'm not that far from New York, so I'll prolong my stay east and meet you. Is that okay?"

"That's perfect. I'll make the arrangements, and we can meet and stay at one of the casinos Chief Hightower owned. Thank you for this, Papio; thank you very much."

"No problem, sir. But I do have a question."

"Yes?"

"This is rare for you, isn't it? I mean, you are not known for leaving Miami too much. As a matter of fact, in all my years of dealing with you, I have never even heard of you leaving your estate. Won't this be kind of dangerous for you?"

"Sí, I do have many enemies out there who would love to take advantage of this opportunity, but as I stated, it is very important to me that I go and pay my respects to my friend. So it's well worth the risk. That, combined with the fact that I have every confidence in Castro and his abilities to keep me safe for my brief stay in New York. Though I am not comfortable leaving my highly protected estate, this has to happen. If it's meant for my demise, then so be it. So, I will give you a call in a few days to give you the arrangements once they're made. Good day, Señor Papio," Mr. Suarez said and ended the call.

Papio hung up the phone and sat there thinking. Thinking about how he once again got over on the Cuban drug lord and wondered how he would be pushing his luck by attending the Seneca Indian chief's funeral. If Mr. Suarez ever found out that Special was still breathing, he would definitely lose his head. To make matters worse, Papio now had to attend the funeral of the man he also deceived, all in the name of love.

Special came into the living room of their suite and saw Papio seated with a funny expression on his face and asked what was wrong with him. After he explained, she sat down next to him, sighed, and said, "You got to do it, Clyde. I mean, you have to finish the play. If you don't go, then, that Cuban may get suspicious and start looking into shit."

"I know. I just can't help but think I'm pushing my luck with this shit, though. I mean, with my debt cleared with

Mr. Suarez, all I wanted to do was stay the fuck away from that fool for the rest of my days."

"In a perfect world that would happen, baby, but the life we lead it just ain't meant to be that way."

"Fuck. Check it; Kango will be here in a little while. I need to make a few more calls to check on some shit, so you might as well get fresh 'cause I think he's going to take us out and about so we can go over everything."

"All right. I want you to know again how much I appreciate you for what you did for me, Clyde. If it wasn't for you, I don't know how I'd be living right now. Fuck, I'd most likely not be living at all. I love you, Clyde."

He smiled and said, "I love you too, Bonnie. That love is the reason why I got down like I did. I don't regret it one bit. Let's just hope and pray that shit never comes to light. 'Cause if it does, we're going to either have to run for the rest of our lives or go to war with some high-powered mothafuckas."

He smiled at her and shook his head. She said, "I was thinking the same thing, Clyde."

Chapter Twelve

After enjoying one of the best seafood meals they'd ever had, Kango and Steven took Papio and Special past the Federal Reserve Bank of Boston that sat on Atlantic Avenue, then showed them the route they would take once the robbery was complete to the first vehicle where they would switch SUVs. Less than five minutes from the first switch, they showed them where the next SUV would be parked for their final switch. Papio didn't have any negative feelings toward anything he'd heard so far, so he gave Special a questioning glance to see if she had anything to say.

"What do you think the take will be with this one, Kango?"

Steven answered for him. "I've done the homework on this, and this Federal Reserve Bank holds anywhere from forty to sixty-plus million in its safe weekly. Thursdays, they're usually closer to the sixty-plus million. That's why tomorrow morning by 10:00 a.m., that will be the best time to move. We're not hitting the bank clerk drawers, only the safe. Two will hit the safe and two watch everyone inside while we do the takeover."

"No driver?" asked Papio.

"Yes, I've found a dependable driver from the Hyde Park area."

Shaking his head, Papio said, "Not feeling no new nigga, Steven. What's up with that?"

"What other choice do we have? Going in three deep is too risky."

"True. But dealing with someone new is riskier."

"We're open for any ideas you have on this one, Papio. This has to go down tomorrow, so we can all take a much-needed break because the heat has been turned up considerably. That's one of the reasons why we chose Boston. Though we've made plenty of moves on the East Coast, the authorities are shaken way left, and Boston would be unlikely on their lists of our targets. That, plus we've never hit a Federal Reserve," said Kango.

Papio silently sat as they drove back toward their hotel. He then said, "This new man you're using to drive, you also know you're putting him in the mix about the device, right?"

"Not really. I figured when we pull up in front of the bank, one of you in the backseat could activate the device, then give us the go once everything has been deactivated. He doesn't have to know anything about the device."

"It's just not sitting right in my gut, Kango."

"Are you good with this guy, Kango?" asked Special. "I mean, is he like close to you guys?"

"If you're asking me whether he's expendable, then, yes, he is, Special."

"That's that, then. We're using him because he knows the area the way we need him to, which is cool. Once we get to the last switch, I'll do him; then we switch and get the fuck up outta there. Problem solved."

"Yes, problem solved and more money for us to split," said Steven.

"I like that too," said Kango.

"So now it's robbing a Federal Reserve Bank, plus adding a body? Come on, let's look at this all the way. Are you sure this fool hasn't bumped his gums to anyone about what we're going to put down in the morning? I mean, we could put this down, pop him, and get the fuck out, only to find out later he told his girlfriend Suzy Q., and then we'd be fucked, or should I say, *you* guys would be fucked because if he ran his mouth, *you* are the ones who are at risk."

"I understand that, Papio, and he hasn't been told anything as of yet. I just told him to remain ready for my call and not to tell anyone about me or what we're going to be doing," said Kango.

"How did you hook up with this dude?" asked Special.

"Through a friend in the NY. A solid Brooklyn cat I know from way back."

"How will this Brooklyn cat feel when he hears about his friend's untimely death?"

Kango shrugged and said, "I think once he receives the nice chunk I'm going to lay on him, he won't have any problems with the loss of that particular friend."

"You think?" asked Special.

Kango smiled. "I like you, Special. One moment, please," he said as he pulled out his phone and called his friend in Brooklyn. When the line was answered, Kango said, "Treez, my man, how it goes your way?"

"I'm straight, Kango. What's up with you out there in Beantown?"

"So far, so good."

"No problem with my mans, huh?"

"Kinda, sorta. I was wondering how good you were with your man; you know what I'm saying?"

Treez was silent for a moment; then he realized what Kango was asking. He said, "We good. We were upstate, and he wanted to be a part of my way of living, but he didn't have what it takes to bang Nine Trey. So I looked out for him and kept him safe."

"So, he's not a part of the family?"

"Nope."

"So?"

"So, make sure you come holla at Treez when everything is everything, Kango. And make sure when you holla at Treez, you holla right. Ya feel me?"

"Indeed. I'll holla at you," and he hung up the phone.

Kango turned and faced Papio and Special as they pulled in front of their hotel. "He's expendable."

Special smiled and spoke for her and Papio. "Then, we'll see you guys bright and early in the morning!" They all started laughing.

"I really like your lady here, Papio."

"Yeah, I know. You keep repeating that, Kango. Just remember that she is *my* lady. Big emphasis on *my*, ya dig?"

Kango raised his hands for peace and said, "Now you know I'd never disrespect you, Papio. Kingo would break my neck for that. You're considered family."

"That's right. Just had to make sure we're clear."

"Understood. So, it's a go?"

"As the lady said, we'll see you guys bright and early in the morning!"

The next morning, Steven picked up Special and Papio in the front of their hotel and drove them to a run-down neighborhood in the Roxbury area. They parked in front of a house that looked like if the wind blew hard enough, it would collapse. Five minutes later, Kango and a small, funny-looking, light-skinned brother came out of the house and got inside of the SUV. Without a word being said, Steven pulled from in front of the house and drove for fifteen minutes to another neighborhood that looked a little better than the neighborhood they had just left. He pulled into a garage that he opened with the garage door opener he had clipped to the sun visor of the SUV.

They all got out of the truck and went inside of the home where Steven and Kango had been staying while in Boston. It was ten minutes after nine a.m., so there was no time for small talk or introductions. Kango went into the bedroom and returned with black camouflage army fatigues for each of them. They all dressed silently. Steven gave each of them a pair of latex gloves, and some flesh-colored ear mikes. Everyone miked up and did a check to make sure they were all on the right channel. Once that was complete, Kango pulled a large duffel bag from behind the sofa and started issuing out the weapons they would use. Each member of the crew would have two 9 mms with two full 18-round magazines. Then Kango spoke for the first time since they entered the home.

"No assault rifles because I don't want to take the chance of someone noticing us as we exit the vehicle or the bank when we're leaving. So the pistols will suffice. Special, you and I will hit the vault while Steven and Papio hold everyone in place. K. T., you will keep an eye on the streets. Make sure you watch up and down Atlantic. The SUV we will be using is tinted so you can be comfortable watching all round you. You see anything remotely looking like police, you alert us on your ear mike. Understood?"

"I got you."

Special eyed K. T. and could tell he was cool, and that relaxed her as she checked her weapons.

"You know the route we drove last night, so there's nothing to speak on as far as that's concerned. Once we get inside of the vehicle, I want you to ease away from the curb and blend with traffic real smooth-like. No rushing. Once we make the switch, then we can put a little speed to the situation so we can make the final switch and be in the wind." Kango checked his watch and saw that it was now 9:30 a.m. "Any questions?" When he saw that there weren't any, he smiled. He reached back inside of the duffel bag and pulled out four more folded duffel bags and tossed two of them to Special. "Let's go have a good morning!" They all filed out of the house back into the garage and inside of the SUV. It was time to make it happen.

Twenty-five minutes later, K. T. pulled in front of the Federal Reserve Bank of Boston. Each member of the crew had on skull caps covering their long hair. Papio had his long ponytail stuck inside the back of his fatigues as was his custom when he did a bank job. Kango checked his watch and saw that it was 9:57 a.m. and gave a nod to Steven, who was in the backseat. Steven pulled out the device and turned it on and flipped the switch that would deactivate the bank's alarm and surveillance systems, making them totally blind. The red light on the device switched to green, and at 9:59 a.m., Kango said, "Let's get it!" Each member climbed out of the SUV and calmly walked inside of the Federal Reserve Bank without a sideways glance.

As soon as Kango was inside, he yelled for everyone to get on the floor and put their hands where they could see them. He proceeded toward the vault, followed closely by Special. Steven went straight to the security guard and disarmed him and laid him on the floor. Papio stood in the center of the bank and aimed both of his pistols at everyone who was lying down all around him. The takeover of the bank went as smooth as they always went with the help of the device. There was no rushing, and everyone inside of the bank was held under control. Papio could tell they were terrified, and for some reason, that gave him one hell of an adrenaline rush.

Two customers of the Federal Reserve Bank of Boston picked the wrong time to do some banking. Thanks to a heads-up by K. T., Papio met them as they entered the bank and quickly led them to the middle of the bank so they could lie down and join the other customers who were currently being held hostage.

Five and a half minutes later, Papio saw Special coming from behind the counter struggling with the two duffel bags, so he stepped to her quickly while mouthing in his ear mike that he was going to take the bags while she watched his back. She confirmed, and they made the switch and began to exit the bank, followed closely by Kango with Steven bringing up their rear.

Once they were all inside of the SUV, K. T. eased away from the curb just as he had been told to do, and they were on their way to the first switch. Five minutes later, K. T. came to a stop on the side of a dark brown Lincoln Navigator, and they all switched from one SUV to another. This time, K. T. added a little speed as he drove toward the last switch location.

Steven was listening to a police scanner and heard the alert go out finally about the bank robbery. He smiled when he heard the description of the first SUV they had already switched from. *So far, so good,* he thought as he set the scanner on his lap and reached between his legs and passed Special a silenced .380-caliber pistol. Special checked to make sure that there was a live round inside of the chamber and gave a nod to Papio, who had been watching her silently. She smiled and winked.

K. T. came up behind the last switch and just as he put Navigator in park, Special leaned up and put the .380 pistol point-blank on the back of his head and pulled the trigger. K. T. fell forward with his head on the steering wheel. Kango quickly pulled him back so he wouldn't sound the horn, and they all calmly stepped out of the Navigator and climbed inside of a new Mercedes-Benz SUV and left the murder scene without anyone noticing them.

Twenty-five minutes later, they were back in the home where they had started this mission. Each wore a smile on their faces as they began to relax and unwind. No one was going anywhere for the next twenty-four hours, so they all made themselves comfortable. The city of Boston was about to become hot as a firecracker, so they would patiently wait out the heat for a day or so and then make their exits from the state. Mission complete.

Chapter Thirteen

The Federal Reserve Bank of Boston was swarming with FBI agents. Highly pissed-off federal agents. None of them could believe that a bank in their city had become an addition to the list of bank robberies that had been committed across the United States. Special Agent in Charge (SAC) of the bank robbery division, Agent Broddick, couldn't believe that this had happened. Especially since he thought he had chosen the right banks to cover in the city. For some reason, he never thought the bank robbers would have the balls to rob a bank so close to the downtown area. His anger had him red-faced as he marched around the bank watching as his agents questioned the many witnesses that were in the bank while it had been robbed so damn easily.

He pulled one of his agents away from a witness and asked him, "Anything so far, Robert?"

"Nothing so far, sir. The same MO as all of the other jobs we've been briefed on. They seemed to be in no rush whatsoever and were extra calm as two of the robbers hit the vault and cleaned it out. Each witness I've spoken with has the same statement, real calm and cool customers as they easily did the job."

"We checked the surveillance tapes and nothing. How in the fuck are they doing this shit?" SAC Broddick wondered aloud in his heavy Bostonian accent. "I mean, the manager of the bank hit the silent alarm as well as two of the bank tellers; yet, no alarm sounded until at least fifteen minutes after the fuckers had left the damn bank! And to think I've had extra men posted all around the fucking city watching banks, and I didn't pick this one because of the location being so close to downtown and a fucking police station, for God's sake."

"No need to beat yourself up on this, sir. I mean, we made all of the logical decisions for our surveillance teams. They just got lucky. Sooner or later, their luck will run out."

"Fuck! East Boston Savings, Century Bank & Trust, and First Republic Bank were the ones I felt positive if they tried us in Boston would be the ones they would hit."

"We might as well put teams on Cathay Bank and Boston Private Bank & Trust now."

"For what? They're fucking gone, and I highly doubt those cocky bastards would have the balls to try us again. But you're right. Put teams on it. I want an agent inside every one of those fuckers as well. For now, though, I want this fucking city locked down. These fuckers are out of towners, and I want the train station, airports, and every fucking place we can think of to have our men there on full alert. I want this fucking city locked all the way down. I want every snitch, CI, or source we have to be put on full alert. I want these bastards. They cannot make it out of Boston, Robert. Get on it."

"Yes, sir," the agent said as he went to go make the calls his boss told him to make.

By the time they finished counting the take from the Federal Reserve robbery, they were all extremely tired. It took them a little over three hours to count $57 million. Special sighed and wore a satisfied smile on her face as she thought about the $14.1 million they were each getting for the robbery.

Not bad at all, she thought as she stared at Papio, who had a strange look on his face. "What up, Clyde? You look spooked."

"We all should be spooked right about now. The Feds are sure to have this entire city on lock. Sitting here like this, waiting for them to cool off may not be the best move."

"What you thinking, Papio?" asked Steven.

"I'm thinking we need to get the fuck out of this city as soon as possible."

"I feel that, but how? If the city is on lock, they will be looking for anyone who fits that out of town look, and we definitely fit that description," said Kango.

"First, we need to split up. Moving in a group is not the way to go. I think me and Special should head back to our suite. Then we fall back and try to figure a way to get the fuck out of Boston."

"If you guys don't mind spending some change, I think I know a way we can ease up out of this bitch quite comfortably," said Special.

"How's that?" asked Papio.

"You two stay here, and me and Papio will head back to the room and make the arrangements for us to get out of here tomorrow morning or the afternoon, at the latest. When we get back to the hotel, I'll call and order us a private jet to fly us up out of this bitch. Once everything has been arranged, I'll order a limousine to come and pick us up; then we'll scoop you two and have the limo take us to the airport and drive us right to the jet so we can take to the friendly skies without being seen by too many people. I mean, do you think the Feds would expect for four bank robbers to fly private out of here?"

Kango smiled and said, "I like it."

"Bold move," said Steven.

Papio smiled at his woman and said, "Brilliant, Bonnie."

"I know. You guys get packed up and be ready. We'll hit you once everything is set in motion. I've flown on a few private jets in my time, and I know Delta Private Jets, XOJET, and Blue Star Jets are the easiest to reserve. One of them should be pretty easy to secure a flight to the west."

"The west? Why fly all the way out there?" asked Kango.

"I think that's an excellent idea. We need to get the device to Fay anyway," said Steven.

"And for real, we need to get as far away from the East Coast as possible."

"That's right. When we land, I'll also have another limo there waiting for us so we can slide on into L.A. and get the fuck out of Dodge."

"Like I said, fucking brilliant, Bonnie. Come on, let's bounce so we can make it happen. I trust you guys will be able to dispose of everything?"

"No problem. I'm going to leave that to Treez. He needs to earn this blessing we're going to give him."

"I thought he was earning it by keeping his fucking mouth shut about his boy," said Special.

"I'm giving him a cool million. I don't think he will object to coming out this way to get rid of these guns and picking up his money. Shit, he can keep them if he wants," said Kango.

"Smart. That way, everything is tight."

"Exactly. You guys can take the ear mikes and dispose of them at the hotel. We'll wipe down the house totally and be waiting for your call."

"What about the Benz truck?"

"Leave it at the valet. By the time they realize it's been sitting there, it won't matter," said Kango.

"Not good. They could line us to the truck and then pull up our names from the hotel. Plus, there may be cameras at the hotel," said Papio.

"Looks like Treez not only gets a cool million, he also can come up on a new Benz SUV if he wants," said Steven.

"That means one of you guys will have to take us back to the hotel. That's one hell of a risk," said Papio.

"Not really. That truck is clean, and we won't have anything on us that will give us away. We'll keep the ear mikes here and get rid of them. We'll be clean as a whistle as we roll. Remember, the Feds are looking for four or more, not three. Come on, let's do this," Kango said as he stood.

Special paused and stared at Papio. Papio returned her stare for a moment and read her mind. "I know there's plenty of trust in this room, and I mean no disrespect, Kango, Steven, but—"

Kango laughed and said, "Don't even think that shit, Papio. Another twenty-eight million isn't worth ruining a friendship, my brother."

Papio nodded and smiled as he led the way toward the garage.

Agent Robert Diddle came running back inside of the Federal Reserve Bank waving his arms toward his superior, SAC Broddick. When he was standing in front of him, he spoke urgently. "Sir, I think we have a lead! A dead man was found in a Navigator not more than five miles away from here."

"What makes you think this dead man has something to do with this bank being robbed?"

"The officer on the scene said the man was shot point-blank in the back of the head and was wearing a pair of latex gloves with what looks like an ear mike inside of his right ear."

SAC Broddick smiled and said, "Let's hit it then!"

Both of the FBI agents rushed out of the bank and climbed into a black Chevy Tahoe and sped toward the crime scene which was less than ten minutes from the bank. When they arrived at the scene, the local police had the entire area roped off with yellow tape. The agents jumped out of the SUV and quickly stepped to the crime scene officer and asked him a few questions. After finding out that the victim was a local thug from the Hyde Park area, both agents sighed, hopeful that this could be a lead that will bring them to the elusive bank robbers.

"Okay, run a check on this joker and see what you can find out. See if he has a girlfriend, wife, mother, cousin—whoever—and see if he ran his mouth about his business. This looks like he was used as a driver and then eliminated because he could ID these bastards. They're good, but they finally fucked up. They now have murder added to their long fucking list of bank robberies. If this pans out, we may be the ones who can bring this crew down. Get on it!"

"Yes, sir!" Agent Diddle said as he pulled out his phone and started making calls.

Special's plan worked to perfection. The crew was delivered right to the front of a private jet owned by Blue Star Jets. The limousine driver helped her out of the car and assisted the men with their luggage onto the luxury G-5 jet. Once they were on board, they were treated with the very best service by an attractive flight attendant. Once they were airborne, they all wore smiles of relief and watched from their windows as they departed the East Coast. Special had called Poppa Blue and had him arrange everything for her so none of their names would be on anything just in case the Feds somehow found out about three men and a lone female who flew out of Logan

International Airport on a private jet. There would be no way they could trace it back to them or Poppa Blue because he used one of his many aliases for the purchase of the jet and limousine ride. With a sigh of relief, Special reclined her soft leather seat back and placed her right hand on Papio's.

"We're good, Clyde; we're all good."

"Yeah, and I think it's time we lie the fuck down for real this time. No amount of money is worth losing everything we already got."

"You got that shit right. I mean, we got way more than we ever thought anyway."

"So it's time to live and enjoy our lives."

"Uh-huh."

Papio thought about Brandy and figured now was a good enough time to drop the bomb on Special. At least, she wouldn't go the fuck off on him on this jet with Kango, Steven, and the flight crew who could hear her. He squeezed her hand and said, "I want to thank you, Bonnie."

"Thank me for what?"

"Thank you for being my rider, for loving me, and for real, not sweating me about Brandy. You haven't asked me once about my trip to OKC. I just knew you would grill me on that shit and be salty at a nigga."

"For what? I already know you fucked her, Clyde. You a tender-dick nigga when it comes to her. It is what it is," she said and shrugged.

He didn't care for that 'tender-dick' remark but let it slide because he knew she was about to become extremely pissed and hurt. He sighed and said, "There's some shit I need to get at you about, and it's real important."

Special turned in her seat and stared at him for a minute and said, "What? You didn't end it with her?"

"She's pregnant, Bonnie, and the baby is mines."

Special stared at him for a minute and then shook her head and spoke through clenched teeth. "You're one smart-ass pretty nigga, Clyde. Telling me now while we're on this jet was the best fucking thing you could have ever done. Any place else, and I would be slapping the fuck out of your ass right now."

"Come on, Bonnie, it's not like I planned this shit to happen."

She held up her hand in his face and said, "Stop. No more. Not now. We'll deal with this shit when we touch the west."

"But we—"

"But we my ass. I. Don't. Want. To. Talk. About. This. Right. Now. Clyde." She snatched her hand out of his and turned and stared at the clear blue sky as the jet cruised smoothly through the air. She stayed that way for over an hour because she refused to let Papio see the tears as they fell from her eyes.

Chapter Fourteen

SAC Broddick was sitting in his office totally frustrated with how it seemed as if the crew who robbed the Federal Reserve Bank not only committed another perfect robbery but also were able to make a clean escape out of his city. He was positive that they were in the wind, long gone from Boston. If they were as smart as he thought they were, they wouldn't be returning to Boston any time soon, especially to rob another bank. His chance at bringing down this evasive crew has come and passed him by, and that hurt. He was still holding onto hope, though. If something could pan out from the murdered driver, they may be able to get a lead on this crew, and if that happened, he didn't give a damn how far he would have to travel to bring this crew down. He would go to hell if need be to get them. By coming to Boston, robbing the bank successfully, and committing a cold-blooded murder was a blatant slap in his face, and *no one* slapped him without him slapping back.

Harder.

There was a knock at SAC Broddick's office door. He yelled for the person to enter, and as soon as he saw the look on Agent Diddle's face, he knew his chances of catching this crew had diminished even further. Fuck!

"Talk to me, Robert."

"Not much to tell, sir. We went and spoke to the victim's, one Kevin Turner's, mother, who knew nothing about him being involved with any bank robbers. Neither did his sister or his girlfriend. Kevin, known as K. T. on the streets, did some time in upstate New York for robbery back in 2007. He'd been home for three years working odd jobs here and there. No known heavy association with anyone around the city. This crew knew what they were doing. By eliminating him, they left nothing for us to go on. Hopefully, we'll get lucky, sir, and they will slip up while trying to get out of the city."

Shaking his head, the special agent in charge of the bank robbery division heavily sighed as he sat back in his seat and said, "It's done, Robert. They're gone, in the wind, with over fifty-plus fucking million dollars."

"How can you be certain of that, sir? It's only been a little over twenty-four hours. They could still be trying to lie low, hoping for the heat to die down before trying to get out of the city."

"That's some wishful thinking, and I pray to God you're right. But my old gut here is telling me they made every move right from the bank job to the murder of this Kevin Turner guy to their escape. I'll tell you this, though. Whenever those bastards do slip up and get caught, I'm going to be standing front and center watching their execution because they all deserve to burn in hell!"

The Blue Star Jet's G-5 touched down perfectly at the Burbank airport, then taxied slowly to the designated area where a stretched Range Rover limousine was idling, waiting for the passengers from the G-5 to deplane. Ten minutes after the jet came to a halt, the passengers were all seated comfortably in the back of the limousine as the driver left the airport. No one said a word until they were on the freeway headed toward the Westin Hotel where Papio and Special still had a suite. There was a collective sigh of relief from each member of the crew. Though they made it out of Boston, they still felt they wouldn't be out of the woods until they were safely on the ground in Los Angeles, California. Now, that they were, everyone wore smiles on their faces.

"I have to say it again, Papio, your woman is one smart lady!" Kango said and started laughing.

"Yes, she is. You made this go really smooth on several accounts, Special. It has truly been a privilege working with you," added Steven.

"Thank you, gentlemen. Now we can proceed to fall way back and let things get considerably cooler before any further adventures?"

"That is correct. I think a well deserved vacation is called for," said Kango.

"That's real. Check it; we'll take care of the jet and limo, and you can take care of your mans in the NY, and all will be good," said Papio.

"That's fine. As a matter of fact, that has already been taken care of. When Treez arrives at the house, he'll see a cool million dollars waiting for him, along with the tools we left for him to keep. So I'm sure he will be more than satisfied."

"That means we did a great job, and all is good," said Special just as the driver of the limousine pulled in front of the doors of the Westin Hotel. "Okay, gentlemen, this is our stop. Enjoy your ride down to sunny San Diego and give your cousin Fay our regards."

"Will do. However, I think it would be less of a risk if we left you with the device. No need for us to travel with it any further."

Special nodded her head as Kango gave her the small garage door opener-looking device. After putting the device inside of her purse, she shook each of the Jamaicans' hands and stepped out of the limo, followed by Papio, who grabbed their bags from the driver, then tipped him a hundred-dollar bill before entering into the hotel.

When they made it to their suite, Special stripped off her clothes and went into the bathroom to take a shower. Papio took her silence toward him as a blessing because he wasn't in the mood to beef with her, but he knew it was about to go down, so he figured while she was in the shower, he would take this time to make some calls and get some stuff out of the way.

He called Brandy and checked on her to make sure she was OK. He then promised her that after he left New York, he would come through and spend a few days with her in Oklahoma. This excited her because she wanted him to help her with rearranging one of the rooms in his home for the baby. That put a smile on his face. Being able to be a part of her pregnancy meant a lot to him since he wasn't able to be there with Special when she had his son, so he wanted to make sure that he enjoyed this entire experience with Brandy.

After ending the call with her, he called his money man, Quincy, and let him know that all was good, and he wanted him to get with him so he could give him his cut of the money they had just made. He also gave Quincy instructions on how to deposit the money and let him know that he was done making any moves for a good while.

"So that means the mighty Papio has retired, right, dude?"

"It means I'm taking a well-deserved break. I got all the money I need. I made my goal and some, so it's time to enjoy it. But you know how I rock. I may call you in a day or so out of boredom and tell you to hook me up with a move, so stay ready so you won't have to get ready, white boy!" They both started laughing. After ending the call with Quincy, Papio called his mother and gave her the news about Brandy's pregnancy.

"Oh, mijo, this is so wonderful! My God! Have you told Special? I know she will be very angry and hurt by this news."

"Sí, Mama, she is both. But what could I do? Keep this from her?"

"No, you did the correct thing, mijo. She will get over this because she loves you. I know this for certain. But you will have to be patient with her because this will take some time because she will look at Brandy being pregnant as a betrayal on your part."

"But how, Mama Mia? I mean, she knew I was messing with Brandy, this wasn't something I planned on."

"Sí, but that is how she will look at it. Let her be angry. Do what you can to be nice, and she will get past this. Trust me, mijo."

"If you say so, but you know I'm not one to have a lot of patience."

"This is true. But in this case, you must have the patience because you too love that woman. You love her more than you love Brandy. That's obvious. So you have no choice unless you'd rather be with Brandy than Special. You and I both know that's not truth, right there, sí?"

He smiled into the receiver of his phone and agreed with his mother. "Sí."

"Okay. Now you tell Special that I expect for her and Li'l Pee to be here soon. I'm missing my mijo, so get him to me."

"I'll let her know, Mama Mia. I should be home later this evening or tomorrow afternoon at the latest."

"That is fine. Love you, mijo."

"Love you too, Mama Mia," Papio said as he ended the call.

He then called Mr. Suarez to let him know his business had been handled, and he would meet him in New York when he requested his presence. After confirming everything with Castro, he hung up the phone feeling some kind of way. He couldn't put his finger on it; it just felt strange. He didn't know if it was the fact of him attending the funeral of the man he betrayed, or the thought of the ruse he was pulling over Mr. Suarez. He knew for a fact that if this ever came out, the shit was going to hit the fan big time. That thought sent chills through his entire body.

As he got off the phone, Special came out of the bathroom and into the living room of their suite, looking gorgeous as always in a pair of shorts and one of his wife beaters. She stepped barefoot to the couch and sat down next to him and folded her arms across her chest.

"Oh shit, here we go," he said to himself as he stared at her.

"This shit hurts, Clyde. I mean, it really fucking hurts. I'm the one. I'm the one who has your child, and I should be the *only* one! The thought of you having to be tied to that old bitch for the rest of her life because of her having your child hurts me so deeply that I hate even thinking about that shit."

"Do you want to end what we got, then, Special? I mean, if this fucks with you that much, then I will not fight you on this. You know how I feel about you and Li'l Pee. You two, along with Mama Mia, are my everything."

"See, that's just it. Right now, we're your everything, but in a few short months, we won't be! You will have an addition to your life. Two of them! Brandy and her child will also become your everything, and I can't stand it!"

He stared at her and calmly asked her again. "Do you want to end it, then, Special? Because Brandy is having my child. I'm not trying to be cold with you; just stating how it is and how it's going to be. I love Brandy; never said I didn't. But I don't love her as much as I love you. I am *in love* with you, and that's what the difference is. Brandy having my child will not take away from my love for you or Li'l Pee one bit. Yes, I will love my child by her just as much as I love my son. But that will not ever interfere with what we have. It's you I want to wake up with every single morning, Special. It's you that has my heart. So, it's up to you to decide what you want to do. I'm about to go shower and get dressed. Q. is coming through in a little while to get the ends and take care of them for me. You give Poppa Blue his 10 percent, and I'll take care of Q."

"Yeah, I figured we'd get down like that. That was a nice move we took down, Clyde. I'm going to miss that shit for real."

"Me too, but there comes a time when we got to hold up and look at shit. Like right now, we got way too much in front of us to be still taking all of these risks with shit being so damn hot."

"I know."

He stared at her for a moment and said, "Do you love me?"

"Don't ask me something you already know the answer to, Papio."

"Tell me."

"No."

"Why?"

"Because I'm hurt. You make me feel as if you betrayed me. I don't do betrayal well."

Thinking back to what his mother had told him, he shook his head and said, "I cannot change how you feel, but believe me, I never wanted or tried to betray you in any way. This is just as much of a shock to me as it is to you. I love you, Special, and as long as you stick with me, there is nothing in this world we can't get past together. You're my Bonnie, and I'm your Clyde. Don't you forget that shit."

"Ugh! I'm about to go see Poppa Blue and then hit the Sunset Plaza and tear up that trendy two-mile stretch of stores and eat me an expensive meal at one of those fly-ass restaurants. After spending a big chunk of money on some fly shit at some of those exclusively pricy boutiques, hopefully, I'll feel better."

"If you say so," he said as he pulled off his shirt and began walking toward the bedroom of the suite.

"Clyde?"

He stopped, turned, and faced her. "What up?"

"I love you."

"I know," he said and turned and went into the bedroom with a smile on his face.

She sat there with a goofy grin on her face and shook her head and thought, *No, that mothafucka didn't just say that shit to me and walk away. Ugh! I hate his ass!*

Chapter Fifteen

The last two years had been the best years of Papio's life. For once, everything was going his way, and it looked as if it would continue to go his way. His money was where he always dreamed of it being, and his personal life was fucking great! Special was happy, Brandy was happy, his mother was happy, and he was totally content. He had two adorable children that he loved with every ounce of love his heart possessed. Brandy gave birth to a beautiful baby girl who just turned 2 years old the day before Thanksgiving. Bredeen Mia Ortiz was his princess, and Li'l Pee was his prince. Life was good. After all he endured, from the drugs, robberies, scams, and murders, here he was sitting on the balcony of Special's place in Marina Del Rey two days before Christmas without a care in the world. No debts to worry about, no stress about where his next move was going to come from; no worries.

Yet, he knew that it was way past time for him to make the decision he'd been dreading for a long time now. He wanted to marry Special and make their family complete the right way. But hurting Brandy like that was something he couldn't bring himself to do. Though neither of them was putting any pressure on him, he knew Special well enough to know that it was fucking with her mental every time he chose to fly out to Oklahoma City to spend time with Brandy and Bredeen. The passion she showed him every time he returned from a trip told him that she was extremely insecure about Brandy. Though she portrayed as if it didn't bother her, he knew better.

Brandy, on the other hand, knew her position in his life and would continue to play her part in his life as the mother of his daughter and his side chick. She was content because she knew if she pressed for more, she would lose him, and that was something she feared more than anything else in the world. Papio knew that and had taken advantage of that, but now, he felt it was time to man up and make the right decision.

He sighed and went back inside the condo to speak with Special and share his thoughts about their future. When he entered the bedroom, he smiled when he saw his son sleeping peacefully in his spot. He heard the toilet flush and sat down on the end of the bed and waited for Special to come out of the bathroom. When he heard the shower start running, he smiled and slipped off his boxers and went to join her. What better way to start the morning than some great sex with the woman who owned his heart?

Special was stepping into the shower stall when he entered the bathroom and joined her. Without a word being said from either of them, they began to wash each other, soapy hands running over each of their bodies turning the cleansing from innocent to passionate almost instantaneously. Their mouths met, and tongues quickly entwined. He began to finger her pussy slowly, turning the heat up in the shower several degrees. She reached for his hard dick and slowly began to stroke him. Their oral efforts soon had them ready for what they knew would be some explosive sex. Every time they had sex, it was explosive. There was something about their chemistry that neither could explain. They were a perfect match, and nothing would ever change that.

After they both came groaning and moaning each other's name, they finished by washing each other again and got out of the shower, drying each other off. When they came out of the bathroom, their son was sitting up in their bed rubbing his sleepy eyes.

"I'm hungry, Mama. Can I have cereal?" Li'l Pee asked as he focused on his parents.

"You sure can, my li'l man," Special said as she stepped to him and scooped him off of the bed.

"Don't you have to use the bathroom, Li'l Pee?" asked Papio as he stepped toward the dresser so he could choose some clothes to wear for the day.

"Um-hm," Li'l Pee said as Special set him down so he could use the bathroom. At three and a half years old, Li'l Pee was so smart that he made Papio feel as if he could do no wrong. Proud was an understatement when Papio thought about his son. He loved him to death.

"So, now that we've started this morning off properly, what do you have planned for the day, Clyde?" Special asked as she sat on the end of the bed and began to put lotion on her smooth, caramel skin.

"Brandy and Bredeen's flight arrives around three, so I'm about to head out to my place and get Mama Mia, then come back and pick them up and take them Christmas shopping. You wanna come with us?"

Special frowned and said, "Nah. I'm going to take Li'l Pee over to spend some time with Bernadine and Poppa Blue. It's been a minute since he's seen them, and I know Bernadine wants to give him his Christmas stuff."

Li'l Pee came running out of the bathroom. "I washed my hands, Daddy! Can I have cereal now?"

Laughing, Papio said, "You got it, champ; come on." He scooped his son in his arms and carried him into the kitchen.

After pouring him a healthy size of Froot Loops cereal, Papio returned to the bedroom and said, "It's time we make things right, Special."

"What are you talking about?"

"I know you're not digging everything with me and Brandy. You don't say shit, but I can tell. I'm letting her know today that it would be best if she went on and started living her life; life without me being in it. I will always be there for Bredeen and do my best to coparent with Brandy, but I cannot continue with this back and forth."

Special gave him that smile of hers that drove him crazy and asked, "What are you saying here, Clyde?"

He smiled and said, "I'm saying I love you, and I want you to be my wife." Before she could say a word, he pulled out a small red ring box. "Will you marry me, Special?"

Special stared at the box for a moment, then looked at him with tears in her eyes and said, "Only if it's a monster Oprah diamond in that there box, mister."

Laughing, he handed it to her and said, "Well, open it up, and let's see if we can make Oprah proud."

Special opened the ring box and gasped when she saw the sparkling 17-carat diamond and platinum ring. "Oh! My! God! Damn! Clyde! You did that shit for real! How much did you spend on this Oprah diamond?"

"First off, does this mean you will marry me or what, Bonnie?"

She held the ring out toward him so he could place it on her ring finger. Once it was firmly on her finger, she sighed and let the tears slide down her face as she nodded and said, "Yes yes yes! Yes, I will marry you, baby!" She then gave him a long, tender kiss.

When they were done kissing, he said, "I'll never tell you how much I paid for that there Oprah diamond, Special, but I will say this . . . Kim Kardashian's ring that Kanye gave her ain't got shit on that one. No way I'm gon' let Kanye outdo me. I'm too damn fly for that shit."

"You know I love you, you cocky-ass nigga! Damn, you did that shit!" she yelled as she jumped around the room, staring at her wedding ring, which cost Papio over $15 million. After a few minutes, she calmed down some and said, "Seriously, though, thank you, Clyde. Thank you for stepping up to the plate and being the man I knew you could be. I won't front, I have been battling with myself ever since Bredeen was born. I couldn't bring myself to try to force you to choose between Li'l Pee and me. I would never try to separate you from your daughter. Never. But every single time you went out to visit them, all I could think about was you out there doing family shit, and worse, fucking Brandy."

"I know."

"I never once asked, but I knew, and I could tell it was driving you nuts, so I knew sooner or later, you would decide, and I prayed every single night that when you did make that decision, it would be me that you chose, me and Li'l Pee."

"It's always been you, Special. You own my heart, and Brandy knows that. She knows that no matter what, she will always remain an important woman in my life. Believe me, she earned that spot way before she ever had Bredeen. I will make sure that they are always straight financially, and I will always be there for my princess. The only thing that's changing is I will no longer be fucking Brandy. I'm going to let her go so she can find some happiness in her life. She deserves that."

"For a coldhearted gangsta, you are one sweet man, you know that, Clyde?"

"I wouldn't say that. It's just time for us to move forward. All of us. Me holding Brandy back was selfish, and with all the good fortune we've had, it would be flat-out wrong for me to keep her locked down like that."

"You're right. Don't get me wrong here. You know I'm 100 percent with this decision. But don't you think telling her this right before Christmas is like bad timing?"

"When you are telling someone important in your life that it's over, is there *ever* a good time?"

"I know, huh? Okay, Clyde, do it your way. Let me get dressed, so I can hurry up and go show off this monster rock to Poppa Blue and Bernadine."

"Yeah, you do that. I'll get Li'l Pee and dress him while you get yourself right. Mama Mia wants us all at the house for dinner tomorrow evening. Make sure you tell Poppa Blue and Bernadine that they're invited."

"Will do."

Papio smiled and said, "You do know that that Oprah diamond is twofold, right?"

"What you talking about, Clyde? Twofold?"

"Yeah, twofold. That's your wedding ring *and* your damn Christmas gift. That piece there set a nigga back some serious loochie!"

"Nigga, you got over a hundred million in several accounts overseas. You better stop playing! Shit, your interest alone on your ends can pay for this. You better have me something real fucking fly the day after tomorrow, you pretty-ass nigga," she said with a mock attitude as she stepped into the bathroom.

"What about me? What you gon' get me for Christmas?" he yelled from the bedroom.

"Wait until the day after tomorrow and see!" she yelled back.

Papio was smiling as he went to the dining room to clean up the mess he knew his son made while eating his cereal.

Papio hated how they had to wait outside for Brandy and Bredeen to come out of the airport, but since 9/11, this was how it was with the damn TSA. Mama Mia was just as anxious and excited about seeing her granddaughter as he was. His anxiety about telling Brandy it was over for them was overridden by the happy feelings of seeing his daughter, even though he had just spent two weeks with them for Thanksgiving. He loved his princess, and he couldn't wait to give her a kiss and a tight hug.

Papio checked his watch for what seemed like the fiftieth time in the last twelve minutes as he and his mother stood next to his Aston Martin. Since he knew they still had a few more minutes before Brandy and Bredeen would come out of the airport, he took this time to inform Mama Mia of his decision to marry Special.

When he told her, she smiled knowingly and said, "It took you long enough. I was wondering when you do this, mijo. Brandy is a good woman and a great mother to my granddaughter. I love her so. But she isn't the woman for you for the long ride. Special is. I've always known that. Brandy does too. Her fear is losing what little of you that she does have. So when you tell her this decision, you make sure you let her know that no matter what, she will always remain close to your heart. She knows this, but she will need you to reassure her 'cause she will be heartbroken, mijo."

"I know, Mama Mia, I know. I don't want to hurt her. She doesn't deserve that. But she doesn't deserve being treated the way I've been treating her, either. Me coming spending time with her and Bredeen monthly, acting as if we're this happy family ain't right. I love them both, and there's nothing in the world I will not do for them. But I cannot keep living like this. I thought it was cool, and I could keep it up as long as Special didn't trip out on me, but the longer I thought about it, the more it became clear to me it was time to let Brandy go."

His mother patted his hand and said, "You doing the right thing, mijo. Wrong time but the right thing. You tell Brandy this after Christmas, not before, you hear me?

Bredeen will pick up on any bad vibes, and I don't want my granddaughter to have a bad Christmas, sí?"

"Sí, Mama Mia," he said with a smile on his face as he looked up and saw Brandy coming out of the airport with Bredeen in her arms. He was so focused on Brandy and his daughter that he didn't pay attention to the tall brother carrying their luggage walking beside them.

When they were standing in front of each other, Brandy gave Bredeen to Mama Mia who quickly embraced her grandchild and gave her a tight hug. Brandy smiled at Papio and said, "Hi, Daddy." She hugged him, but it wasn't the type of hug he was accustomed to. Something wasn't right, but he couldn't put it together just yet. Brandy pulled from his embrace and said, "Daddy, I have someone I'd like for you to meet." She turned to her left and said, "Devin, this is Bredeen's father, Papio Ortiz. Papio, this is Devin Johnson."

Papio noticed how nervous Brandy was all of a sudden, and it hit him like a slap in the face. Brandy and this nigga were a couple! *Now ain't that a bitch!* he said to himself. He reached out his hand and shook hands with Devin and said, "Pleased to meet you, Devin. Welcome to sunny California."

"The pleasure's all mine, Papio. I've heard a lot of good things about you."

Papio sized Devin up. About six foot two or six foot three; bald fade; broad shoulders; looked to be in good shape . . . *Yeah, the perfect square type o' nigga Brandy needs in her life,* he said to himself. "That's what's up. Come on; let's get this luggage in the car so we can head on out to the house."

"Um, excuse me, Daddy; can I speak with you for a moment?" Brandy asked as she pulled him to the side and said, "I reserved us a hotel because I didn't know how you would take this. I didn't know any other way to break this to you, Daddy, so I thought by bringing Devin out here with us, it would be the easiest way. I've been seeing him for the last six months. We've never had sex, though, Daddy. He's never been to your home. I told you I would never disrespect you, and I kept my word. But it's time for me to move forward with my life. I can't keep up with how things have been going with us, Daddy. I love you and—"

Papio smiled as he put his index finger of his right hand to Brandy's trembling lips. "Stop. It's all good, Brandy; trust me, baby, it's all good."

"Are you sure?"

"Brandy, I couldn't be surer of anything else in this world. All I want is for you to be happy. You do know I got to check this cat's temperature to make sure he's worthy enough to be around the two most important females in my life in Oklahoma City. I love you too much to do anything less, you feel me?"

Brandy sighed, and a single tear dropped from her eyes as she smiled and whispered, "Thank you, Daddy."

He kissed her on her cheek and said, "You're welcome." He then bent toward her ear so only she could hear him and then said, "That pussy still and always will belong to me, you hear me?"

She nodded her head, smiled, and looked directly into his light brown eyes and answered him honestly. "Always, Daddy, always."

"*That's* what's up. Now, come on. You guys aren't staying in any damn hotel. Let's get your stuff loaded up. We got some Christmas shopping to do!" He then grabbed his daughter out of his mother's arms and gave her a kiss and a hug and said, "Welcome to California, princess!" His daughter smiled brightly at him and kissed him. *Yeah, looks like my luck is definitely holding up,* he thought and smiled as he gave Bredeen back to Mama Mia and helped Devin load their luggage in the car.

Chapter Sixteen

Mama Mia went all out for their Christmas Eve meal. Everything from a fried turkey, stuffing, macaroni and cheese, green beans, yams, to some of her most exquisite Mexican dishes. This was her first Christmas Eve dinner she ever cooked for anyone other than herself and Papio, and she wanted to make sure she did a good job, which she definitely did. She had a packed house, and she was excited about that. Poppa Blue and his wife Bernadine, Quentin and his girlfriend, Special and Papio, her grand-children, plus Brandy and her new friend were all in attendance, and she hoped and prayed everyone would be impressed with her cooking.

While Mama Mia was busy fussing around in the kitchen making sure everything was in order, everyone else was in the living room having a drink and chatting, getting to know one another. Special was busy flaunting her monster diamond engagement ring. Though Brandy was now involved with Devin, she couldn't help but feel a pang of jealousy when she saw that huge rock on Special's wedding finger. She cut her eyes at Papio, who quickly dropped his eyes.

No wonder you accepted Devin so easily. You are one smooth customer, Daddy, she said to herself. She smiled and congratulated them both on their engagement, and there was a sigh of relief all around the room.

Quentin, being the one never to think before he spoke, blurted, "Well, that's a relief! I just knew it was about to get *L.A. Basketball Wives* up in this bitch!" Everyone started laughing.

"You are the smartest dumb white boy I've ever met in my life, Q.," Papio said playfully.

"Hey, that's my guy you're insulting there, Papio," said Daun, the latest edition of Quentin's trophy arm pieces.

"Yeah? He may be your guy, but he's still a dummy!" Everyone laughed some more.

"Call me what you like, but thanks to this dummy, your money has been making more than you've ever dreamed of, dude. All of the hard work we've put in over the years has finally paid off. Now, look at us, living the good life. Not bad for a dumb white guy from Sherman Oaks!"

"Q., you really are funny. You know I need to holla at you myself. I need some of those good investments too," said Special.

"Hey, what am I over here, chopped liver?" asked Poppa Blue with a smile on his face.

"Stop it, you know I was just clowning, you old fart. I'd never trade you for anything in this world."

"Yeah, right!"

"Mmm, so, what do you do exactly, Quentin?" asked Devin.

"I'm an investor as well as an attorney at one of the most prestigious law firms in Los Angeles."

"What type of law do you practice?"

"Some civil law but mostly real estate law is what has earned me my vast fortune. Some think the market is down out here in California, but it's doing quite well, actually," Quentin said as he sipped some of his martini.

"And your investing, I'm sure that adds quite a lot to your fortune, especially if you're as good as you said you are."

"I hate to toot my own horn here but . . . TOOT! I am the shit!" Everyone burst into laughter at Quentin's silliness.

"So, what do you do out there in Oklahoma City, Devin?" Quentin asked as he took another sip of his drink.

"I work for the Federal Bureau of Investigations."

Quentin damn near spit out his drink and quickly put his hand over his mouth before speaking. After dabbing his mouth with a napkin, he stared at Devin and said, "Are you saying you're an FBI agent?"

"Yes."

There were a few minutes of uncomfortable silence before Papio started smiling and asked, "What division of the FBI do you work for, Devin?"

"Bank Robbery Division. I was previously in the Fraud department but recently transferred to my new post."

With his poker face on, Papio smoothly said, "I see. So, tell me, how did you meet Brandy?"

Way to change the subject real smooth-like, Papio, Poppa Blue said to himself as he continued to listen to their conversation while at the same time trying to see if this Devin guy was on some other shit. *A fucking FBI agent. Damn, Brandy, you fucked up,* he thought.

Devin smiled at Brandy and didn't catch the enraged look on her face as he said, "My job sent me to the FCI where Brandy works to interview some well-known bank robbers to see if we could get some help for the rash of bank robberies we had been having across the country."

"Yeah, I heard about that on CNN, but it's like all of a sudden, those guys just stopped robbing banks and credit unions and called it quits," said Quentin.

"Indeed, it seems that way. But criminals of that nature never quit. These guys are smart, though, so one never knows."

"You were saying how you met Brandy?" Papio asked again as he shot Brandy a withering look.

"Yes, after I concluded my interviews, Brandy was assigned to me to show me around the prison. We had lunch, and from there, just started to get to know each other better."

"I see."

"Okay, guys, you can do all that chitchatting. I'm about to check and see if Mama Mia needs any help in the kitchen. Special, why don't you go upstairs and check on the kids. I'm sure they're about ready to get up so they can eat," Bernadine said as she got to her feet.

Special was stunned and getting pissed off, but she knew better than to say anything. This was for Papio to handle. "Okay, come on, Daun; help me with the kids."

Daun stood and said, "Sure, Special," and followed Special out of the room.

After the ladies left the room except for Brandy, Devin said, "I hope there isn't a problem, Papio. I've been a perfect gentleman with Brandy, and I will continue to be good to her for as long as she will let me."

"Nah, there's no problem, Devin. I mean, it's kind of strange that Brandy would get involved with an FBI agent, but as long as you keep her happy, it's all good."

"Why is it strange for her to be involved with an FBI agent? It's not like she's a criminal, is she?" Devin joked.

Papio stared at him and in a serious tone said, "Nah, she's no criminal, but I am."

Now it was Poppa Blue's turn almost to spit out some of the drink he was drinking. He quickly wiped his mouth and warned Papio. "Now, Papio there's no need to—"

Papio raised his hand to stop Poppa Blue and said, "Hold up, Poppa Blue. This man is about to be spending a lot of time around my daughter and her mother. He needs to know the real about me and my get down. I think I said that wrong, so let me clear it up for you, Devin."

"Please do."

"I assume Brandy here didn't tell you how we met?"

"No. Actually, she speaks very little of you other than you're a great father and supporter of her and Bredeen."

"I see." *Good point for your ass, Brandy,* he said to himself. He then continued, "Well, we met while I was serving a thirty-year sentence for distribution of cocaine."

"Thirty years? Wow."

Laughing, Papio said, "Yeah, that's about how I felt when the judge slammed me with all of that damn time. Luckily, I had some superior lawyers, and after serving only three years of the thirty they gave me, I was released. Exonerated of all charges. The day I received my immediate release, Brandy and I met and clicked, and the rest is history."

"You're one very lucky man, Papio. Most men who get that type of time normally never get that type of action with the courts."

"True. But most men don't have the type of lawyers I do. Anyway, that's what I meant when I said I'm the criminal of the family. Since my release, I've been able to take the money I saved during my drug-dealing days and invest wisely, thanks to my man, Q., here, so now, I'm sitting lovely and no longer have to participate in that illegal life."

"Like I said, you're one lucky man."

"I make my own luck, Devin."

"And how's that?"

"By making sure every single move I make is calculated to a tee. I made a mistake once; only once. I never make the same mistake twice."

"Lucky *and* smart. Very rare."

"Yeah, I'm one of a kind, huh, Brandy?"

"Um, yes, Daddy," she answered sheepishly. She stood and grabbed Devin's hand and said, "Could you guys excuse us for a few minutes? I need to speak with Devin alone."

"No problem. Me and the fellas are going to sit here and drink some more before Mama Mia calls us to eat. Take your time," Papio said as he relaxed back in his seat and watched as Brandy led Devin out of the living room and up to the guest room. Once they were gone, Papio downed the rest of his drink and said, "Fuck."

"That is *exactly* the same thing I was about to say, dude," said Quentin.

Poppa Blue lit up a cigar and sighed. "You handled that very well, Papio. For a minute there, I thought you were about to get goofy with it."

"Nah, I had to check his temp and see what he was really on. Being real with him lets him know I ain't hiding shit. I'm an ex-dope boy, plain and simple."

"You think he has gotten at Brandy for any other reason?" asked Quentin.

Papio shrugged and said, "Too early to tell."

"I can tell you one thing, though," said Poppa Blue.

"What's that, OG?"

"Brandy sure as hell didn't know what he was an FBI agent."

"She had to! I mean, you heard the dude say he went to the job to interview bank robbers. What, you don't think they told her who he was when he went to the prison? I highly doubt that shit," said Quentin.

"You obviously didn't pay attention to her when he said what he did for a living. Her reaction was pissed off with a capitol P. I'm willing to bet a nice chunk of change that right now she is giving that Feebie the blues up there."

"She better, because she already knows what she's going to get from me after this evening is over," Papio said as he went to the bar and poured himself a drink. "Bringing a mothafucking federal agent to my mothafucking house. That bitch has lost her fucking mind!"

Poppa Blue was wise with the bet he was willing to make because just as soon as Brandy had the door closed behind her and Devin inside of the guest room, she hissed, "You're a fucking FBI agent, Devin? Really? *Six months!* We've been dating for *six* months, and the entire time you've been lying to me. How fucking dare you!"

"Not true, Brandy. I didn't lie to you. I told you I worked for the federal government as an investigator, and that was why I was at the prison to get profile makeup on some of the bank robbers incarcerated there. Now, I never told you I was an actual agent, true, but I never lied to you."

Brandy gave him a look of total disgust and said, "I cannot believe you did this to me. You let me bring you out here to meet Papio, and then you spring this shit on me. Ugh! My God, do you know what you have done?"

"No, I don't. What's wrong? Papio doesn't seem to mind what I do for a living, so why are you making such a big fuss about this? I mean, your daughter's father was rather straight forward about his life, past as well as present. So why are you acting this way, Brandy?"

"Because you betrayed me. You had me thinking one thing, and you aren't the person I thought you were. I can never be involved with an FBI agent!"

"And why is that? Are you a criminal like your baby's daddy said he was?" he asked sarcastically.

She smiled and said, "I think you need to pack your bags, Devin. Hopefully, there will be a room available for you until you're able to catch a flight back to the city."

"Come on, Brandy, don't be this way. I didn't mean to insult you or lie to you. If Papio isn't troubled by what I do, why are you?"

"You *lied* to me. I don't know you, Devin. You're not the man I thought you were. Now, please, after dinner, get your stuff ready, so I can call your ass a cab so you can get the fuck out of my baby daddy's house!" She turned and stormed out of the guest room and bumped right into Special. They stared at each other for a moment, and then they both gave each other a nod and smiled.

"You go, girl," said Special as she turned and followed Brandy downstairs so they could enjoy their Christmas Eve dinner.

Chapter Seventeen

Even though there was some serious tension at the dinner table between Brandy and Devin, everyone still enjoyed the delicious meal Mama Mia prepared for them. Once everyone had their fill of her scrumptious meal, they went into the living room and let the kids open up some of their gifts. Papio, Brandy, and Special all watched with pride as Bredeen and Li'l Pee tore open their gifts and started playing with all of the toys their parents bought them. This was the first Christmas holiday that Papio was able to spend with both of his children, and he liked how he was feeling. One thing was for certain . . . He loved his family, and no matter what, he wanted to feel this way every year.

"Okay, since my shorties are having a ball, I guess it's time to spread some more love around this place," Papio said as he stepped around Bredeen and Li'l Pee and grabbed two small boxes from under the Christmas tree. He sat back down and gave Brandy a rectangular-shaped box and said, "Merry Christmas, Brandy." He then gave the smaller square box to Mama Mia and said, "Merry Christmas, Mama." He watched with pride as the women quickly opened their gifts.

Brandy put her right hand across her heart and gasped loudly. "Thank you, Daddy! This is gorgeous," she said as she stared in awe at the 7.5-carat diamond and platinum necklace.

"Here, let me put it on you, Brandy." After he closed the clasp on the necklace, everyone in the room was smiling. The sparking diamond necklace was the shit.

"Okay, you do know I am like real jealous over here, Clyde," Special said with a smile on her face.

"You know you need to quit that, girl, especially with that crazy-sized rock you sporting on your finger," Bernadine said, laughing.

It was Mama Mia's turn to gasp loudly as she opened her box and saw a pair of 3-carat diamond hoop earrings. She quickly pulled them out of the box and put them through her earlobes. "How do they look, mijo?" she asked with a smile on her face.

"Beautiful, Mama Mia; just as beautiful as you are. Merry Christmas," Papio said sincerely.

All of the women inside of the room gave the typical response of *aaaaw!*

"Okay, my turn," Poppa Blue said as he pulled out his wallet and gave Special three tickets.

She accepted the tickets and screamed! "YES! Thank you for this, you old fart! Thank you so much!" she screamed as she stared at the three floor seats to the Lakers/Heat game.

"You're welcome, Special. I know you're a diehard like I am, and I thought this would be the perfect gift for you and Papio here. I would love to join you two, but my loving wife here has me committed to spending Christmas Day with my in-laws, so be thinking of me when you're sitting next to Jack at the game tomorrow. Hopefully, you can bring us some luck since Kobe won't be playing this year."

"I know, that sucks, but it don't matter. You know we bleed purple and gold!" Special said, smiling.

"Damn, Poppa Blue, how in the heck did you pull off some floor seats next to Jack for the Christmas Day game?" asked Papio.

Poppa Blue grinned as he chomped down on his cigar and said, "Never question Poppa Blue's get down, young man. When you've been down as long as I have in this city, there's nothing I can't get my hands on."

"I know that's right, OG. Okay, Special, I know you thought I left you out. You love staying in a nigga's pocket, but you know I have no problem keeping that smile on your face. You ready for your gift, baby?"

"You damn skippy!" she said, grinning like a little girl.

Papio went inside his pocket and pulled out a small piece of wrapping paper and gave it to her. "Here you go, Bonnie. I hope you like it."

Special stared at the piece of wrapping paper for a moment. She could tell something was inside of it, but for the life of her, she didn't have a clue about what it was. She quickly opened it and screamed, "NO! Where? Where is it, Clyde?"

Papio started laughing, and so did Quentin. "Why don't you go to the window and take a look outside, Special," Quentin said as he smiled.

Special jumped from her seat and ran to the picture window and screamed! "I got the brand-new Mercedes Benz SUV! Yes!" She then ran outside, and everyone got up and followed her and watched as she used the key that Papio had given her to disarm the alarm to her new Benz SUV. She jumped inside and blew the horn as she started it up and quickly pulled out of the driveway, disappearing down the street.

"Now, where in the hell is that crazy woman going?" Poppa Blue said, smiling and shaking his head.

"Stop that, Poppa. Let the girl enjoy herself," Bernadine scolded.

Before anyone could say anything else, a cab pulled in front of the house, and they all watched in silence as Devin came out of the house carrying his bags, looking dejected. He stopped in front of Brandy and was about to say something, but before he could speak, she held up her hand and said, "Goodbye, Devin. I hope you have a Merry Christmas." She then turned and went back inside the house.

Laughing, Papio said, "Yeah, bye, Devin. Merry Christmas!"

"That's cold, dude; that's real fucking cold," Quentin said and started laughing with him.

Papio shrugged and said, "It is what it is," and started laughing some more as a pissed-off Devin jumped inside of the cab and left his home. "Now, where the hell did Special go?" Papio asked.

"Beats me, but it's cold out here. I'm going back inside," Poppa Blue said as he led the way back inside of the house so they could enjoy the rest of their evening.

Once they were all back inside, Papio stared at Brandy. He could tell she was sad, and that bothered him. "Check it, Brandy. Let me holla at you for a minute," he said as he led her into the media room.

Before he could say a word, she said, "I'm sorry, Daddy. I didn't know that that prick was an FBI agent. If I had, I would have never started seeing him, and I damn sure wouldn't have invited him out here to your home. You know I know better than that."

"Yeah, I know you better, baby. But why did you dismiss him like that? I thought you were digging him."

"How can I dig a man that doesn't keep it all the way real with me? You may have kept things from me in the name of your business, but to my knowledge, you've never lied to me. I respect that, and I can never respect a man who doesn't keep it real. If I have to be by myself for the rest of my days, then so be it 'cause I will never settle for less."

"One thing for sure . . . You won't be by yourself, baby. You're too damn gorgeous for that shit. But check it, do you think that fool got at you for you, or was he trying to get at you to try to get in my business?"

"I honestly don't know, Daddy. I mean, he never once asked me about you or anything like that. I never even told him your name. I referred to you as my daughter's father whenever I spoke about you. Plus, he's in the Bank Robbery Division, so that shouldn't be any concern of yours, Daddy. You don't rob banks, Daddy." She paused and saw the funny look on Papio's face, then asked, "*Do you?*"

Papio smiled and said, "You know me, baby. I'm a modern-day pirate. I do whatever it takes to get the bread. But don't trip. I'm retired now, Brandy. It's all about being here for my family and making sure those two kids in there get every break in life that I didn't have."

With tears in her eyes, she said, "I'm so proud of you, Daddy. You made it; you really did it."

"Yeah, Brandy, I did it. So, I want you to live, baby. Live your life the way you feel you need to. Don't worry about me being salty at you 'cause I refuse to deny you your happiness. I'm sorry I couldn't be the man you needed me to be."

"Stop that. You are all the man I need you to be. You are a real man in every sense of the word. Now your means of acquiring your money was outrageous, but besides that, you are all man, and I love everything about you. You are caring, considerate, loving, generous, and you tell no lies. I respect you, Daddy, and I will never stop loving you. What you and Special have found is special, so treat her how she deserves to be treated, Daddy, 'K?"

"I will, Brandy. I love her. She completes me and makes me whole. The love I have for her and you are two different types of love. If she wouldn't have come into my life, it wou—"

Brandy put a finger to his lips and stopped him from saying another word. "Shhh, it wasn't meant for us to be, Daddy. I'm okay with that. You gave me Bredeen, so I will forever have a part of you."

Special had tears in her eyes as she eavesdropped on Papio and Brandy's conversation. She couldn't stand it any longer. "Okay, you two. You're really like killing a bitch here. Damn you, Clyde, will you kiss this gorgeous woman? She loves you, fool, give her that; she deserves it." Special was smiling as she saw the shocked expression on both of their faces. "Kiss her, I said!"

Papio bent and gave Brandy a tentative kiss on the lips and stopped.

"Nah, scary-ass nigga, I mean a *real* kiss!"

Brandy smiled and said, "I've never seen Daddy so nervous! Look at him, Special. He's scared to death. Come here, Daddy. I think I know what she wants to see," Brandy said as she pulled his head down to her face and gave him a fierce and passionate kiss that lasted nearly an entire minute. When she pulled away from him, she said, "I'm gonna sure miss that tongue, Daddy."

"You don't have to miss it, Brandy. That is, if you don't mind making love to a married man when he comes to your town to see you and Bredeen."

Now it was Brandy's turn to have the shocked expression on her face. "You mean you would actually give your husband *permission* to be with me whenever he comes to Oklahoma City, Special?"

Special shrugged and said, "Girl, it would only be a matter of time before he did that shit anyway. It's not like I don't know y'all fuck every time he goes out there."

"True. But you're not married."

"So what? Plus, it's kinda hot knowing you turn him on the way you do."

Laughing, Brandy said, "Now, how do you know how I turn him on?"

Special laughed and pointed toward Papio's manhood and said, "Girl, would you look at all that hard dick right there. That ain't 'cause of me. It's because of you!"

"Come on, Special, you're killing a nigga here," Papio said, totally embarrassed.

Special stared at Papio, the man she was going to marry, the man she loved more than any other male on this earth next to her son and Poppa Blue, and said, "I want you happy, Clyde. I want to keep you happy for the rest of your life. If permitting you to be with Brandy when you go OT, then that's nothing to me. You can never be with any other woman unless we're together. So, Brandy is the exception to the rule. You with that?"

He smiled and used one of her favorite expressions. "You damn skippy!"

They all started laughing.

"Wait a minute; did you say he couldn't be with any other women unless he was with 'me'?"

"Yep. That's one of the things we have in common, Brandy. We both love pussy." Special noticed the excited look on Brandy's face and smiled. "Remember Inga, Clyde?"

Already knowing where Special was headed, Papio could barely contain the excitement in his voice when he answered her. "Yep."

"I think Brandy here is a little curious. What you think?"

Papio smiled at Brandy and said, "I don't know, Bonnie. That may be a bit too much for her."

Brandy blushed a crimson red and said in a hushed tone, "Oh my God, I am soooo wet right now."

"Shit," said Papio as he watched Special step to Brandy and put her hands on the sides of her face and gently kissed her once, then twice. The third time, she slid her tongue inside of Brandy's mouth. When Papio heard Brandy deeply moan as she kissed Special back, he looked toward the ceiling and said, "Thank you, Father. Thank you for blessing me with this!"

The women stopped kissing and started laughing.

"Are you ready for your Christmas gift, Clyde?" asked Special.

"Baby, you don't have to give me shit. What you just gave me just made this Christmas the best one of my fucking life!"

Special stared at Brandy for a moment and then said, "Ya think?" She then pulled the thin spaghetti straps off of Brandy's dress and exposed both of her firm breasts and lowered her mouth to her right nipple and began sucking on it tenderly. Brandy moaned loudly and placed her hand on the back of Special's head as she sucked away on her breast. Special stopped, and Brandy pouted. "Go get rid of our guests while Brandy and I get warmed up for you, Clyde. *We're* your gift for Christmas, and I promise you, this Christmas will be one you will never forget." She then went back to sucking Brandy's titties, and Papio darted out of the room to tell his guests that they had to get the hell out of his house!

Chapter Eighteen

Papio was lying flat on his back with Brandy on his left and Special on his right. Each one of the gorgeous women had their hands on top of each side of his chest. He had a huge smile on his face as he stared at the ceiling and thought back to the glorious night he had with the ladies. It all seemed so surreal to him now as he closed his eyes and relived the greatest sexual night in his entire life.

After Papio had hurried everyone out of his house and assisted Mama Mia with the kids, getting them bathed and prepared for bed, he rushed to his bedroom to see something he never thought he would ever see. Special was on her back while Brandy had her face stuck between her legs, sucking on Special's clit, giving her extreme pleasure. Special's moans and groans drove him mad with lust as he quickly undressed and got onto the bed with the ladies.

Brandy stopped her oral ministrations on Special's pussy, raised her head, and smiled at him and shyly said, "Hi, Daddy. You wanna help me out here?" She smiled as she dipped her head back between Special's legs and resumed eating her pussy.

Papio sighed as he turned and began kissing Special passionately. Special was in heaven as she kissed him back hard and reached for his very hard dick and began to stroke him slowly. The combination of their kiss and Brandy's wicked tongue on her pussy drove her to a very intense orgasm that made her stop kissing Papio and scream out loud.

"Oh! Fuck! My! God! I'm! Coming!"

Papio put his mouth onto her to quiet her. He didn't need for his mother to think something was wrong, so he kept kissing her until her orgasm subsided. He then got up from the bed and went and turned on the MP3 he had connected to his surround sound system in the room and put his playlist on shuffle so all of his favorite slow jams could be their theme music for the rest of the night. "All The Places" by Aaron Hall started playing as he eased back onto the bed and rejoined the ladies.

Brandy came from between Special's legs and smiled at him as she gave him a tender kiss so he could taste and savor Special's pussy juices. The smell of Special's pussy on Brandy's lips acted as an aphrodisiac to him and made him feel as if he were ready to explode and come all over both of them.

Sensing his excitement, Brandy quickly removed her mouth from his lips and slid down to his dick. She then began to give him some head, and his mind was reeling as she sucked him so good. He closed his eyes and didn't pay attention as Special slid down and joined Brandy by sucking on his balls. She had his legs raised in the air, and for a moment, he thought this couldn't be happening to him—no way! Special and Brandy both sucking him up at the same time! No-fucking-way! But it *was* happening, and he *loved* this shit! When he felt one of the women's tongue slide on in and all around his asshole, he came so hard that his come spurted salvo after salvo inside of Brandy's mouth, and she eagerly swallowed every last drop. Special, who was the one who had brought him over the top with her oral ass play, slid her mouth back to his balls and began to suck them again. He moaned and couldn't believe that after coming so hard, he was *still* maintaining a monster erection. An erection that Brandy was ready to feel inside of her hot pussy. She quickly stopped sucking his dick and mounted that nice size of man-meat and began to ride him slowly.

Special had moved away from his balls just in time because Brandy was so hungry for the dick that she hadn't paid her any attention. Special got to her feet and stood to the side and watched them fuck. This scene was so hot that as she stood there, she started rubbing and playing with her clit to get off as she watched her man, her fiancé, get served some good pussy by the mother of his daughter. Papio's eyes were closed, and he held onto Brandy's hips and pulled her down hard on his dick trying to get as deep as he could every time she came down on him.

When Special started coming, she moaned loudly, which made him open his eyes and stare at her. Realizing what she was doing, he removed one of his hands and reached out to her. She came and climbed on top of his face so he could suck her soaking wet pussy and finish bringing her off. She was now facing Brandy as she continued to ride Papio's dick, and they began kissing each other. All of a sudden, all three of them starting coming at the same time, and their screams would have been heard all throughout the house had the music not been playing. The last thing Papio remembered before he fell asleep was R. Kelly's song from his *Black Panties* CD. "Crazy Sex" was playing, and he smiled because he felt that song was so fitting at that time.

Now as he lay there with both of his women on each side of him, all he wanted to do was stay in bed all day long. He never wanted this to end. But he knew he would have to get up soon and go downstairs so he could watch his children open up the rest of their gifts since Mama Mia refused to let them open everything last night. The gifts they already opened were from the family, and the gifts they would open this morning would be from Santa Claus. That was Mama Mia being in the Christmas spirit, and he knew better than to miss that. He turned and looked at the clock and saw that it was almost seven in the morning, so he figured he had a few more minutes before he heard his mother screaming his name, telling them to come downstairs.

Might as well take advantage of this time, he thought with a smile on his face as he turned and kissed Brandy on the lips and then did the same to Special. He then turned and rolled on top of Special and started rubbing on her pussy as he kissed her. Sleepily, she responded by sticking her tongue inside of his mouth and opening her legs for him so he could stick his early-morning hard dick slowly inside of her.

She moaned, and Brandy opened her eyes and smiled sleepily at both of them and said, "You want more, Daddy?"

Papio nodded his head as he stroked deeply inside of Special. "Yeah, baby, Daddy wants more."

Brandy slid over next to Special and started sucking her titties and said, "Then more Daddy shall have."

Mama Mia, Brandy, Special, and Papio all watched with smiles on their faces as Bredeen and Li'l Pee happily opened the gifts that Santa had brought them. Papio never knew how good it would feel to see everyone he held dear to his heart so happy.

"Now, this is what life is all about. My money is right, my family is good, and everyone is happy. That's what's up," he said to himself as he sat down next to Li'l Pee and started showing him how to operate one of the remote control cars Santa had brought him. He was interrupted by his cell phone ringing. When he saw the 876 area code number on the caller ID, he wondered who would be calling him from Jamaica.

"Hello."

"Papio, what is it like out there, mon?" asked Kingo.

"Everything is good, Old Dread. What's good with you?"

"I'm good, mon, real good."

"I know that's right. Merry Christmas, Dread."

"Come on, mon; you know me don't celebrate no pagan holiday like that. Me just happy to be alive and well on this day."

"Yeah, I hear you. Wait! Hold the fuck up! I didn't push no damn five to accept this call!"

"No, you didn't, did you, mon?" Kingo said, laughing.

"Aw, hell nah! Don't you tell me you're out?"

"You saw me number on your screen, didn't you? Yes, my friend. Kingo no longer locked in a cage, I'm a free mon, and let me tell you, it feels real good to be home."

"When the hell did you get out? And why in the fuck didn't you call me sooner, Dread?"

"I've been home a few days. I've been at the immigration spot in Mississippi for six months, but they finally got my papers correct and let me go the other day. I'm sitting here at me castle with my wife, brother, and other family enjoying the free life here in Jamaica, mon."

"Now, *that's* the business! Dread, you just really made my day even better."

"Good. Now, when can yu find some time to fly out here and spend some time with me? We have lots to talk about, mon."

"Man, I wish I could hop a bird out there today. But you know that's not happening. I got the family here, and we're all enjoying the holiday."

"Why don't you bring Special out here and bring in the New Year with me, mon? We can bring in the New Year the right way as free men."

"I'm with that. Hold on for a sec and let me get at Special about it." Papio pulled the phone away from his face and asked, "Special. Did you have anything planned for us for the New Year, Bonnie?"

Shaking her head no, she said, "Uh-uh. Just thought we'd all go out somewhere and have a good time. Why?"

"My man Kingo got out, and he's invited us to Jamaica to bring in the New Year. You with that?"

She smiled at him and said what he knew she would. "You damn skippy! Nothing more fly than sitting on a fly beach chilling for the New Year."

"That's what it is then." He then gave Brandy a look and said, "What about you, baby? You wanna fly out there with us? I'm sure Mama Mia won't have a problem keeping Bredeen for us."

Brandy looked toward Mama Mia with a questioning look. When Mama Mia gave her a nod yes, she smiled and said, "I'd love to, Daddy."

Papio nodded, then put the phone back to his ear and told Kingo, "Yeah, we're coming. I'll get at my mans and have him set up some flight arrangements and get back with you and let you know when to expect us, Dread."

"No-fucking-way, mon. This here trip is all on Kingo. I'll take care of everything and get back with you. How about in a day or so? That way, we can talk business for a day or so and get things in order, then party like never before Jamaican style, mon."

"That's cool. But check it, Brandy is going to come too. Is that cool with you?"

"Brandy? As in Mrs. Wickerson Brandy?"

"Yep," Papio said with a smile knowing what his mans was thinking.

"Whoa, mon, you got it like that now? You got both your women on the same page like that, mon?"

Laughing, Papio stared at both Special and Brandy and said, "Yep. As a matter of fact, Dread, I do. So make sure you have a big-ass bed for us!"

"Oh, my mon, ya never cease to impress Kingo! I think Fay will be disappointed when she hears you are not only bringing Special, but also your other woman as well."

"It's all good. You know me. I'll find some time to take care of that too!"

Laughing, Kingo said, "I bet you would do that too. You come to Jamaica to tear down the romping shop, huh, mon? I love it! Okay, I'll give you a call in a day or so to let you know when you can fly out to me, mon. Later."

"That's what's up. Later, Dread," Papio said as he ended the call. *Damn, Kingo coming home makes things even better. Life is so fucking good. My luck seems to be getting stronger and stronger,* he thought . . . but little did he know his luck was about to make a turn . . . for the worse.

Since Poppa Blue gave Special three tickets for the Lakers/Heat game, Special asked Brandy if she would like to join them to watch the Lakers try to upset the two-time NBA champions without Kobe Bryant. Brandy, being a diehard Oklahoma City Thunder fan and an avid Miami Heat hater, quickly agreed to join them. After making sure the kids were fed and settled, the three left the house to head downtown to the Staples Center to watch the Lakers/Heat Christmas Day game.

The game was much better than anyone expected. Nick Young, one of the new Lakers, was giving his all, and the Lakers were holding their own against the reigning champs. Papio sat in the middle of his ladies with Special on his right and Brandy on his left, seated right next to the famous actor Jack Nicholson, who never missed a Lakers game, and who was known as the number one fan of the Lakers. Brandy was so excited to be sitting next to Jack she could barely contain herself. Every time Jack fussed at a referee for a call he disagreed with, she fussed right along with him. Which, after the third time doing this, Jack turned toward her, smiled, and gave her a high five. It was the highlight of the day as far as Brandy was concerned.

In Miami, Castro, Mr. Suarez's right-hand man, was sitting in his room watching his Miami Heat slug it out with the Los Angeles Lakers. Castro was glad that Mr. Suarez was busy entertaining his son and his family in the family room enjoying Christmas dinner. This gave him the time alone he needed to watch his beloved Miami Heat. Right after LeBron James made a spectacular slam dunk over Pau Gasol, the cameraman zoomed in on Jack Nicholson, who was extremely pissed that the referee didn't make a charging call against LeBron. Castro's eyes grew wide as he stared at the television. He wasn't focused on Jack Nicholson; he was staring at Papio and the woman that was sitting to his right. He couldn't believe what he was seeing, but he was so happy. He quickly hit the DVR and replayed the dunk of LeBron again so he could pause the TV at the right time. When he paused it, he confirmed what he thought he saw originally. That slimy prick Papio finally fucked up. He lied! He didn't murder that bitch Special like he told Mr. Suarez he did.

Castro started laughing loudly because he just received the best Christmas gift ever. And it was all thanks to Papio. Because he knew without a doubt once he told Mr. Suarez of Papio's betrayal, he would then be given the green light to end that no-good prick, Papio's life. He smiled as he stared at Papio on the TV screen sitting next to Special and said, "It's going to be a pleasure to kill the two of you snake mothafuckers."

Chapter Nineteen

Papio, Special, and Brandy arrived at Sangster International Airport in Montego Bay, Jamaica, at 1:25 p.m. Each somewhat tired from the long layover they had in Dallas-Ft. Worth but still excited to be in the beautiful country of Jamaica. Once they made it through customs, they quickly stepped outside in the hot, tropical heat to be greeted by Kingo, Steven, Brad, Macho, Kango, Fay, a female who looked like a younger version of Fay, and two more Jamaican men that Papio had never seen before but who he quickly realized were Kingo's personal security.

The security men stepped up to them and took their luggage and loaded them into the back of a brand-new Challenger Jeep SRT 8. Kingo was standing in front of a brand-new AC Zagato 378 GT. The new Corvette was shining brightly under the hot Jamaican sun. After hugging each other in a manly fashion, Kingo smiled and directed each of Papio's females toward one of the four other expensive sports cars that were lined up in front of them. Kango and Special got inside of a new SRT Viper. Kango quickly let the top back down once they were inside. Steven led Brandy to a new Hennessey Corvette and dropped the top as well. Brad and Macho got into the new Dodge Challenger, while Fay and the other female got inside of the Ferrari 458. The small convoy of expensive vehicles then sped away from the airport led by Kingo's security in the Challenger Jeep.

Once they were on their way, Kingo explained to Papio that it would be a forty-five- or fifty-minute drive from Montego Bay to his home in Negril. "Even with such speed at our disposal, it will take us some time because of the hillside and cliffs we must navigate to my hometown. So, tell me, mon, how you do that with Special and Ms. Wickerson? Truly amazing, even for your standards, mon."

Laughing, Papio said, "Actually, Dread, I can't even front on this one. It wasn't my doing. It was all on Special. She made it happen, and I was just as shocked as you were when it went down. She gave me the best Christmas present ever. She has accepted me and Brandy, as well as agreed to marry me."

"Whoa, mon, stop that. You lie! Marrying you and letting you keep taking Brandy to the rompin' shop? No way!" roared Kingo.

"For real. She knows whenever I go visit Bandy and my daughter, odds were high I would still fuck, so she said we might as well fuck her together, so whenever I go out there without her, she won't be ripping because Brandy not only belongs to me, she belongs to both of us."

"Both of you? You mean—"

Papio cut him off with, "Yep, that's *exactly* what I mean. We are in a three-way relationship, and let me tell you, Dread, though that shit may be every man's fantasy, that shit is really fucking draining! Shit, they kept taking turns sucking me up on the flight over here! When I was too tired to play, they went into the bathroom and took each other for a trip on the Mile High Club. They're both insatiable! I got to hurry my ass up and separate them before they give me a damn heart attack!"

Shaking his head, Kingo said, "Only you, mon, only you could ever do something like that."

"Yeah, you right! So tell me, how does it feel to be free and back in your homeland?"

"It feels fantastic, mon. I mean, the love I have here is wonderful, and to be back with me family makes my heart beat stronger than ever."

"The love, huh? You got so much love with the security guys around? I see they're packing some serious heat. What's up with that?"

"Longtime war with certain Rude Boys out this way, mon. One can never take anything or anyone for granted in Jamaica. That's the quickest way to lose head. Kingo remains safe at all times. My family is strong in these parts, but my enemies are no slouch. Since I've come home, there have been several threats toward me safety."

"If it's that serious, then why did you come back? I mean, you could have gotten your visa and stayed in the U.S. since your wife is American."

"First, me had to take care of some things here at home. I plan to take Melkely back to her home so she can spend time with her family. I had to move her here for the time being while I finished the time because I didn't want to take the chance of something happening to my queen while I was away. Now that I'm back, we are planning on making a move to America before Valentine's Day."

"Where?"

"Miami. That's where Melkely is from, and that's where a lot of my business is based at. I have plenty Rude Boys and Haitians on my team out there. It's time to get things back how it's supposed to be, mon."

"What are you talking about, Dread? You're home, and you're obviously not hurting for anything. What you got cooking?"

"I'm the top-rankin' Rude Boy, Kingo, mon. I rule the empire me built from the ground up. My brother has done well making sure the finances remained intact, but it's up to me to rule. He's not built for that kind of power."

"So, the moves he's made with the device was to make sure things were good with you on the money tip?"

"Right, mon."

"What kind of moves will you be making when you hit Miami? Please don't say more banks because that heat is too intense, even though it's been over two years since the last get down. The Feds are still trying their best to figure out how all them banks and credit unions got hit. We all agreed it was time to let that device remain dormant."

"This is true. That device was the best thing that could ever happen for us. But, no, mon, Kingo king of the drug trade as well. Parts of Miami belongs to me. But since I've been gone, people have took it upon themselves to try to rid Kingo of his territory. I let them in, and they got greedy, and now they don't want to relinquish what was given to them. So my Rude Boys out there are waiting for Kingo so we can take back what belongs to us."

"So, you're telling me your ass is fresh out of doing damn near twenty years, and you're about to jump right back into the mix and most likely go to war with some heavyweight types to reclaim your throne?"

"Yeah, mon, that's exactly what Kingo is telling you."

"Damn."

Laughing, Kingo said, "No worries, mon. Kingo got everything under control. But I'm going to need your help some."

"For what?"

"The Cubans."

"Come on, Dread, don't tell me you got beef with Mr. Suarez?"

Kingo raised his right hand from the steering wheel and turned it side to side and said, "Some, but nothing that cannot be dealt with in the right way if we talk. The thing is, he has sent word that he doesn't have any

interest in talking to Kingo, and that's not good. Me Rude
Boys are waiting and watching, so Kingo need to have
this meeting. I will not nor cannot lose face with me Rude
Boys. That would show weakness and then bring new
trouble my way as well as to me family."

"So you want me to get at Mr. Suarez to see if he will
have a sit-down with you?"

"Yeah, mon; that's it, and that's all."

"What if I get at him, and he still refuses to meet with
you? Then what?"

Kingo slowed the turbo-charged sports car down as he
made a hard right turn headed up a cliff and gave Papio a
one-word answer.

"Murder."

"Damn," Papio said as he let his head rest on the back
of his seat.

Mr. Suarez sat back in his seat and watched for what
seemed like the thousandth time Papio sitting in between
Special and some other good-looking black woman. It
had been over three days, and he still refused to believe
that Papio would have betrayed him this way. He sighed
and called Castro into his office so he could give him the
orders that he knew Castro had been dying to hear. He
respected Papio, and he didn't want to end his existence,
but he had no other choice for his betrayal and disrespect
to his longtime friend, Chief Hightower; he had no other
choice but to order his death. There was no way he could
overlook this. When Castro entered Mr. Suarez's office,
he wore a grin as he stood and waited for his boss to
speak.

"I don't want anything extravagant done with this,
Castro. Neat, clean, smooth. Find him and kill him."

"Sí, Mr. Suarez. And the woman?"

"The same. She shouldn't be too hard to find now that they are obviously an item. Handle them both as quickly as possible, Castro, so we can put this behind us."

"Sí."

As Mr. Suarez stared at the TV screen, he said, "I find it almost unbelievable that he had the gall to betray me this way. After all of the chances I've given him, it amazes me that he dared to try to play me this way."

"It isn't a shock to me, sir. I mean, I feel he crossed us in several ways, but you have that generous streak in you because you're a fair man, so you continued to find a reason to spare that cockroach's measly, pitiful life. And for your generosity, he gives you more betrayal. It's going to be my pleasure to blow his brains out. As you ordered . . . neat, smooth, and clean, sir."

"Leave for Los Angeles immediately and get this done. I need you here with me. Those Jamaicans are also aggravating me, so it's time to prepare for that situation as well."

"Sí. The security here is secure, and there will be no way these gates can be penetrated. Our security system is one of the best in the world. Yet, I will still send for more men to roam the grounds while I'm away."

"Thank you, Castro," Mr. Suarez said as he turned in his seat at his desk and stared out the window wondering how things would play out with those crazy Jamaicans. Problems. *There are always problems,* he thought as he continued to stare out the window.

Papio couldn't believe the size of Kingo's home. It was not a mansion. It was indeed a fucking castle! It was huge and looked like something out of a medieval movie. What amazed him, even more, was the security that roamed the grounds with some heavy artillery. It looked like AK-74s and AR-15s strapped around their shoulders as the long dreads were posted almost everywhere you looked.

"Damn, my mans Kingo don't be bullshitting," Papio said to himself as he got out of the car and followed Kingo inside of the house along with everyone else. Once they were inside, he was hit with the strong smell of some serious ganja, and he started laughing. "Damn, Kingo your people don't be playing with that smoke, huh?"

"You know we Jamaicans don't play when it comes to the ganja, mon. You wanna smoke some?"

Papio held up his hands and said, "Maybe later. Right now, I need to go get showered and fresh, you know?"

Before Kingo could respond, his wife stepped into the room and said, "I finally get to meet the one and only Papio. Welcome to Negril. Welcome to my home," she said as she stepped to him and kissed him on his cheek and a tight hug.

Papio smiled at Melkely and said, "It's a pleasure, Melkely. I feel as if I've known you for years after all of the stories I had to listen to when me and Kingo were cellies. Let me introduce you to my girls." Papio turned toward Special and Brandy and introduced them to Kingo's wife.

Melkely laughed and said, "Excuse my laughter, but you did just say 'your girls,' correct?"

Before Papio could respond, Special answered for him. "Yes, you're correct. We're his girls. We both have children by him, and we both are madly in love with him. We belong to him as he belongs to us. Right, Brandy?"

Brandy smiled brightly and said, "Right!"

Kingo roared with laughter, and everyone in the room joined in. Everyone, that is, except for Fay. Kingo noticed this and teased his first cousin. "Don't be a hater, Fay. Maybe Special here will let you have some more of Papio before he goes back to America."

Fay wore a pout on her face as she stared at Papio and thought about the marvelous sex they had with each other when they were in San Diego a few years ago. She shook her head and smiled at Special. But when she spoke, she spoke in patois, so no one could understand them but the family. She said, "That gorgeous American woman won't share him with me, mon. Especially since she shares him with the other gorgeous American woman. He has too much going on for old women like me. But you know I never give up! I may have a trip with him to the rompin' shop before he leaves me country!"

Everyone who understood her started laughing. Fay's daughter shook her head and said in English, "You need to quit teasing, Mother. He is a handsome man who obviously can handle more than one woman." She stared at Special and stated boldly, "Do you think he can handle more than two at one time?"

Special smiled as she stared at the pretty, dark-skinned woman and said, "Keily, isn't it?"

"Yes."

"You're a pretty little thang, and if my man cannot hang, then I'm quite sure I can take up any slack. So let's play that by ear, huh? Right now, though, I'm sorta tired and need a shower to get myself together. On top of that, I'm hungry!"

"Okay, mon, let me people show you to your room. I gave you a large room on the third floor since it will be three of you. When you are good and fresh, come back down, and we will eat, drink, and enjoy the rest of this glorious afternoon," said Kingo.

"That's what I needed to hear," Special said as she followed one of the long-dreaded security men as he led the way toward a grand spiral staircase.

Papio's cell phone started ringing, and when he checked the number and saw that it was a Miami area code, he stopped and called Kingo, pointed to his cell, and said, "It's the Cubans."

"Aaah, now is a good time to talk, mon."

Papio told Special and Brandy he would be up in a few; he had to take this call. Upon hearing him say Cubans, Special's radar went up, and she gave him a quizzical look. "Just asking for a favor for Kingo, Bonnie. We're good."

She gave him a nod and continued up the stairs.

Papio stepped next to Kingo just as he answered the phone. "What's up, Castro? What do your flunky ass want now?"

Castro smiled into the receiver as he got into the backseat of the SUV that was taking him to Miami International for his flight to Los Angeles. "I just wanted to give you a heads-up since I'm a fair man who loves a challenge."

"What the fuck are you talking about, clown? I don't have time for games, chump; spit it out."

Laughing, Castro said, "I sure hope you have this much spunk when I get ready to blow your brains out, you filthy piece of shit. I've been given the green light to come and take your life, Papio. So get ready. I'm on my way."

"Get the fuck outta here. Let me speak to Mr. Suarez, you bitch," Papio said, thinking that Castro was shooting the shit as they always did when they spoke to each other.

"No more speaking to Mr. Suarez, bitch. Your time of doing that is over. For your betrayal, you have been given a death sentence, and I'm the man who is going to serve you that sentence. So stay ready. As I said, I'm on my way, bitch. Oh, and make sure you tell your bitch, Special, she's getting it too since your ass was unable to handle your business when given a chance."

Papio stood there with the phone to his ear stunned and realized that somehow, he had fucked up. Fucked up majorly.

Castro loved the silence and savored it for a full minute before speaking. "I know you're wondering how we found out that you betrayed Mr. Suarez, so let me put you up on that before I go. I have a flight to LAX I'm hurrying to catch. When you go to the Lakers game, it isn't always wise to have the best seats in the house, you fucking dummy! See you soon, bitch. Stay ready because I'm on my way!" Castro said, laughing as he hung up the phone.

Papio stood there with his phone in his hand, and for the first time since he knew him, Kingo saw fear on his young friend's face. "What's good, mon? You look like you got bad news. Talk to Kingo."

"It's all bad, Kingo. All bad. Looks like we both are going to have to go to war."

"With the Cubans?"

"Yep."

"Fuck 'em, mon. War it is then."

"Yeah, fuck 'em," Papio said as he realized that his luck had finally changed.

For the worse.

Fuck!

Chapter Twenty

Papio tried his best to have a good time with Kingo and his family, but he couldn't shake the feeling that everything he had worked so hard to achieve was about to be snatched from him. He didn't fear death because that's life; we all live to die one day. But he did fear not being able to watch his children grow up. He feared leaving his children without a father. He feared for Special and Brandy, as well as his mother. Never in his life would he want anything to happen to any of his loved ones because of the moves he chose to make. His mind was everywhere, and Kingo saw that he was stressed and kept giving him a reassuring nod every time their eyes met. Once everyone had consumed enough liquor and weed, Papio, Special, and Brandy called it a night and went to their room for some serious sexing. Even the great sex he had with the two beautiful women couldn't take his mind off of what lay ahead of him.

He knew he had to make sure that everything was in order in case of his demise. He slid out of the bed while Brandy and Special were sleeping soundly and grabbed his cell phone and called Quentin. He quickly explained to Quentin what was about to go down and made all of the necessary arrangements so that if something did happen to him, Brandy, Mama Mia, and his children would be secure financially. With that done, he went back to bed and tried to get some sleep, but sleep eluded him because the fight inside of him refused to give up.

"Okay, you got everything straight with Q., now you got to come up with a way to get rid of Mr. Suarez. The only way to do that is to murder that fat fuck. But, damn, that is one hard-ass task," he said to himself as he stared at the ceiling.

Special sleepily opened her eyes and saw that Papio was awake and watched him for a few minutes without him knowing it. Something was wrong. She could see it in his eyes, she thought, as she sat up and pointed toward the bathroom and whispered, "Follow me, Clyde." She then eased out of bed and led the way to the bathroom. She turned on the shower and stepped into the hot water and waited for Papio to join her. Once he was inside of the shower stall with her, she gave him a hug and a kiss.

"Talk to me, Clyde. Something is up. You haven't been the same since after we first got here. Even when we were freaking, I could sense your mind was somewhere else. What's wrong, baby?"

He stared at her for a moment and sighed. He knew he couldn't keep this shit from Special, but there was no way he would tell Brandy. She wasn't built for what lay ahead because his mind was made up; he wasn't going down without one hell of a fight. If that fat Cuban fuck thought he was going to lie down, he didn't know how Papio got down, and that was going to be a fatal mistake on his part, he thought as he stared at the woman he hoped to marry real soon. "Check it, Bonnie; we fucked up. I got a call yesterday from Castro, Mr. Suarez's number one flunky. He has been given the green light to lay us down. They know you're alive."

Her eyes grew wide as she asked, "How?"

He shrugged his shoulders and said, "The bitch said some shit about when I go to a Lakers game, it isn't wise to have the best seats in the house."

"Shit. That means they must have seen us sitting next to Jack at the fucking game. Now, what kinda fucked-up luck is that?"

"I know. But it is what it is."

"So, how are we going to move, Clyde? We can't sit back and wait for them to move on us."

"I know. We have two options. One, we shake the spot and find somewhere to live and watch our asses and pray we can shake that fat fuck. And when I say we, that means *all* of us. Me, you, Mama Mia, Brandy, and the kids."

"And two?"

He stared at her as the water continued to spray over them and then said, "We take that bitch to war and get his ass before he gets us."

Special smiled at her man because she had those same thoughts going through her head. "I'm not much for living my life on the run from some Cuban fuck who thinks he's the 2k Scarface. He has the money and the power to track us down eventually."

"Exactly."

"And I don't like playing defense."

"Me neither."

"We got money and some power of our own at our disposal."

"True."

"Let's take it to that bitch, Clyde. Let's take it to him as hard as we can and kill that mothafucka and whoever rides with him."

He kissed her hard for a full minute, then pulled from her and said, "That is what I was hoping you would say. But before we move like that, we have to secure Mama Mia, Brandy, and the kids. I don't want to send Brandy back to Oklahoma because they know about my spot out there."

"What about the house in Dallas?"

"You know that spot is janky to me, Bonnie. I got hit twice in that bitch, and I am not trying to press my luck."

"You may have got hit twice, but you survived both attempts on your life there, so stop tripping. That is a spot they will never think to look for you or the family."

"True. But I'd still rather put them somewhere else."

"We can move them to my place in Hancock Park until everything is everything. Mama Mia and Brandy can take care of the kids together and be safe. No one knows about that place but Poppa Blue, you, and me. Bernadine doesn't even know about it. The security is top flight, and the neighborhood is gated. They'll be fine there."

He nodded his head and said, "I like that. Okay, in the morning, we get at Poppa Blue and have him go scoop Mama Mia and the kids and get them situated at your place."

Shaking her head, she said, "Nah, Clyde, we get at him now. He needs to move them as soon as possible. You don't know if they have someone on the house already."

"You're right. That bitch Castro did say he was getting ready to catch a flight to LAX. I thought he was wolfing, but he may have been serious. Fuck, I should have already gotten at you with this. Come on; we got some calls to make."

They got out of the shower, and both slipped on some clothes real quick and quietly left the room and went downstairs to the living room, both with their cells in their hands. While Special called Poppa Blue and woke him so she could explain what she needed, Papio called Mama Mia and woke her.

When she answered the phone, he said, "I want you to wake up, Mama, and listen very carefully to what I'm about to tell you, sí?"

"Sí, mijo. Is something wrong?"

"Sí, something is very wrong, but I don't want you to worry about it. I need for you to take care of my kids.

Poppa Blue is going to be there within the next hour or so, and I need you to pack your stuff and the kids' stuff and go with him. He's going to move you and the kids to Special's house down in Los Angeles. You are to stay there with the kids until Brandy comes and joins you there. Mama, this is very important. I cannot explain everything to you, but I need you to understand that I have some serious issues with some men that may try to hurt you and the children once they see they cannot find me. So, it's crucial that you stay there with Brandy and the kids until I tell you otherwise. Do you understand what I'm saying?"

"Sí, I do. But what about you, mijo? Are you going to be all right?"

"You know me, Mama. I'm going to take care of everything so I can get you right back to your home, so you can play with your grandkids and take care of your flowerbeds and stuff."

"Bah. I know you are trying not to scare me, mijo, but I will do as you tell me. I can call you and check on you?"

"Sí. But when and if you need to leave the house, I need you to call Poppa Blue. He will make sure everything you and Brandy need for the kids and each other will be taken care of."

"Okay, mijo. Let me get to packing. Call me as soon as you can, sí?"

"Sí. Brandy will be there with you the day after tomorrow. We will spend New Year's Eve here as planned; then she will fly back to L.A. I love you, Mama Mia."

"I love you also, mijo. Please be careful."

"Always, Mama," he said as he ended the call and stared at Special as she was speaking to Poppa Blue.

"Running ain't what either of us wants to do, Poppa Blue. Right now, we don't have a fucking clue about how we're going to move. Our priority is getting Mama Mia and the kids secure. Once you handle that, then we will plan from there. We're safe out this way, and Kingo will keep us that way. So we're going to stay out here until we decide on how we gon' move on those Cuban mothafuckas."

"That makes sense. Damn, I feel like a fucking jerk for giving you those tickets."

"Shut up, old fart, and get your old ass moving. I need you to get Li'l Pee, Bredeen, and Mama Mia like now. You know damn well no one could have predicted no shit like this happening."

"Special, as soon as you called me and told me about this shit, I was already dressed and walking out the fucking door. I'm already on the freeway headed to Riverside."

She smiled into the receiver of the phone and said, "Not bad for an old man."

"I'm a vet at this gangsta stuff, youngin, and don't you ever forget that shit."

"How can I? You trained me."

"That's right, I did. I gave you all the game you needed to make it in this cold world. Now, I'm about to lay some more on you and your man. To kill that Cuban, you are going to have to find his weaknesses."

"I know that. The thing is, how will we be able to find out what his weaknesses are?"

"When I first got word a few years back that they were looking for you, I done some checking on him, and I think I have a few aces up my sleeve that can come in handy for this shit. He has a son who is married and lives in Orlando. A square son that wants nothing whatsoever to do with his father's lifestyle. We may have to snatch him and use him as some leverage against the Cuban."

"We? There is no way I'm letting you get anywhere near this shit, Poppa Blue. I—"

"Shut the fuck up, Special! I promised your mother that no matter what, I would always take care of you, and I will go to my grave keeping that promise. So shut up and listen."

Tears slid down her face as she thought about her mom and understood more than ever that Poppa Blue was not only a friend and business associate, he was her father—the only father she'd ever known.

"Like I was saying, that could give us some leverage, but leverage is only going to buy us time. We need to find a way to kill that fucker. And that's what's going to be the most difficult. He rarely leaves his estate, and that place sits on thirty acres and has a security system out of this world."

"And from what Papio said, he has at least ten men around the house at all times."

"If there's a will, there's a way. You go on and get some rest. We'll piece this shit together and make it happen one way or the other."

"We don't have any other choice, Poppa Blue," Special said seriously.

"I know, baby girl, I know. One thing for certain is an added plus. Papio's ties to that Jamaican may be what can help us end this shit. He is a powerful dread for real and not to be taken lightly. What makes him a true blessing is he has a strong presence in Miami."

"How the hell do you know so much about Kingo?"

"Special, Special, haven't you realized that when you move, I check everything around you inside and out to make sure you're good? When you told me about going to Jamaica to see this Kingo, I did my thang and checked into him with some of my people, and I found out everything I needed to know about his ass.

"Fucking right, I am. But, baby, believe this . . . Just as I'm good, your man's friend is strong. He may be our only way of ending this shit. I'm sure Papio knows this already because that youngster is sharp as a tack. You did good by falling for him. He's a good man."

Special smiled and glanced at Papio as he stood at the bar pouring himself a drink. "You fucking right he is. Okay, we're about to lay it back down. Text me when you have Mama Mia and the kids secure at my place."

"Will do."

"Bye," Special said as she ended the call. She went and joined Papio at the bar and told him what Poppa Blue said.

"I was already thinking along those lines."

She nodded and said, "Poppa Blue said you were sharp as a tack and figured you were already on top of that."

"No doubt. When I told Kingo about this shit, he said 'Fuck 'em. War it is.' See, he has a lightweight beef with the Cubans already. Mr. Suarez has refused to meet with him so they can come to some common ground about shit out there in the MIA. Time is of the essence with this, so Kingo has to address this situation. Now that he sees the Cubans are a threat to me, he is ready for war. I swear I love that old dread, Special."

Kingo started laughing and said, "And me swear me loves you too, mon. But tell me why you no sleep. You in my home totally safe. That bloodclaat Cuban will never come harm you here in my homeland. Go. Go back to bed with your women, mon. We talk business tomorrow. Tomorrow, we end the year the right way. Then, the New Year starts, and we do war and make everything right. Ya hear me, mon?"

Papio smiled at his friend and said, "Yeah, I hear you, Dread. I hear ya."

"Go then, mon," Kingo said, smiling at them as Papio grabbed Special by the hand and led her back to their bedroom, both feeling somewhat better than they did when they first came down those stairs.

Chapter Twenty-one

"You did what!" screamed Mr. Suarez. "That was not only arrogant of you, Castro, but that was also extremely stupid! You cannot give a man like Papio any advance warning when threatening his life. Not only have you taken away the advantage we had over him, but you have also now given him an edge against us."

"Sir, I highly doubt if Papio can ever have an edge against us. He knows he cannot win, so if anything, all he will do is run for his life. And that is obviously what he is doing because no one is at his home. He's moved his mother away in fear for her life. The coward can run, but he cannot hide. I will find him, sir; my word to you, Mr. Suarez."

"You don't understand, Castro, and I am very disappointed in you. You should have known better than calling him, telling him you were coming to take his life. A man who feels he is backed in a corner will come out like a cat trapped, clawing with all that he has. What if Papio decided to go to the authorities? Did you think about that?"

"And tell them what, sir? That we are planning on killing him? I highly doubt that. He no longer knows anything about any of our business, so he has nothing to tell them."

"This is true. But you still have put him in an advantageous position over us. He can become the aggressor if he chooses to now because of your cocky behavior. I don't

like that. I want you back here ASAP. Now, Castro, do
you hear me? Catch the first plane back here."

"I need just a few more days to check with some of
our contacts out this way, sir. Give me forty-eight more
hours, please."

"No. Get back here no later than tonight. I have this
business with those nappy-headed Jamaicans to deal
with, and I need you here. We'll get back to Papio later,"
Mr. Suarez said and hung up the phone. He wondered
if sending Castro after Papio would come back and
haunt him. He then grabbed the phone and called his
son in Orlando. When his son answered, Mr. Suarez
told him, "Benito, I have been having some issues with
some unsavory characters, and I may need you to move
your family here to my estate until this situation can be
resolved. How soon can you get out here?"

"You know I have nothing to do with your business,
Father. I am not about to take my kids out of school and
bring them to your home. I will not scare them that way,
nor will I let your business affairs effect my life. I have a
job and work that is very important."

"Don't be a fool here, Benito. My enemies are your enemies, no matter how straight forward a life you choose to
live. I wouldn't be able to live with myself if something
happened to you, your wife, or my grandchildren because
of my affairs. Please, reconsider and stay with me for a
while. You can make it seem as if you're coming to stay
for a vacation."

Laughing, Benito said, "There is no way that Monica
would believe me or go for that, Father. She too has a job
and responsibilities to take care of. Do what you must as
I am sure you will to keep your business away from my
family and me. Happy New Year, Father, and goodbye,"
he said and hung up the phone.

"You stubborn fool!" Mr. Suarez yelled as he hung up the phone and sat back in his seat frustrated. He sighed and thought about things for a few minutes and came to the conclusion that his son and his family should be safe. It was not like any of his enemies knew where he lived. He had kept that a well-guarded secret for many years. So far, no one had ever made an attempt on his son's life, so everything should be fine with Benito and his family.

The stresses he was dealing with because of these Jamaicans was making him panic, and there was no room for any of that. He had to remain focused so he could deal with this situation properly. The Jamaicans had to be dealt with, and just as soon as Castro returned, he was going to make sure that they *were* dealt with . . . in a deadly fashion. He was not comfortable with his current position, nor was he used to feeling as if he were being hunted. *He* was the hunter, and he would do whatever was necessary to capture his prey.

Papio woke up on New Year's Day with a monster hangover. The Black Jamaican Rum wasn't no punk, he thought as he got up and went into the bathroom to a wonderful sight. Special and Brandy were inside of the Jacuzzi tub kissing each other passionately. He smiled at them as he turned and used the bathroom to relieve his early-morning hard-on. When he turned around, he watched in fascination as the women stood in the tub and stepped out and walked toward him. They grabbed him and pulled him into the bedroom where they got onto the bed and made love to him. When they finished, they returned to the bathroom and turned on the hot water to warm the water back up so they could bathe. After bathing, Papio sighed because it was now time for him to tell Brandy that she would be returning to L.A. without them. He knew she would have a lot of questions, and he hoped he would be able to convince her that everything was okay because he didn't want to spook her.

"Thank you for this trip, Daddy. This is the best New Year's I've ever had in my life. I cannot believe how much fun I've had the last few days. Kingo sure knows how to throw a party. Whew, that rum still has me buzzing," said Brandy as she sat at the dresser picking out some underwear.

"I'm glad you had a good time, baby. That's what it's all about, you being happy. Check it, though. You are going to have to fly back to L.A. without me and Special. We got some business that needs to be taken care of out here with Kingo. I don't know how long it will be, so I want you to catch a flight out in the morning, okay?"

"I understand, Daddy. I'll spend the last few days of my vacation with Mama Mia, Bredeen, and Li'l Pee. We can take the kids to Disneyland and Knott's Berry Farm. I'm sure the kids will love that."

Shaking her head no from the other side of the room, Special said, "There's no time to bullshitting here, Clyde. We need to serve her the real, so she can be on point."

Brandy looked at the two of them with a puzzled expression on her face and asked, "Is something wrong, Daddy? Special?"

Seeing that Papio was hesitant, Special said, "Yeah, some shit is real wrong, Brandy." She then told Brandy everything that was going on and gave her the full rundown on what happened with her, Papio, and the Cubans. She left nothing out, and this pissed Papio off because he was not used to having Brandy in his business. But he silently fumed as Special finished telling Brandy that their lives were in danger, and the best thing that they could do was to have her move to Special's home in Hancock Park and stay with Mama Mia and the kids until they figured a way to kill the Cubans to end this entire ordeal.

When she finished, Brandy stared at both of them for a few minutes with a terrified look on her face. "I understand everything you've said, Special, but there is no way I can stay in L.A. I have a job that I am expected to return to. I can't just stay in L.A. for God knows how long until you guys get this business taken care of. I'm not a part of your lives in that way, so no one would come after me or Bredeen." She paused and stared at them some more and then asked, "Would they? Would they harm my daughter, Daddy?"

Papio took a deep breath and spoke the truth because he never lied to Brandy when it came to the gangsta shit. "I honestly don't know, baby. They could be just after Special and me, or they could be on some wicked shit and try to get at me through my family. That's why we have Mama Mia and the kids already moved to Special's place. I would have preferred not to put you in this mix," he said as he shot Special a fierce look, then continued. "But since Special decided to serve it all, I have no choice but to keep it one hundred with you. This shit can get ugly, so before I let that happen, I have to take every precaution to keep you and the kids, as well as my mother, safe. You can't go back to Oklahoma, Brandy. I know you have a job to go to, but that job won't matter at all if you are no longer living. Can't you take a leave of absence or something without raising any eyebrows?"

"I suppose I can, but that doesn't mean you will have everything taken care of promptly, Daddy. I cannot take too long off before my superiors can my ass."

"Girl, fuck that damn job! You know how much money we got. You don't need to worry about your damn job! You got to worry about remaining alive! We got you financially; you already know that. Once this shit is handled, either way, you and the kids, along with Mama Mia, will be taken care of. If we die, you will be good. If you die, you won't be good at all. So dead the square shit, Brandy. That's who you are. I understand that, but that's not who we are. This is the life we chose, and you are a part of that life, whether or not you want to be. This is as real as it can get, and we are going to make sure that we do what needs to be done to bring this shit to a close just as soon as we can."

"Even if it means the two of you dying?" Brandy asked with tears sliding down her face.

This was exactly what Papio was hoping to avoid. The soap opera shit.

"Yeah, even if it means Papio and me dying. Because if we die, then you and Mama Mia and the kids will be safe. As long as we're alive and they're looking for us, my son, your daughter, and Papio's mother's lives are in danger. We aren't going to take any chances on that shit happening, so it's all out on those fucking Cubans, baby. Win or lose, it has to be this way. I, for one, don't give a fuck about my life one bit when it comes to the well-being of my son. You have become just as special to me as Papio in a very short time. We're family now, Brandy, you hear me?"

Nodding her head, she answered her lover in a determined voice. "Yes, I hear you, Special. We all we got. I got it. I will do what needs to be done. I will stay with Mama Mia and the kids at your home for as long as it takes."

"Good. That's my girl. Now, let's go down and have some breakfast and enjoy the rest of this day."

"Have you spoken to Mama Mia since they moved to Special's house, Daddy?"

"Yeah, they're good. The kids have been keeping Mama Mia busy, and she loves the indoor pool Special has, so all is good."

"And no one knows where this house is except for Poppa Blue?"

"Yep."

She sighed and stared at them for a minute and then said, "You need to hurry up and kill those bastards because this shit is scaring the hell out of me."

Special smiled at Papio, and they both said in unison, "You damn skippy!"

Chapter Twenty-two

Papio, Special, and Brandy stood outside of Sangster International Airport and were saying their goodbyes, each of the women was teary-eyed, and Papio was trying his best not to let a tear drop from his eyes because he knew he would hear it from Kingo's ass. This was a sad moment for them all because none of them knew if this would be the last time that they saw one another. Brandy smiled sadly at Papio and said, "You don't have to keep the tough-guy look on your face, Daddy. I know you're feeling just as emotional about all of this as we are. Now gimme a kiss so I can catch this bird back to L.A."

He smiled at Brandy and gave her a tight hug and a tender kiss. He put both of his hands on the sides of her face and stared directly into her soft brown eyes. "I love you, lady. You've helped make my life extremely pleasant. You are a special woman to me, Brandy. If something does go left, never forget that my love for you was really real."

Shaking her head, she said, "You have never lost since we've met, and I don't want you even thinking about losing now. You hear me, Daddy? Win. Win by whatever means you have to. Come back to your family and me. We need you." She turned and faced Special and added, "Both of you. We all we got, remember? I love you both." They grouped together and had a group hug and shared kisses with Brandy. Then Special and Papio took a step back and watched as Brandy grabbed her bags and entered the airport.

Kingo sat in the backseat of his security's SUV and shook his head. "Only Papio could pull something like that one there off, mon. I admire that man deeply."

"Admire my ass, mon! That is one lucky mon. I envy him!" said one of the security guards as they watched as Special and Papio returned to the SUV.

Once they were on their way back to Kingo's home, Kingo said, "I've made the arrangements for the next phase of things, mon. Me Rude Boys in Miami have checked on what you told me, Special, and all that pans out. Mr. Suarez does have a son who is happily married living in Orlando. He's a lawyer and works for a law firm located in downtown Orlando. He handles what you Americans call the civil law. That's when he sues people, correct?"

"Yeah, that's it, Dread. So what's the plan?"

"Keily will fly to Orlando. She has an appointment set up with the attorney Benito Suarez to discuss a lawsuit she wants to file. She will be accompanied by one of me Rude Boys in Orlando. She will get me what I need for the meeting I am setting up with Mr. Suarez."

"I thought you said they refused to meet with you," said Papio.

"He has, but he won't when we speak. Me Rude Boys have made some aggressive moves on several of his main operations in Miami, and right now, he is feeling the pain of losing quite a lot of product. The heat that is coming along with this should have him ready to talk to Kingo."

"Okay, you set up a meeting, then what? You do him right there or what?" Special asked anxiously.

Kingo smiled at her and said, "Be calm, dear. Everything will take its course. Kingo is a top-rankin' Rude Boy, but me a fair mon. I will give him the chance to dictate his own fate. I will come with an agreement to back off of him with war and not take all of me turf back from his fat, grubby hands. I will let him have a substantial area where he can still make money."

"You're doing this if he will back off of us?" asked Papio.

"That right, mon."

"So, if he doesn't agree, then you do him?" Special said hopefully.

"Me God! You are ready for the murder to happen, I see, Special."

"You damn right! That fat fuck has a hit out on me and my man's life, Kingo. He has to fucking go."

"Me understand you, but I have to do this me way, understand?"

She nodded but didn't speak.

"If he agrees to me terms, then we will shake hands on it, and all will be good. He will be shocked to learn that we are friends, and I'm pretty sure when he sees that this can save him money and war, and the attention of the FBI, he will back up."

"And if that cocky bastard doesn't back up?" asked Special.

"Then you get what you want, Special. The murder. We will meet in a place where we both feel is safe, and no attempts can be made on either of our lives and take things from there."

"I have a few questions about this, Dread," said Papio.

"Talk to me, mon."

"First of all, your ass just got outta the Feds. How in the fuck are you going to make it to Miami for this meeting?"

Laughing, Kingo said, "Come on, mon, everyone knows there's no problem getting into your country. That's the easiest thing of all out of this. Next question, mon."

"If he doesn't agree, then when can we move on him to bring this to an end?"

"He doesn't agree, then I will show him a picture of Keily with his son. I will also show him a picture of

Benito's family. His son at the junior high school he attends. His daughter who goes to the nursery school not far from the law firm where he works, and of his wife while she is at home watering their grass in their front yard, clearly showing their home address. I've touched every base here, mon, so it will be up to Mr. Suarez to accept this offer or not. The choice will be his to make. And I will make it quite clear that if we leave that meeting without an agreement to my liking—which can only be that the hit has been called off of both of you, his son and his family will be slaughtered in such a brutal fashion there would be only closed caskets for their funeral."

Special looked at Kingo, astounded at the raw animalism in the man's face. For an instant, his hard brown eyes flashed with the glint of incalculable malice. She knew right then that Kingo wasn't faking or giving weak threats. He was dead serious, and for the first time since Papio had told her about the hit on their lives, she felt pretty damn good that everything would turn out in their favor.

She smiled at Kingo and said, "Okay, I am really feeling this, but I have to say this, Kingo. If he doesn't go for the threats or promises about his son's family, when will you move on him?"

"That will be determined at a later time. First, we see how meeting goes and take it from there."

"I want to be in on it, if and when you have to move on that fat fuck. I want to be one of the people who helps plug that fuck and as many of his men as possible. No one puts a hit out on me and my man without feeling that shit from me up close and personal-like."

Laughing, Kingo said, "If it comes to that, you have my word you will be able to participate in taking the lives of Mr. Suarez and his men."

"Check it; I think we're way ahead of ourselves here, Dread. I feel your get down, and it sounds like a good script for real. But I don't think you're going to get that meeting you want."

"Why not, mon? Me already told you what type of damage me Rude Boys are doing to him at this time."

"True. But Mr. Suarez doesn't do meetings like that. If he were to agree to a meeting with you, it would be nowhere other than his estate. And the security he has there is top of the line; basically impenetrable. I know you ain't trying to have no meeting at his place. That would be suicide, Dread. I've dealt with that Cuban piece of dirt for years, and I know how he moves. If he agrees to meet with you, he will send his number one flunky, Castro. He will then have Castro relay everything to him and then tell you whether he's with it or not. That fool is super cautious and never slips. He rarely leaves his estate. Shit, he fucked me up when he had me meet him in NY to attend that funeral a couple of years ago. Though your plan sounds good, you will have to prepare for that play by Mr. Suarez."

Kingo nodded and thought about what Papio told him for a moment, then said, "If that's the case, then so be it, mon. Either way, he will have to make the decision, and we go from there. Me Rude Boys are on deck ready for whatever I tell them to do. If we have to take it to him, we take it to him real hard, even if it means invading his estate and getting him there. Nothing is impenetrable, mon, not when me men have the will to get the job done. And me Rude Boys have the will of coldhearted Jamaican killers."

"So when will this take place?" asked Special.

"Me Rude Boys have already made their moves, so I'm giving Keily time to get there and get everything with Mr. Suarez's son; then I will make the call and set up the meeting. We'll fly out to Miami when I have heard from Keily, and she has completed the task I've given her."

"We?" Papio and Special asked in unison.

Laughing, Kingo said, "Sure. I know neither of you would want to miss the look on Mr. Suarez's or his number one mon's face when he sees you with me for the meeting. That should be priceless, mon."

Papio thought about that and all of the slick back-and-forth talk he and Castro shared and started to laugh. "You're right. That would be priceless, and I wouldn't miss that meeting for anything in the world."

"Me neither. Plus, while I'm out there, I can get at my mans Scrape. Back when I first heard about the Cubans putting that hit out on me for those Indians, I went to Miami and made some offensive preparations of my own. I have some serious dudes out of Opa-locka that may be of some assistance, if needed."

"Opa-locka, you say? Mmm, that could be a good one for me. That's one of the areas where Mr. Suarez is trying not to lose. Are your men loyal, Special?"

"Actually, it's one man, and, yes. Scrape is very loyal to me. He has a team of some of the most ruthless niggas in Miami. He has already been compensated, and when I call, he will do as I ask him to."

"Good, very good. Okay, that's it, then. Since we have a few days in between, I think we should enjoy some more of this wonderful Jamaican weather and go Jet Ski and have some fun in the sun."

Special smiled and said, "I'm with that. I need to do something to keep my mind off this business."

"Me too. Let's get with it so you can show me what you working with, Old Dread," Papio said and smiled.

Laughing, Kingo shook his head and said, "You still got to try to outdo me, huh, mon? You couldn't do it on the weight pile or the pull-up bar when we were at El Reno, and you won't be able to do it here in me homeland."

"Let's get with it and see, then, Old Dread."

Special laughed and said, "I sure hope Melkely will be joining us, 'cause I am not interested in you two beefing out there in the water trying to outdo each other."

"As a matter of fact, me wife and me cousin Fay *will* be joining us. So we shall have good time," Kingo said and sat back in his seat and smiled. "Life is good, mon; life is really good."

"Life will be even better once we get this shit straight with those fucking Cubans," said Papio.

"You ain't never lied," Special said.

"No worry, mon. We will take care of the Cuban situation and continue to live good and enjoy life. That's me promise. Me and my family look at you two as family, and we will never let family down. Trust that, mon."

Papio smiled as he squeezed Special's hand and said, "I do trust you, Kingo. I wouldn't be putting my life or Special's life in your hands if I didn't. I know one thing, though. If this meeting doesn't go as planned, then it's a must we take them down, Kingo. However it has to get down, we will have to end the existence of Mr. Suarez and his main man."

"If it comes to that, mon, then end their existence we shall do," Kingo said seriously.

Special noticed the return of that animalistic look in Kingo's eyes and felt confident that everything was going to be okay. That man is a cold-blooded killer. There's no faking in his ass at all. She smiled at that thought and felt relieved because it looked as if everything would work out in their favor. God, she prayed, it would.

Chapter Twenty-three

Poppa Blue couldn't believe what he heard from Special. When she finished breaking down everything to him about Kingo's plan, he was amazed at their good fortune. But he was still worried about this working out as they all hoped it would, so he voiced his concerns.

"This sounds solid, and with the power Kingo possesses, it should go right. But we need to put some contingency plans in place. You know how I get down, Special. I want to be prepared for any surprises."

"I feel that, but there is no running, Poppa Blue. Either we handle this shit this way, or we war and take that fuck out. Papio and I aren't going to live our lives running."

Poppa Blue sighed. "Stubborn as ever, I see. You need to be prepared to do whatever it takes to keep you breathing, and if that means leaving the U.S., then so be it. Do not tell me what you and Papio *don't* want to do, dammit. There's more to this that just you two and what you two want. You have two kids involved in this. Papio's mother is involved in this. Shit, Brandy is even thrown into the equation now. This has more to do with the survival of everyone, not just you and your man, Special," Poppa Blue said in a stern voice.

Properly scolded, Special said, "I understand that. Why can't you understand that we'd rather be dead than not to be able to live right and be there with the kids? Moving somewhere and living with the fear of a hit being made on us any day won't be living right, Poppa Blue. It will be living scared, and we can't live like that. I'd rather be dead. I know if something does happen to me or Papio, the kids will be taken care of because you, Bernadine, Mama Mia, and Brandy will be there to make sure that Li'l Pee and Bredeen will be properly taken care of. That gives me solace and peace of mind, so I can focus on dealing with this shit aggressively. That's the only way this shit can be handled, for real."

"Parts of what you just said are true, but you forgot one major fact in all that."

"What's that?"

"If something happens to you, then there will only be Bernadine, Mama Mia, and Brandy to help take care of the kids because you gots to know damn well that if those fucking Cubans harm one hair on that head of yours, I am going all-out until I breathe no more. Vengeance will be mine if they hurt you, Special."

She sighed and said, "I didn't forget that, Poppa Blue. You know I already know how you rock. That's another reason why we have to do it this way. No contingency shit. It is what it is. If Kingo's move works, then it's all good. If not, then we go after the Cubans with all that we got, plus with what Kingo has. That should be enough to get the job done. If not, then shit is going to get real bloody. 'Cause if we go down, we're going down swinging. If the Cubans choose to play it the hard way, then that's how we'll play it. I promise you this . . . If the Cubans choose war when everything is all said and done, Mr. Suarez will say they don't play fair because we're going to do everything—I mean *everything* it takes to win this shit."

"I hear you. So when does this shit get started?"

"Kingo's men have been tearing up every operation that the Cubans have going on in Miami. He's waiting for his men to let him know when they can set up a meeting with Mr. Suarez. Once he gets that set, we're flying out to Miami for the sit-down."

"Please tell me you and Papio aren't going to attend that damn meeting, Special."

Laughing, she said, "Now what fun would it not be if we didn't come face-to-face with the men who want to take our lives from us? Come on, old fart, you know it as well as we do . . . That's the gangsta way to deal with this shit. The Cubans underestimated us. They didn't think we'd have this type of muscle behind us. The looks on their faces when we enter the room will be worth any risks involved."

Poppa Blue sighed and said, "I give up. Whatever you say, Special. Hit me when you get to Miami and keep me informed on everything."

She smiled into the receiver of the phone and said, "Will do, you old fart. Love you, Poppa Blue."

"I love you too, Special."

"Those fucking Jamaicans have hit another warehouse of our drugs, Castro! This shit has to stop! We cannot keep losing the coca like this. This has gotten too expensive, and at this rate, we won't be able to supply our people on the East or West Coasts."

"I understand, sir. I have ordered two more teams out to get right at the Jamaicans. If they want war, then we will give it to them. I've made a call for more men to be flown in from Cuba. I have ears on the streets, and I will soon learn more of the whereabouts of the Jamaicans and where they store their drugs. We won't burn down their places; instead, we will take their drugs from them to make up for what has been destroyed in our warehouses."

Shaking his head, Mr. Suarez said, "No, that is not the way to handle this. It will continue to get too hot in the city, and we will continue to lose money. The Jamaicans are strong and have shown they are prepared for war. To handle this correctly, we need intelligence and patience. Not brute force. We will have to take the head before we can conquer their body."

"To get at their leader, we would have to get men into Jamaica, and from what I have been told, that would be impossible. He lives on the outskirts of Negril in a fucking humongous castle set high in the cliffs."

"You don't seem to understand, so let me explain so you can see this clearly. We agree to have a meeting with this Kingo. During this meeting, we find some common ground even if we have to relinquish some real estate."

"That would make us look real weak, sir; I don't think that would be a wise move. We show those dreaded niggers some weakness, they will pounce on us again sooner or later."

"No weakness when trying to maintain peace. War is expensive, and neither of us is in this business to lose money . . . only to make a lot of it. That's the common denominator in all of this, Castro. Money. Never forget that."

"I understand, sir."

"As I was saying, we have this meeting, and we find some common ground. We will in no way make the negotiations seem as if we are giving up anything easily. We do that, then they will see through what we're doing."

Castro smiled at his boss as he realized what Mr. Suarez was telling him.

"I can tell by the smile on your face you realize where I'm headed with this, huh?"

Castro nodded and said, "Sí."

"Good. Once the meeting has concluded, and everyone is in agreement that we will stop the war, then we will let things fall into place and start recouping from our losses, meanwhile gathering all of the intelligence needed on that Kingo character. When the time is right, then we will strike."

"And take the head from the body," Castro said, smiling.

"Exactly. We must outthink our adversary to conquer them. So, set up a meeting. You, of course, will be speaking on my behalf because there is no way I will give this cockroach the honor of being in my presence, even for a meeting as important as this."

"I understand, sir."

"If there is anything you feel the need to discuss with me during this meeting, then call me, and we will proceed from there."

"I'll get right on top of this, sir. I have one more question."

"What is it, Castro?"

"Will you let me resume the hunt for Papio and Special after this meeting with the Jamaicans?"

Mr. Suarez sat back in his seat in thought for a moment and then said, "I don't know why, but for some reason, the respect I have for Papio and the courage he possesses has given me pause. I know for a fact that he has crossed me several times, though I don't have the proof. He killed Lee in Oklahoma. He has stolen from us to obtain his freedom. He betrayed me and my longtime friend Chief Hightower by not taking Special's life. That, alone, should make me want him dead. Not to speak of the money he accepted from the chief and me for the debt I squashed. There is absolutely no reason why I should stop you from hunting him down and murdering him and Special as painfully as possible.

"But, but I am ordering you to stand down on Papio. Though he has betrayed me in almost every way, I respect him. I admire his courage and how he stands on his principles. He didn't kill Special just to betray me. He didn't do it because he is in love with her. So, in essence, he risked his life and all that he has gained, all in the name of love. Call me an old fool or an overly romantic from the old school, but I understand and respect the decisions he's made. So we're going to deal with this Jamaican situation; then we will get with Papio and give him another chance to do right by paying handsomely. That should help with some of the money we've lost with this damn Jamaican business."

Castro frowned and couldn't believe what his boss was telling him. "Can't we punish him physically without killing him? I mean, to make sure he understands that he cannot keep crossing us, sir?"

"You really dislike that man, don't you, Castro?"

"Sí, sir, I really do."

Mr. Suarez sighed and said, "I'll tell you what. Let's get the meeting with the Jamaicans put to bed; then, we will sit back down and revisit this conversation. For now, I need you focused on the tasks at hand."

"Understood, sir. I will let you know once everything is arranged."

"You do that, Castro."

"Everything is set, mon. Keily has successfully handled the business, and we now have in our possession some pictures that will show Mr. Suarez that he is not as untouchable as he thinks he is," Kingo said as he sipped some Black Rum as he waited for his wife to let them know their dinner was ready.

"When do we leave for Miami?" asked Special.

"In the morning. Since I have to go an around about way for my reentry to America, I will be leaving later on tonight. By the time you arrive in Miami, me Rude Boys will be waiting to pick you up and take you to the Ritz Carlton, where the meeting will take place."

"So, you've already spoken to the Cubans?" asked Papio with a serious look on his face.

Kingo nodded. "Yeah, mon. Me Rude Boy number one in Miami has spoken with Castro, and like you said, *mon,* Castro will be representing Mr. Suarez at the meeting."

"Told you."

With a shrug of his broad shoulders, Kingo said, "No problem, mon. Our point will be made. Me confident that everything will go the way we want it to. And if not, then we war. If we war, we take it to them hard and do brutal things to them and their entire operation. From what I've been told, they want to come to a peaceful conclusion, so thangs should go smoothly."

"All right then, it is what it is. I know one thing. I will be paying real close attention to this Castro fool. If he even looks like he is on the bullshit, then I'm blowing his brains out right then and there," Special said menacingly.

Laughing, Kingo said, "Whoa, there, gangsta, calm down. Trust me; there will be no shooting inside of the Ritz Carlton. What you tinking? You trying to get us all locked up in the bing?"

"Shit, that's what silencers are for. I can get at Scrape and have him hook us up with some. So if we need to move like that, we can lay all they ass down right there."

"Not good, Bonnie. Even with silencers, it doesn't mean they won't be strapped to the tee, and a shootout in some place like the Ritz will equal too many police and jail. We'll have to play it smoother than that. So if you don't think you will be able to remain calm during the meeting, then maybe you shouldn't be there," said Papio wisely.

"Humph. You know better than that."

"Okay, then, we be calm and see what they have to talk about. If they speak it right, then all will be good. Me personally don't think they'll object to anything once we show our hand. But before that, I want to see how they want to move. So we will let the meeting take its course. Remember, we have the upper hand, so there's no need to let emotions run wild here," said Kingo.

Both Special and Papio nodded their heads in agreement.

Melkely came into the living room and announced that dinner was ready, so they all adjourned to the large dining room where a long dinner table was set with an array of Jamaican dishes. Jerked chicken, jerked beef, several different seafood dishes, rice bread pudding, and some of the juiciest fruit Special ever tasted in her life. They enjoyed their meal, drank, and had a nice evening laughing and talking . . . Each with thoughts of how things were going to turn out in Miami the next day.

Chapter Twenty-four

Special and Papio arrived at Miami International Airport and met up with one of Kingo's Rude Boys, Mikell. Mikell took them straight to the Ritz Carlton Hotel and led them right by the front desk straight to the elevator bank. He was a quiet man who said few words, but both Special and Papio could tell by his precise movements he was a serious dread who was all business.

Once the elevator stopped on the ninth floor, Mikell stepped out first, checked to his right and left, then gave them a nod and led them down the hall toward the room where they were to stay until the meeting was to be held. He stopped in front of a room and stuck a key card inside the door slot.

Once he had the door opened, he took a step back and said, "You are to wait here until you are called, mon. When you get a call, come down to the eighth floor and go to room 8004. Then we go from there."

"Understood," Papio said as he walked past Mikell and entered the room, followed by Special.

After Papio closed the door, Special went and sat down on the bed and sighed. "I don't know about you, Clyde, but I'm a nervous fucking wreck here."

"I won't front and say I'm not, but I am confident that Kingo will make shit right, one way or the other; so, it is what it is, baby. Might as well relax until we get the call to go join the party."

"Relax? How in the hell can I relax right about now?"

He shrugged and said, "You got to do something to keep your mind off this shit."

"Like what?"

"Why don't you give Brandy a call and talk to Li'l Pee. I'm sure that can take your mind off of things for a minute."

"Yeah, I do need to speak to my little man," she said, smiling as she grabbed her purse and pulled out her phone. "After I finish talking to Li'l Pee, why don't you come over here and let me suck that dick. I'm sure that will help keep my mind off the business too."

"Call my son, Bonnie, with your silly ass," Papio said, laughing as he stepped toward the minibar to pour himself a drink.

"I ain't playing, Clyde. When I get nervous, I get horny, so get ready for a quickie," she said as she dialed Brandy's cell number.

Papio was shaking his head as he watched her call their son.

One floor under Papio and Special, the meeting between Kingo and Mr. Suarez's main man, Castro, was about to begin in suite 8004. Castro and two of his men arrived at the same time as Kingo and one of his men. As they were entering the suite, Kingo's other associate joined them. Kingo gave him a questioning glance, and Mikell gave him a nod letting him know that Papio and Special were secure upstairs.

Once everyone had made themselves comfortable, Kingo stood and reached his hand out toward Castro and said, "I hope we can come to a positive agreement here today, mon."

Shaking hands with Kingo, Castro said, "I hope so too. Violence only causes death and loss of money. I'm sure you'd agree that neither are good for business."

"This is true. So let's get to the business, shall we?"

Castro nodded.

"At this time, me Rude Boys are in control of Liberty City, Little Haiti, and Carol City. We have other business interests in North Miami, Atlantic City, Opa-locka, and Overtown. This is where the problem lies with us. Your hold in Opa-locka, North Miami, and Overtown needs to cease or at least give me Rude Boys room to make money. The days of you locking down those areas are done. I cannot let me men continue to lose money like this because it has gotten to a point where it is causing conflicts within my organization. I am not a greedy mon, but I am not in this business to lose money or have friendships that have lasted many decades become ruined behind others trying to overstep their bounds because they cannot get money within boundaries where they should be able to. I tried to contact you all when I first came home to rectify this situation in a peaceful manner hopefully. But you refused to meet with me. So to get your attention, I ordered the attacks against you and your properties. Now that I have your attention and you know where I stand, I need to see if you can rectify this predicament."

Castro waited a few minutes as he processed what he heard, then said, "I have been authorized by Mr. Suarez to find a peaceful solution to this problem. What you are asking is that we relinquish all of our interests in the areas you mentioned?"

"No. Just give me room so me men can make money. As it is now, your men are locking everything down, and that cannot be any longer."

"I see. So as long as we allow your men to operate in Opa-locka, North Miami, and Overtown, then you'd be willing to end this beef?"

"Yeah, mon. You show me that respect, then everyone good. We all eat, and we all enjoy life with no problem. I have heard rumors that you Cubans were possibly tinking of moving toward Carol City and Liberty City. That too cannot happen at all. We give no ground on the territories we run flat-out."

"So you want us to share our territories with you, but you can't share any of your territories with us? That doesn't sound fair at all, Kingo. Why can't we eat in the areas you mentioned?"

"Because you've never ate there. Why now? We let you in now, you may try to take over later. We've always ate in the areas where you are controlling. We helped your way in during my absence because it was beneficial for all parties. You got stronger, and you slowly pushed me men out, which has caused the conflict. We will not make that mistake again."

"I need a moment to call Mr. Suarez to let him know of this because I'm not sure if he will find this acceptable."

"Do what you must. Please understand, mon, this is the only way that anyting can be resolved."

Castro nodded as he stood and stepped away from Kingo and pulled out his phone and called Mr. Suarez. When he had his boss on the line, he quickly told him what had been said and how Kingo refused to give any ground on the territories he had under his control. "I told him that I needed to speak with you before I made a decision on this, sir."

"Remember what we discussed a few days ago, Castro?"

"Sí, sir."

"Then agree for the peace, and we will proceed from there. You have done well by showing some resistance. This will play right for us at a later time," Mr. Suarez said as he hung up the phone.

Castro returned to his seat and said, "As long as you give your word that there will be no more destruction of our properties or attacks on our men, then we agree to your terms. The streets have gotten extremely hot, and that is bad for business. Mr. Suarez doesn't want you to take this as weakness on his part; instead, he would like to think that you will see it as a good business move for both sides."

Castro stood and reached his hand out to Kingo, and they shook on it to seal the deal. "Then it's agreed. We shall have peace and good business."

"Agreed," said Kingo. He paused and then turned and gave the nod toward Mikell who quickly pulled out his phone and called Papio and Special and told them that it was time for them to come and join the meeting. After Mikell put his phone back in his pocket, Kingo told Castro, "There is one more matter that needs to be addressed, a matter of extreme importance to me. It's a personal matter to some people who I consider me family as well as business associates."

"Does this concern the business we've discussed?" asked Castro puzzled.

"Yeah, mon, it does. Only because lives are at stake with me people who has helped me family make a whole lot of money. That, combined with the fact that I consider them me family as well makes this a sticky situation that I hope we can make right."

"I'm confused here. Who are these people, and what have we done to them for this to be brought up?"

Before Kingo could say a word, there was a knock at the door. Kingo gave Mikell a nod to open the door, turned back, faced Castro, and said, "You are about to have the answer to your question in one moment."

When Castro turned toward the door of the suite and watched as Papio and Special entered the suite, his eyes grew wide, and he began to shake his head. "No-fucking-way! This fucking nigga-prick mothafucka is connected with this fucking dread-headed nigga. No-fucking-way!" Castro said to himself.

Seeing the shock on Castro's face made Papio smile as he strolled into the suite and stood by Kingo's side with Special right next to him staring at Castro as if he was a piece of shit. "What up, Castro? Bet you didn't think you'd be seeing me at this meeting, huh, chump?"

Kingo raised his hand and said, "No insults, Papio. We here to address this right, mon." He then told Castro, "I know of the hit you have on these two people, and I am respectfully asking you to call it off. These two people are like me blood. Even more important, we make a lot of money together, and I cannot have anything happening to them."

"You're asking us to call off the hit on these two—or what?"

Kingo stared directly into Castro's brown eyes and said, "Or everyting we agreed to a few minutes ago is null and void, and we go all-out war. No harm can come to these people. They are very important to me and my family. So, do you need to make another call, or can you make this decision?" Kingo asked sarcastically.

Castro gave both Special and Papio a look of disdain and sighed. "Yes, I need to call Mr. Suarez again because this may change things. Papio has not only disrespected Mr. Suarez, but he has also taken money from him and a close friend, a *deceased* close friend of Mr. Suarez, so I don't have the authority to make this decision."

Papio couldn't help himself. He had to give Castro another jab. "Well, make the call, you flunky mothafucka. It's not like we ain't got better shit to do." Papio then looked at Kingo and said, "Sorry, Dread."

"You are a mess, mon, but me love you to death."

Furious, Castro stood and again pulled out his phone and called Mr. Suarez back. When he told his boss of the latest turn at the meeting, he was surprised to hear Mr. Suarez burst into laughter.

"Only Papio! Oh my God! Only Papio would have the allegiance with the fucking Jamaicans we are beefing with. This is fucking hilarious." After he calmed down some and stopped laughing, he turned serious and said, "Tell Kingo that we will call off the hit on their lives, but I want my money returned to me. Not only the money Chief Hightower and I gave Papio, but the money he is responsible for. Since Papio has helped Kingo make so much money, then there shouldn't be a problem with Papio giving me the five hundred million he was responsible for me losing. If I cannot have all of my money in a timely manner, then the hit goes back on them, and if it's war they want, then it's war he will get. This is not negotiable. I want what was taken from me. Period. There will be no more need to call me back, Castro. I'll see you when you return," he said and hung up the phone.

Castro had a smile on his face as he returned to his seat, and that smile on his face made Papio and Special's stomach turn into knots. *Oh, shit,* they both thought as they waited for the Cuban to speak.

"I have been told to tell you that Mr. Suarez will call off the hit on both Papio and Special. He wants to bring this business to an end on a positive note with you, Kingo."

Kingo smiled and said, "That is the best ting I've heard all day, Castro. Please tell Mr. Suarez that I tink everyting will be fine with us from tis point on, and I appreciate him making this wise decision."

Castro nodded and then said, "There is more to this, though. Papio took money from Mr. Suarez, and Mr. Suarez wants that money back within a timely manner."

"Tell him he'll have the million Chief Hightower gave me within twenty-four hours."

Smiling and shaking his head, Castro said, "It's more than just a million dollars, Papio."

Papio thought about it and remembered that Mr. Suarez had thrown in several more million to sweeten the deal on him hitting Special. Then he said, "No problem. I will have the three million to him in a day."

"Papio, I'm surprised at your selective memory. Mr. Suarez wants the money you were responsible for him *losing* to gain your release from the federal prison. He wants you to repay your debt, or the hit goes back on your and Special's lives." Castro stared at Kingo and added, "He also said if he doesn't receive his money, then war it is, and there will not be any discussions on this matter again. So if Papio repays his debt, then everything is good, and we can proceed. If not, then it's war, and the hit goes back live."

Kingo looked back at Papio and asked, "How much you owe, mon?"

Papio stared at Castro who was smiling, truly enjoying this moment, and thought, *Fuck!* He showed no emotion on his face as he answered Kingo.

"About five hundred million."

"What? How the fuck do they expect us to come up with that kind of loot in a timely fucking manner? As a matter of fact, what exactly *is* a timely fucking manner any fucking way?" asked Special.

Castro shrugged and said, "I have no idea. I was told not to call back anymore, so I guess Mr. Suarez will be in contact with you one way or the other."

"Fuck you, Castro. Fuck you and your boss. Tell him I said I need by the end of the summer, and he'll get every penny I owe his ass." He faced Kingo and said, "I'd never let you fuck up your business behind any of my moves. I got what it takes to get him the money, so that's what we're going to do."

Kingo nodded but didn't say a word.

Special realized Papio was talking about the device and knew that it was about to get real wicked with the banks and credit unions again because they were about to put the device back in play, big time.

Damn.

Chapter Twenty-five

Papio and Special arrived at LAX after a long, somber flight from Miami. Both were thinking the same thing, but neither wanted to speak about what had to be done.

Special smiled brightly as she stepped out of the airport and saw Poppa Blue standing in front of her new Mercedes Benz SUV. After giving Poppa Blue a tight hug, she quickly hopped inside of her SUV while Papio and Poppa Blue loaded their luggage inside of the truck.

Once they were on their way, Poppa Blue said, "I must say, I am extremely happy to see both of you back here in sunny California. That shit with the Cubans had me totally stressed."

"You? Humph. That's all that's been on my brain. We're not out of the woods yet, though. We still got to come up with $500 million by the end of the summer," Special said as she turned onto the 405 freeway.

"I've been giving that some serious thought, and with over a two-year layoff, it should be good to start making those bank moves again. The Feds most likely think it's a wrap, and everyone is living good off their riches from all of those robberies."

"That may be true, Poppa Blue, or they could be lying in the cut waiting for us to get back busy," said Papio. "It doesn't matter, though, because that's the only way we can come up with that loot by the end of the summer. My thing is, the faster, the better. So I need you to start checking into the banks and credit unions we can hit that will give us the biggest payoff. That way, we can still be able to break you off your 10 percent and get closer to our goal."

Shaking his head, Poppa Blue said, "That 10 percent shit is done. Whatever you make off the moves, you keep it all so you can get them fucking Cubans off your and Special's ass."

"That's what's up. I appreciate that. I'll get at Q. and have him get on the business as well. I'm pretty sure he'll be with the same thing as you, and that's love. But when everything is everything, we will still make things right. That's just how I get down, Poppa Blue."

"I respect that, Papio." Poppa Blue asked Special, "Where are you headed to, girl? This isn't the way to your house. Mama Mia and Brandy both are anxious as I don't know what to see you guys."

"I'm starving. The entire flight, all I was thinking about was one of those juicy steaks from Mastro's Steakhouse. We need some substance so we can think and plan properly."

"So, a juicy steak will give us that substance?" Papio asked with a smile on his face.

Laughing, Special said, "You damn skippy!" as she exited the freeway headed toward Beverly Hills where Mastro's Steakhouse was located.

By the time they finished their meals, everyone was stuffed and seemed more relaxed. Papio sighed and said, "Damn, Bonnie, that was a good idea you had about coming here to eat. I do feel a little better. My head has a million different things bouncing around, but now, for some reason, I'm like more focused."

"I know what you mean, baby. But shit is going to get wicked real quick. By the time we hit a bank or two, even if the Feds have backed off, they will get right back on high alert and be watching every damn bank around the country."

"I was thinking the same thing," said Poppa Blue. "So maybe we need to switch shit up some. I mean, other moves can be made besides banks and credit unions."

"We need $500 million, Poppa Blue. What other lick can bring us that type of money faster than hitting banks?" asked Special.

"Jewels. Remember that first move you did to check on the device?"

"Yep."

"That was over a $10 million lick. It may not be as much as the banks and credit unions, but it damn sure won't hurt."

"I'm feeling that. Get on it. But the first two banks we hit have to be some nice ones. So if it does get extra hot, we can slide back in the cut while they're focused on the banks and then hit a bunch of jewelry licks to keep ends coming in. I want to be able to drop those bitch-ass Cubans a nice chunk as soon as possible," said Papio as he pulled out his credit card and gave it to the waiter to pay for their meals.

"What about Kingo and his family? Are they going to assist in this business?"

"Yeah. Kingo told me whatever I needed from him as far as help with the moves, he would make sure Kango and his crew would be with it. He also offered to give me a hundred mill. But there was no way I can take that from him. He's not hurting, but fuck that; this is our shit, and we will get them their fucking money. As far as I'm concerned, we're starting at zero because I'm not giving them none of the money I have now. I worked too fucking hard to get that paper, and I am not about to break myself to pay this debt back. They will get they money, but if they get stupid, and for some reason, we can't meet that deadline, then it's war. And that's when I will call on Kingo. Those Cubans showed that they don't really want beef with Kingo. That was a sign of weakness to me."

"Mmmm, that's interesting. Give me a replay of exactly how that meeting went down," said Poppa Blue as he sat back, stuffed, in his seat, wishing he could smoke a cigar right then, but knew he couldn't because it was against the law in California to smoke inside any buildings.

Papio and Special took turns replaying what had taken place at the Ritz Carlton in Miami. When they finished, Poppa Blue sighed and said, "I have never dealt with Mr. Suarez or any of his people, but I have heard and watched from a distance how they get down, and this doesn't fit right to me. It doesn't match their get down at all. Mr. Suarez is a shrewd man; a good businessman but also conniving and crafty. From what you two have told me, I feel in my gut that there is something else working in that Cuban's head."

"Kingo feels the same as you do. But he's not worried because if those Cubans break their agreement, he made it crystal clear that it would be war, and they would never have another sit-down to dead shit."

Poppa Blue nodded his head and said, "That's a good move he made. Because I can see those Cubans sticking to the script for a minute and then wait and see if they can catch Kingo and his people slipping. *Then* try to take them out."

"They do that shit, they will be in a whole lot of shit. That Kingo ain't to be fucked with," said Special.

"Yeah, when it comes to the murder shit, he about his work. That's why if it comes to it, I will call on him to get with the Cubans. But for now, we gots to get that fucking money."

Poppa Blue stared at both of them for a moment with a scowl on his face.

"Why are you looking like that, Poppa Blue?" asked Special.

"Yeah, what's wrong, OG?" asked Papio.

"The way I see this shit is two ways it can be handled. One, you hit as many bank licks as you can and get the Cubans their money, or you can say fuck it all and hit the Cubans first and end this shit."

"How in the fuck can we hit the Cubans? Mr. Suarez never leaves his estate and has the top-of-the-line security system in place," said Papio.

"Not to mention about ten men on duty 24/7," added Special.

"If there's a will, there's a way, Special. Never say never. You have Kingo on your side, and if I remember correctly, Special, you paid your mans out there in Miami some good money for some information on Mr. Suarez and his business."

"That's right. Scrape."

"While I'm getting things together for you guys, I think you need to get at your man Scrape and see what he learned about Mr. Suarez. He may have something useful for us."

"Are you saying we should skip the bank moves and just get right at the Cubans and go for the end game with this shit, Poppa Blue?"

"I'm saying let's explore every option before we move. So that way, when we do move, we will be confident that we made the right move. If we can find a chink in the Cubans' armor, I don't see why we wouldn't be able to exploit it and end this shit if we can. Now, if we don't find a weakness, then we're still good with the device because that is the X-factor in all of this."

"I feel you, Poppa Blue, and what you're saying makes perfect sense. I have been so caught up thinking about getting them fools the money I owe them that I haven't even given any thoughts of getting at they ass on some aggressive shit," said Papio.

Poppa Blue nodded his head and said, "Trust me, son, that's *exactly* what the Cubans are thinking as well. They feel you are not in a position of power to even think about getting at them aggressively. Though they know now you have Kingo behind you, they are comfortable that you will do whatever it takes to get them their money to end this thing. Which also makes me think back to what you've told me about that meeting. They may be trying to rock everyone to sleep so when they do get their money from you, they can still put a hit out on you and Special as well as move against Kingo and his people. The more I think about this shit, the more I feel that we should be looking at a way to get at them and end they ass more than getting ready to get all of that heat back on our asses from hitting banks and credit unions."

"Damn, Poppa Blue, you really on some gangsta shit right now. Are you sure some shit like this can be put down against those high-powered mothafuckas?" asked Special.

"Like I just told you, Special, I never say never, and I think anything can be done if one puts enough time and effort toward achieving one's goals."

"I like that shit," she said and smiled.

"So do I," Papio said seriously.

Special pulled her phone from her Birkin bag and started dialing a number.

"Who are you calling, Bonnie?" asked Papio.

"Scrape. Time to see what that two million bucks I gave him has done for me."

In Miami, Mr. Suarez was in a good mood. He knew that Kingo and his crew would think that they gave them what they wanted; therefore, all he needed to do was to bide his time and wait for them to get comfortable.

Then he would strike a deadly blow to all of them. He would make sure he takes the head off before he moved on the rest of those fucking Jamaicans. He needed this time to find out the weaknesses of their leader, Kingo. Once he found a way to touch him, then he would move and end his existence. After Kingo, then he would give Castro the order to go and personally murder Papio and Special. There was no way he would ever let Papio get away with such disrespect. The streets always watched. If he let Papio get away with blatantly disrespecting him, he would seem weak, and that could never happen. His enemies would pounce if they even thought for one minute that Mr. Suarez, the leader of the mighty Cuban organization in Miami, was getting weak. No way could he allow that. Papio would get him the $500 million he owed him. He was sure of that because he knew how Papio worked. But he would still have to die, and it was no one's fault but his own.

Special was smiling as they left the restaurant and got back inside of her SUV. Once they were on their way to her house in Hancock Park, Papio said, "Okay, Bonnie, you've held us in suspense long enough here. What did your mans Scrape have to say?"

"Not much, really. I mean, if you consider the schematics to the high-tech alarm system that Mr. Suarez uses as something."

"Oh my, looks like we may have found a way to get at the mighty Cuban drug lord," Poppa Blue said with a smile on his face.

Papio stared at Special and smiled. "Damn, we may just be able to do this shit, Bonnie."

Special laughed and said, "You damn skippy!"

Chapter Twenty-six

Papio and Brandy spent Brandy's last day in Los Angeles with Bredeen shopping and doing the tourist thing. He took them to the beach for a nice lunch on the Redondo Pier; afterward, they went to Hollywood and spent the rest of the afternoon walking around letting Brandy enjoy spotting her stars' names on the Walk of Fame that were all over the sidewalks of Hollywood. By the time they made it back to Riverside, Bredeen was sleeping soundly, so Papio took this break to have a serious talk with Brandy.

"Check it, Brandy. Shit is real serious. I have six months to get the 500 million I owe the Cubans, or they're going to put the hit back on me and Special. I may have a way of getting the money, but it's going to be heavy work, and, honestly, I don't know if I'm up to it now. It's crazy because all of my life I've gotten money and had no problem doing whatever I had to, to get the money. But here lately, it's like I've lost the hunger to make moves. I'm thinking about the risks involved and worried about something going left, and I end up getting knocked—or worse. This has me baffled for real. But now my back is against the wall, and I have no choice."

"I think the reason why you're worried about the risks involved now is because of your family. Li'l Pee and Bredeen have brought out the fatherly instincts in you, and you don't want to take the risks you normally had no problems taking. So that's understandable, Daddy."

"Yeah, I feel that, but now isn't the time for my fatherly instincts to kick in. If I don't get the ends, they won't have a father 'cause sooner or later, the Cubans will get me, and then it's a wrap. I have another option, but that's even more dangerous than my other option in this shit."

"What's that, Daddy?"

"Saying fuck it all and take it to the Cubans and get them before they get me."

"I know you are going to think I'm stupid here, but bear with me for a moment, Daddy. Why not call the authorities and try to deal with things the right way for once?" Before he could fuss at her for telling him to be a snitch, she hurriedly continued. "I know snitching isn't in your DNA, Daddy, but honestly, that's the safest way to deal with this situation."

Shaking his head vehemently, he said, "That's not my way. When I die, I will be remembered as a nigga who got my money and remained true to this fucked-up game. No dirt will ever be smutted on my name. Snitching ain't an option. Period."

"So it's either try to get the money or war with the Cubans?"

"Basically."

"How will you get the money if you choose that route?"

He stared at her for a moment and then decided, fuck it. He might as well lace her all the way since he was doing something he normally didn't do, and that was putting Brandy in his business. "You remember a couple of years back when they were talking about how all of those banks across the U.S. were getting robbed, and the Feds were clueless about how it was happening without them being able to catch the people who were putting that down?"

"That was you, Daddy? No way!"

He smiled and said, "Yeah, it was me, Special, and some other people making those monster moves."

"You know, I remember watching that stuff on the news thinking I hope to God that you weren't involved in any of that. A part of me felt you were, though. It just seemed like something ingenious you would come up with."

"Well, it wasn't me that came up with this, but it was me putting it down with the help of a solid crew and a special device."

"Special device?"

He then told her about the device and how they paid for it and used it to make all of the robberies they committed to be so easy. "That's how I was able to reach my goal of over a hundred million. That, and some people I thought were loyal who tried to cross me."

"Huh?"

Thinking about how Twirl and Keli tried to get grimy on him pissed him off all over again, but he decided to skip telling Brandy about that. He was keeping it 100 with her, but that was murder, and she didn't need to know anything about that. "Nothing. The thing is, I can get the money with some aggressive moves, but the heat that's going to come with that may be too much for me to handle this time. Shit, we barely got out of that last one we put down in Boston."

Brandy thought about what she heard on the news about that last bank robbery and knew he was telling the truth. After a few minutes of silence, she asked him, "Do you think you could successfully get the Cuban guys if you went at them, Daddy?"

He shrugged and said, "Honestly, I don't know. I know I will have the element of surprise on my side because they're too cocky to think I have the nuts to get at them. That's about the only thing I feel I have on my side for real. If I get at them, I'll only have one shot at they ass. If I miss, it's a wrap. Then, not only will Special and my life be in danger, you, Mama Mia, Bredeen, and Li'l Pee will then become a part of this. The Cubans will go all-out then, and that's what scares the fuck out of me and is making me hesitant with making that move."

"Ever since I met you, all you have ever done was make sure that your every move was made right. You have never doubted yourself. You have to go with the instincts that have gotten you this far, Daddy. No matter what the risk factors are, you have to trust your gut. What is your gut telling you to do?"

He sat there and thought about her question, then answered it honestly. "I want to take it to they ass and slaughter them. I don't want to have this money and good life while having to worry about someone looking to do me and my family in. I'd rather be dead than have to live that way, Brandy."

"Then you have to do what you have to do. Don't start second-guessing yourself now, Daddy. I have every confidence that you can do this and do it right without missing. Make that one shot you got count."

He smiled at her and asked, "When did you get this gangsta, baby?"

With a serious look on her face, she answered him in a firm voice. "The day I drove a minivan full of drugs and money from Niagara Falls to New York City. Daddy, you've trained me every step of the way. You've changed the way I looked at life from that New York trip to now. All I have in this world is my daughter, you, and Special. This entire thing is surreal to me, especially that Special and I part of it. But it is what it is, and I have you. You are the one man I never want to lose, so sharing you with Special is a blessing. Don't let those Cubans take my blessing away from me, Daddy. Get they ass, get them, and end this shit."

Her words floored Papio, and all he could think of to say was, "Damn."

Special and Poppa Blue were having dinner at a nice restaurant called Chart House located in Marina Del Rey, not too far from the condo she owned. When they were finished enjoying some of the best seafood they'd ever tasted, they sat back in their seats full with a million thoughts running through their minds.

"There has to be a way that we can use the schematics Scrape has for me to be able to make a move on those Cubans so we can deliver the death blow to they ass and end this shit, Poppa Blue."

"I feel that, but the question remains, how? How do we get at they ass when they're that fucking secure? Papio says the man never leaves his estate. The same estate that's heavily guarded at all times. Shit, that spot is so high tech that the damn guards don't even roam the grounds.

"The schematics to their security shit won't mean shit for real. We beat the security system, we still got to be able to hit about ten or more heavy hitters. That ain't no easy-ass task, Special."

"Fuck, I know. But it is the only way. Making that money would be next to impossible because of the heat it would bring once we hit a few banks. So, hitting them is the only option."

"What about if we snatch Mr. Suarez's son and his family?"

Shaking her head, she said, "Nah. For one, I don't do the family thing. I don't even want to play that game because if we move like that and miss, then they will come after ours, and that ain't a good look at all."

"You're right. Fuck," Poppa Blue said, clearly frustrated.

"We got Kingo on our side, and that's a major plus. His men will move however he tells them. We just need to find a way to be able to use them and do this shit right because we will only have one chance at them."

"Why not ask Kingo for a loan, and I'll pitch in along with Papio's man, Q.? And with what you both have, we can scrounge up the ends for them. Then we make a few quick bank hits to get some bank and do like I said about hitting some jewel licks. We'll be set back for a minute, but we can make do. When it gets too hot, we'll fall back and hit and move accordingly."

"Nope. There is no way Papio will ever go with that, and to be honest, neither would I. We're not built like that, Poppa Blue. You've been grinding it out in this game too damn long to have to give up all of that money to help us out of this jam."

"This *jam?* That's what you think this shit is, Special? A *damn jam?* Are you fucking stupid? This is your fucking *life!*"

"You think I don't know that shit? And lower your damn voice, you old fart. We're in a restaurant, remember?"

"You listen to me and understand what I'm about to tell your ass. You are *my* responsibility. You are the one child that me and Bernadine have. You mean the world not only to me but also to both of us. Your mother was my world, and I made a promise to her the first day she brought you home from the hospital that if anything ever happened to her, that I would take nothing but the very best care of you. You chose the life, and I couldn't find it in my heart to tell you no. So I schooled you to the rules of the game, and you excelled. So I've kept my promise, and as long as I have a breath to breathe, I will continue to keep that promise to that beautiful woman who's resting in peace. Money ain't shit to me. I have had it all my life, and if I lost everything I got, I would get some more of it one way or the other. I bought a tailor-made suit a few years ago, and you know Poppa Blue don't do the suit thang at all. I have that suit in my closet with the pocket cut out of it."

Laughing, Special asked, "Now, why in the hell would you spend money on a tailor-made suit only to cut the pocket out? That makes no damn sense."

"If you shut up and listen, you'll understand my point."

Special, smiling, made her finger like a zipper and ran it across her lips.

"Thank you. The reason why the pocket is cut out is a reminder to me that I won't be taking anything with me when it's my time to go be with your mother. Hopefully in heaven. The last suit I wear don't need any damn pockets, Special. Money ain't shit to me. When I'm dead, I'm dead."

"I feel that, but you'd be taking away from Bernadine, and I can't let that go down."

"Dummy, don't you know me? Don't you know that I dot all the i's and cross all my t's? When I die, Bernadine not only inherits everything I have, she also collects on a monster fucking life insurance policy. My loving wife will be just fine when it's my time. So don't worry about that shit."

Sighing, Special reached across the table and placed her hands on top of her mentor, father figure, and friend. "I love you to death, Poppa Blue. You've kept your promise to Mama, and she knows it. She also knows me, and she knows I will do whatever it takes to win. I ain't taking a penny from you, nor will Papio take anything from his people. We gon' play this shit out the gangsta way. Neither of us plays fair, so it is what it is. Winner takes all. One way or the other, we're going to get those fucking Cubans and end this shit. Either that, or we're going to be dead."

"If you die, I die, Special. So if this is the call you and Papio are making, then we're going all out."

"I can't change your feelings, so I won't try. So let's think dammit. Let's find a way to get they ass!"

Before Poppa Blue could respond, Special's phone started ringing. When she saw that it was Papio, she smiled and answered.

"Where you at, Bonnie?" Papio asked with an excited tone.

"I've just finished having dinner with Poppa Blue. What's up, Clyde? You sound like you got something good to tell me."

"I do. You and Poppa Blue need to get out here to my spot. We got to talk and start planning how we're going to make that move on those Cubans in Miami."

"What? You done came up with a way to get at them?"

"I didn't come up with shit. Brandy did!"

"Huh?"

"No questions. I've already gotten at Kingo, and he loves it. So hurry your ass up and get to Riverside. We're about to get this shit together, Bonnie. We're about to bring the end game to this shit! Hurry the fuck up!"

Special hung up the phone with a grin on her face. Poppa Blue stared at her for a moment as he watched as she paid for their meal. After she signed the credit card bill and put her card back inside of her purse, she stood and told Poppa Blue, "You better call Bernadine and let her know you'll be late coming home tonight."

"Why? What's up, Special?"

"Papio said Brandy came up with a way where we can end this shit with the Cubans."

"Brandy? What the fuck does that square broad know about some gangsta shit?"

"I don't have a clue. He didn't say. But I do know if she came up with something solid enough to make Papio sound that damn excited, it has to be on point. If my boo-thang has a way for us to end this shit, then I'm going to suck that pussy so good she won't be moving back to Oklahoma. She will stay out here in sunny California with us forever!" Special said and started laughing as she stepped away from their table followed by Poppa Blue.

"You do know that was extremely TMI, Special," Poppa Blue mumbled.

Chapter Twenty-seven

Papio, Mama Mia, and Brandy had just finished bathing and putting Bredeen to bed by the time Special and Poppa Blue made it to the house. Mama Mia spoke to them and excused herself for bed so they would be able to talk about their business. She was confused when she saw that Brandy was joining Papio and the others and thought, *Oh my Lord, they've found a way to corrupt that dear woman. Keep my son and his friends in your hands, Father God,* she silently prayed as she went to her bedroom.

Once everyone was seated and relaxed, Papio smiled and said, "I broke everything down to Brandy. When I say everything, I mean everything from the debt I owe to the Cubans and why, to the device and the bank moves. Since we all know we're not going to pay them Cuban fucks a penny of that 500 million, the only other option is to take it to them and don't miss. Doing that would be no easy task, so that means we will only have one shot at them. I felt that getting at them by attacking Mr. Suarez at his home would be the only way. But since he lives in a fortress-like estate, that seemed impossible. When I told Brandy how you came up with the schematics to the high-tech security system that Mr. Suarez has in place at his estate, Brandy came up with what I feel could be the answer to how we can get in and get at those bastards. It's so fucking simple that I'm surprised none of us came up with this solution. I'll give the floor to Brandy now so she can break it down to you."

Brandy smiled, loving the attention she was receiving as well as the feeling of notoriety she was experiencing by being a part of this entire situation. "After Daddy explained to me about the device, I was puzzled about this ingenious invention. I mean, if this device has been able to disarm silent alarm systems as well as surveillance cameras inside of banks and credit unions all across the United States, then I don't see why the device couldn't be used to disarm the Cubans' high-tech security system that they have in place at their estate. Once you use the device in front of the Cubans' estate, it should have the same effect as it had on the banks and credit unions you all robbed. When the device has manipulated the security system, you all can go in and do what needs to be done with the Cubans. You said that they are comfortable at their estate because that's the last place they feel they will be attacked. So odds are they are relaxed and are trusting the high-tech system that they have in place. Being that lax can be the perfect opportunity for you to end their existence and all of your worries."

"Dammit, man, why didn't I think of that?" said Poppa Blue.

Laughing, Special said, "So fucking simple."

"Yeah, that's exactly what Kingo said when I told him. Check it, Kingo has the men and the firepower we need. Time to dust off the device because instead of using it to get that bread, we're going to use it to get us some Cuban asses."

"You fucking right," said Special.

"I love it. This could work, but at the same time, we still have to make sure we dot all of our i's and cross our t's. We can't take this as an easy move because we still got to be careful," warned Poppa Blue.

"You're right about that, OG. And there is no way we are going to move until we're sure this can pop off the way we

want it to. That's why we're about to get that device and
fly out to Miami and start putting this in place. My plan
is this . . . We go out there and have Special get the schematics from her man. Then we're going to have the
same type of system installed into one of Kingo's spots.
I mean, *everything* from the motion sensors to video
cameras and alarms. Then we'll put the device to the
test to make sure that we got that edge like we think we
have. Once we see that we're good with the device, then
we plan the actual attack on Mr. Suarez's estate. I think
the best way to get at them would be between 3:00–4:00
a.m.; a late-night creep. Get to the Cubans' estate, hit the
device off, and in we go. They have a big wrought iron
gate, but that will be nothing to bypass. Once we're past
the gate, then there are about fifty yards to the house. If
they're slippin' like we think they are, by the time we're
on top of they ass, they won't know what hit them."

"How many men does he normally have there with
him?" asked Poppa Blue.

"Every time I went there, I've seen anywhere from five
to nine, but there could be more. The spot is huge. Kingo
wants us to move with him and twenty of his best Rude
Boys. With me and Special, that's twenty-three of us
armed to the teeth with the wicked shit weapons-wise.
Everything silenced and fully automatic. We hit the
front door blasting everything in our sight until we get to
Castro and Mr. Suarez. Do them and get the fuck up outta
there."

Poppa Blue frowned for a moment and then asked,
"What do you mean blast everything in your sight until
you get to Castro and Mr. Suarez? What else you got
bouncing around in that head of yours, Papio?"

Special smiled because she knew her man better than
anyone else in that room. "He has more money on his
mind, Poppa Blue."

"Huh?"

Laughing and shaking his head, Papio said, "You know me, Bonnie, always got that dollar on my mind. Check it. Every time I went to that house to drop off ends I owed them, Castro always took the money and disappeared. I don't know for certain, but my gut tells me there's a whole lot of loochie in that estate. If we're going to put our murder game down on every mothafucka in there breathing, we might as well get some money out of this shit."

"So, before you do Mr. Suarez and Castro, you want the money?" asked Poppa Blue.

"Yep. Every mothafucking penny."

"What makes you think they'll give it up?"

"When faced with certain death, there's not a doubt in my mind that they will give up everything. Mr. Suarez will feel I'm on some greedy shit and think if he gives me the money, I'll spare his ass. That way, he'll be able to live another day and be able to get his revenge for what I done to him."

"No one will be breathing when we leave that spot, though, right?" asked Special.

Papio stared at her, and in a deadly tone, gave her the answer she wanted to hear. "I have wanted to murder Castro for over ten years. I'll blow his brains all over the place once we get that fucking money."

Special returned her man's stare, and in an equally deadly tone, she said, "And I'll have the pleasure of doing the same to that fat fuck, Mr. Suarez."

Papio nodded and said, "We get money, and we end this shit. Death is coming to the Cubans. There can be no other way to finish this play."

With a determined look on his face, Poppa Blue said, "Let's get crackin', then. Time to make this shit happen."

"Our flight to Miami leaves tomorrow night. When I take Brandy and Bredeen to the airport in the morning, I'll come to your spot, Special, until we fly out. In the meantime, you need to get at Scrape and let him know we'll be getting with him in a day or so. So when we get to Miami, we can get shit started. Kingo will scoop us and take us to one of his spots so we can get things set up. If everything goes smoothly, we can put this shit down no later than a week."

"I love it. This shit is going to work, Clyde. Then we can live our lives and be done with all of this gangsta shit and raise our kids and be happy."

Papio nodded and said, "Yeah, Bonnie, that's the plan."

Special stood and stepped to Brandy and pulled her to her feet and gave her a hug and a tender kiss on the lips. "And to think, I never liked your fine ass. Now I loves me some you! Not only because you're one fine-ass woman, but you've come up with the idea to help us bring all of this craziness to an end. I love you, Brandy. We're family, baby . . . me, you, Papio, Li'l Pee, and Bredeen. You hear me, we're family, baby."

Brandy shyly smiled as she kissed Special back. "I never thought I could be involved in anything as absolutely crazy as this. But it feels right. I knew for a fact that I loved Daddy more than anything in this world and would do whatever it took to keep him a part of my life. But never in my wildest dreams did I think it would be in a three-way relationship! This is ridiculously crazy, but at the same time, it feels right. I love you too, Special. I love you very much. You just make sure you get your ass to Miami and bring my daddy back to me. Keep this triangle we've formed intact, you hear me?"

Special smiled and gave her a nod yes because she was too choked up to answer Brandy.

Poppa Blue stared at the females while they were having their moment and then glanced at Papio and shook his head. "I don't know what you got in you, brother, but whatever it is, I sure wish I had that shit back when I was in *my* twenties!"

Everyone in the room started laughing.

Kingo, Fay, Keily, Kango, Steven, Brad, and Macho were all seated in the living room of Kingo's condo in South Beach discussing what Papio had told Kingo.

"Shit, mon, me think this could work out just fine for all of us. That there device can make it happen. We rid ourselves of that Cuban problem, and all territories belong to you for sure, Kingo," said Fay.

Kingo nodded and said, "This is true. Papio and Special will get out here late tomorrow night; then we start to put everything in order."

"How many men will we need to make this takeover go without a hitch, brother?" asked Kango.

"The last thing those Cubans will expect is for us to make an aggressive move on them at their stronghold, but I don't want to take any chances. I told Papio twenty of me best Rude Boys should be enough to make this go right."

Steven nodded in agreement and said, "Yes, that should be more than enough. Twenty Rude Boys should be more than enough to rid us of these bloodclaats. But I have a suggestion."

"Speak, my cousin."

"Kango, Brad, Macho, and I have worked with Papio as well as Special, and I think we know one another's movements pretty well."

Kingo smiled and finished what his cousin was hinting at. "So, you want to join this takeover and wish for me little brother and me other cousins to join us, correct?"

"Yes. So that will be twenty Rude Boys and the five of us, along with Special and Papio. Twenty-seven killers will be more than enough to get this job done correctly," Steven said confidently.

"Fuck that! Twenty-eight. You're not leaving me out of this kinda fun," said Keily.

Laughing, Kingo turned toward Fay and asked her, "Should we go on and make it twenty-nine, me cousin Fay?"

Fay wore a frown on her face as she shook her head vehemently and said, "Are you gone batty, mon? You know me damn well. I don't want no parts in the violent shit. You all go and have a ball. I'll make sure everything we need is in place so we can make this takeover right. Remember, Fay is a lover, not a fighter!"

Everyone started laughing.

"Agreed. We will put everything into effect and get things prepared for this very important takeover. We're not only doing this for our financial gain, but we're also doing this to help out two very good friends. Papio and Special have helped us gain plenty of riches. That type of loyalty must be matched intensely. We are loyal only to those who are loyal to us, and they have proven theirs."

"True, mon, very true," said Fay. "But I still need to find a way to get me some more of that young man! Whew, just thinking about the last time makes me extremely hot. He worked me over *real good* in the rompin' shop!"

"Mother! You never told me you had some of that delicious-looking mon!" yelled Keily.

"Not your business, daughter. Not your business."

"Humph. Well, I'm making it my business to get me some of him. He's not leaving Miami without taking me to the rompin' shop, I'll tell you that!"

Kingo shook his head and said, "I don't know who's worse off . . . the mother or the damn daughter!"

"Two damn freaky Jamaican women! One old and one young!" laughed Kango.

"One thing is for sure, I don't think Papio will have a problem with either of them," said Macho.

"He might now, but I'm positive Special will be the one who will have the problem!" said Steven.

"Shit, me likes her too. She's more than welcome to join in on the fun!"

Laughing, Kingo slapped his forehead and said, "Please, go to bed. Enough of this. You give me a major headache. Business first, then the talk of the celebration. Sleep well, family. In a few days, our planning begins. The Cubans' demise is on the horizon. Rude Boys of Jamaican descent will run all of Miami!"

Everyone in the room gave a nod of their heads in agreement with Kingo.

Chapter Twenty-eight

Papio and Special spent the day with Li'l Pee. They took him to the park and let him run wild for a little while, then took him shopping. Special loved spoiling her son, and so did Papio. After buying Li'l Pee a bunch of toys and plenty of new outfits, they dropped him off with Poppa Blue and Bernadine and went and enjoyed a seafood meal at a restaurant called Boiling Crab in Koreatown.

Papio checked the time and saw that they were right on time to head out to the airport. He hated how they had to be at the airport two hours before their flight was due to depart. But that's how it was since 9/11. Even though he flew constantly, he still hated the wait. This time around, though, he was ready. When they arrived at LAX and made it through all of the TSA nonsense, he sat down in front of the gate and started looking at something on his iPad. When he started laughing out loud, Special frowned and asked what was so damn funny.

"You know that *Love & Hip Hop* show your ass got me watching?"

"Yeah, and?"

"Ya girl Mimi done went and done a damn sex tape with that fool they said was gay."

"Who, Nikko? You lie!"

"No lie. Here, look for yourself. It's all over mediatake-out.com," he said as he gave her his iPad.

"Oooh, look at Mimi's old ass sucking on that fool's dick! She know she is down bad for that shit."

"Why? Shit, she getting hers in with her dude. It ain't like Stevie J. can be mad. He chose that freaky-ass broad over Mimi, so now Mimi is doing her. Shit, I think it's hot. Why haven't we made one of those sex tapes?"

"You know you are out of your damn mind, Papio. No-fucking-way would I do some shit like that."

"Oh, so now your ass is bashful, huh? Ain't that some shit."

"You know damn well I'm not no bashful-type bitch, but our fucking is for us, not for anyone else."

"I didn't say make a tape and put it on blast like this shit. I said why haven't we made a tape? As in for our enjoyment in private. No way in hell would I do some cornball shit like this and put our shit on blast. I bet that nigga Nikko did that shit so he can have a little more time in the limelight with his wack ass."

"You're probably right. That nigga probably did that shit so he could try to prove he wasn't on the gay shit. Either way, that's some silly shit on Mimi's part. I would never let no shit like that get out. What if Li'l Pee saw it when he got older? That would be disgusting and downright disrespectful."

"I feel you. But like I said, if we got down like that, I would never let it get out. It would be for our eyes only. I bet Brandy would be down for something freaky like that."

Special rolled her eyes and said, "Yeah, because she does whatever *Daddy* says," she said, changing her voice trying to imitate how Brandy sounded.

Laughing, Papio said, "Come on, now, you know you love you some Brandy. Why you hating on your girl now?"

"Not hating, just saying. You have the best in your life, pretty nigga. You got a bad square bitch who loves the fuck outta your ass and would do whatever it takes to keep you smiling. Then you got me, a super bad gangsta bitch that has given you the ultimate male dream come true. Me and a bad bitch loving you together. The flip to that is one bitch is sweet, innocent, loving, and submissive to your ass. Me? I'm the bitch that loves you equally but has to keep your ass grounded before all of this good pussy you getting goes to your fucking head. In other words, *I'm* the one that keeps your ass in check. So if you think your boo-thang would let you make a sex tape, then so be it. I'll be the cameraman for y'all's ass. Shit, I know I'd get off quick watching you fuck the shit out of her pretty ass, Pussy Monster."

Papio smiled and said, "You know I'm feeling that shit. But you need to kill that fucking 'pretty nigga' shit. How many times do I have to tell you about that shit?"

"Whatever."

"When we get to Miami, I'm calling Brandy and asking her if we can make a tape after we handle the business."

"Yeah, I bet your ass is. Whatever."

"When she agrees to let you tape us, she's going to tape me fucking the shit out of you too."

"I wouldn't bet on that shit if I was your ass."

"Hater."

"Freak."

"Your freak."

She smiled and said, "Yeah, mines and Brandy's. You *do* know that you can never fuck with any other bitches, right?"

"Two bad bitches is enough for me."

"Better be."

"Look who's sounding like the hater here."

"Fuck another bitch besides me or Brandy, and you'll see more than some mothafucking hating, pretty nigga!" Before Papio could check her again for calling him 'pretty,' their flight number was called for them to start boarding.

As they began walking toward the gate, Papio smiled and told Special, "For that slick-ass comment, you ain't getting any dick during this long flight to the MIA."

Special laughed and said, "Come on, Clyde, you know I love how we rock the Mile High Club! I'll be nice, baby. Promise, no more 'pretty nigga' remarks."

He shook his head and said, "Just like I said, you freak!" They both were laughing as they boarded their flight to Miami.

Kingo and Melkely were waiting outside of Miami International when Papio and Special came out of the airport with their bags in their hands. Once their luggage was in the back of the Range Rover, they got inside of the SUV, and Melkely eased into the traffic. Kingo smiled at his friends and asked how the flight was.

"It was long, but we made the best of it," Special answered with a wicked grin on her face.

Kingo roared in laughter because he already knew what she meant by that comment. "My God, Papio, you are one lucky gun, mon."

"You know how I do, Dread. Nothing but the best in my life. Now, what's up wit' the business?"

Kingo turned serious and said, "Everyting is set as far as where you two will be staying. In the morning, Special needs to get with her peoples and get us those schematics. Once we have them, we go over everything to make sure it's right as far as the gadget goes. You do have it, right?"

Special patted her Birkin bag and said, "You damn skippy. Wouldn't have left L.A. without this bad boy."

"Good, then everyting is a go. I've had me Rude Boys checking out the Suarez estate discreetly, a few late-night ride-bys to see what it looks like on the late night, and everyting looks criss, mon. Sent me mon through around 3:00 a.m. twice and lights out; totally dark. I cannot believe that Cuban doesn't have any men roaming the grounds."

"He's confident that no one can get to him, and if someone did get lucky enough to make it to the estate, he figures his men will be able to deal with whatever they bring at him," said Papio.

"He doesn't know what we're bringing at him, so someting no mon can deal with. Me Rude Boys bring the fire of death, mon."

"Good. Check it. You know it's like fifty yards from the front gate to the house. Once we get through the gate, we're going to have to make a mad dash just in case someone sees us coming."

"Me have been thinking about that. We use the wire cutta to cut through the iron gate. Big ones, mon, so we will still have the element of surprise on our side. Once we're through the gate, we send half of me Rude Boys to lead the way. Once we see that they have made it to the front of the house, I give the green light to go while the rest of us make the charge to the house. By the time we make it, everything should be going down the hard way. We will be the last to go inside while me Rude Boys secure the house. Twenty of my best men, along with me brother, Brad, Steven, Macho, you two, me, and Keily will be more than enough to get this job done, mon."

"Keily? Did you say Keily?" asked Special.

"Yes. She refused to be left out of the fun."

Laughing, Special said, "I know *that's* right."

Melkely came to a stop in front of an all-white condominium building in South Beach and said, "Well, you two, here you are. Home sweet home while you're here in the lovely South Beach."

"Thanks for the lift, Melkely. Hopefully, after everything is everything, we can go tear down a few of the specialty boutiques I love out here," said Special as she got out of the SUV.

"You're on, Special. I have a few spots that I'm sure you're going to love."

Both Kingo and Papio rolled their eyes and started laughing. "Women!" they yelled in unison.

"Ugh!" was the response they received from both Special and Melkely.

The next morning, Special got up early and called Scrape and told him that she was on her way to get the schematics. She threw on a pair of sweats and a wife beater and left the condo while Papio was still sound asleep. When she arrived in Opa-locka at Scrape's home on 161th Street and Thirtieth Avenue, she smiled when she saw him standing in the doorway of his home talking to a woman who had to be a crackhead. She jumped out of the car and walked up to them and said, "I know damn well you ain't doing what I think you doing, fool."

Scrape started laughing and said, "What, you think 'cause you gave me a nice chunk o' change a few years ago that my grizzle stops? You got to be tripping, Special," Scrape said as he finished the drug transaction with the crackhead. He stuffed the money inside of his jean pocket and said, "Behind the P-Boys don't stop; we rock this shit 'til the casket drop, Special. You already know."

"Whatever, you toothless-ass nigga. Now gimme what I came for. I got shit to do."

"Hold on a sec," Scrape said as he turned and went into the house. He returned a couple of minutes later with a tube in his hand. He gave it to Special and said, "There you go. That breaks down everything those fools got going on, security-wise. I don't know how this shit gon' help your ass, Special; I just hope it keeps your ass safe.

You're real good peeps; would hate to hear something fucked-up happened to your sexy, fine ass."

"You know I got this, boy. Good looking out, Scrape. I mean this shit. You really did me a solid with this right here."

"I wanna know, but then again, something is telling me I don't wanna know how this shit is about to go down."

Laughing, she said, "Trust me; when it pops off, you will know how everything rocked."

"You be careful, Special," he said, genuinely concerned for her well-being.

"You've never seen the monster in me, Scrape. You've only saw this pretty face and all this ass," she laughed as she slapped her backside. "Trust me when I tell you, shit is about to get wild in the MIA, and that bad itch you know and love is going to be the one to come out on top. See ya when I see you, toothless Behind the P-Boy!"

Scrape was shaking his head as he watched Special jump inside of her car and pull out of his driveway. "I know you're a bad bitch and a deadly bitch. I just hope your fine ass hasn't bit off more than you can chew, Special. 'Cause if you have, those fucking Cubans gon' have to deal with me and the rest of the Behind the P-Boys, that's real," he said aloud as he stared at Special's taillights as she made a right turn out of his neighborhood.

Chapter Twenty-nine

It took the entire day for the security technician from Brickshire Security to install the highly sophisticated security system inside of the condominium where Papio and Special were staying. Everything from extrasensitive motion detectors, every window and door wired, and hidden security cameras all around the condominium. As soon as the job was complete, Papio was sitting at the console where the security cameras were located and was staring at every angle of the condominium from the hidden cameras. He was so impressed with the setup that he decided to get this type of security in his home in Riverside as well as the house in Oklahoma City for Brandy and Bredeen.

He smiled at Special as he grabbed his phone and called Kingo and told him to come over so he could be there when they ran the test to make sure the device would be able to deactivate the security system.

After he hung up the phone, he sighed and said, "I sure hope this shit works, Bonnie. If it doesn't, then we're like totally fucked."

"Don't think like that, Clyde. If it don't work, then we do what we got to do and get that fucking money. We're not going to lose, baby, remember that. No matter what it takes, we're going to come out of this shit okay."

"I feel all of that, but a lot is going to come with making that money, and a part of me doesn't know if I'm up to that shit."

"Uh-uh. That type of talk is a waste of time, so dead that shit. For one, this device has made us more money than we've ever dreamed of, and it's not going to fail us now. But if it does, then we will use it for what it was designed for and rob every mothafucking thing we can to get that bread. There's never been any quit in you, and now is not the time to start that shit. So shake it off, baby. We gon' be all right; we don't have no other choice."

Before he could respond, he noticed on one of the cameras that Kingo, Brad, Kango, Steven, and Macho had arrived. He watched as they approached the building, came inside, and walked toward their front door. He then watched another monitor and saw them head toward the elevator bank so they could catch the elevator to their floor. "Damn, that shit is really fly; crystal clear too."

"Shit, it should be. We just spent over fifty Gs on all of this shit. Speaking of that, Kingo will be reimbursing us for this money spent, right? I mean, why do we have to pay for all of this shit?"

Laughing, Papio said, "Since when have you became so damn cheap? You need to quit that shit. If this shit works, it will have been worth every fucking penny of that fifty Gs."

"You're right, but we still need to split the bill with Kingo's rich ass."

Shaking his head, Papio stood and went and opened the door just before Kingo and the crew approached their door. Kingo smiled and said, "Ah, I see someone has had eyes on us, mon."

"Yeah, watched you all the way to the elevator and then saw you when you got off of it. This shit is top notch for real. Everything seems to be working properly," Papio said as he led the men inside of the condominium.

"That's good. Now, let's run these tests. The sooner we know it's a go, the better. Then we will get the Rude Boys ready for this takeover," Kango said as he stepped past his brother and shook hands with Papio. "How ya doing over there, Special?"

"I'm good, Kango. Hey, y'all," she said to the rest of the crew.

After their greetings were complete, Steven said, "Since Kingo has never seen the device work its magic, why don't you and my cousin sit at the monitors and watch as we all go outside and get things started? Then we'll come check every part of the system to make sure it has been deactivated."

"That's a good idea, mon," Kingo said as he followed Papio and sat down in front of the console where the security monitors were located.

Steven, Special, Brad, and Macho all left the condo and went outside and got back inside of the SUV that the crew arrived in. Special pulled the device out of her Chanel bag and turned it on. She waited a few minutes to make sure it was powered up correctly and then flipped the switch to activate it. In another minute or so, the red light on top of the device switched to green.

She took a deep breath and held up her index finger and crossed it with the finger next to it and said, "Okay, here we go. We got the green, so everything should be dead." She pulled out her phone and called Papio inside of the condo. As soon as he answered, she asked him, "What do you see, Clyde?" She held her breath while she waited for his answer.

"I see y'all inside of the truck. Have you activated the device yet?"

"Yep. Okay, hold on for a minute." She motioned for everyone to get out of the truck and follow her. Once they were all out of the SUV, she then asked Papio, "Okay, what do you see now, Clyde?"

"The same thing. Y'all are still inside of the truck."

She smiled and pumped her fist. "Yes!"

Papio smiled, clearly relieved by her emotion and asked, "Does that yes mean that you guys are no longer inside of the truck, Bonnie?"

"You damn skippy! Okay, we're about to enter the condo. Tell me what you see."

Papio watched the other monitor waiting to see if he saw Special and the crew enter the building. When he didn't see them, he asked her, "Are you inside yet?"

"Yep. We're on the elevator now. You didn't see us?"

"Nope."

"That means we're good, Clyde. We're fucking good!"

"So far so good. All right, I'm about to set the alarm and meet you guys outside the front door." He then stood, and Kingo followed him with an amazed expression on his face as he watched as Papio punched in the security code to activate the entire system of the condo.

They stepped outside and closed the door. The crew all wore smiles on their faces as Papio opened the door, and they entered without any of the intruder warnings that should have been going off from the alarm system. Papio went to the wall where the security keypad was mounted and checked to make sure he activated it properly. He saw that it showed that everything should be activated and was on. He turned and walked in the middle of the living room and saw the motion detectors mounted in the far right and left of the living room wall were working and smiled. He then went into the bedroom and raised the bedroom window, and not a sound was made from the security system.

He sighed with relief as he returned to the front and joined the others. "Everything is good; we're straight. Kill the device, Special."

As soon as Special flipped the switch, cutting off the device, a loud screeching and wailing of alarm bells started going off. Papio stepped to the keypad and saw that the security system was fully operational and was informing him that there was motion detected inside of the living room, as well as the bedroom window was opened. He quickly punched in the security code, deactivating the system, and waited for the phone to ring so he would be able to give the proper security password to the security operator that would be calling within the next few minutes. When the call came, he gave the password, and that stopped the security people from summoning the police.

Papio sat down on the leather couch where Kingo was sitting with a smile on his face. "We're good, Dread. It's time to go get them Cuban mothafuckas."

Kingo nodded and said, "Oh yeah, mon. We gon' get them real good."

"When? When are you making this move?" asked Special.

Kingo gave his little brother a questioning look. Kango pulled out his phone and made a call. He spoke in his native patois for a few minutes, then hung up the phone and said, "The Rude Boys are getting everything in order now. They'll be ready to go whenever you want them, Kingo."

Kingo sat back in his seat and said, "Tomorrow night, or morning, however you want to look at it. We let the Rude Boys get ready, and we get all weapons in order. Then we do what needs to be done and bring end to the Cubans."

"*That's* what's up. So since we have another day of rest and relaxation, I don't know about y'all, but I'm trying to enjoy myself. I'm calling your wife up, and she's about to come scoop me so we can do some shopping. See ya later, boys," Special said as she pulled out her phone and went into the bedroom to change clothes.

"Since your girl will be with me girl spending the money, we might as well go have some fun ourselves, mon," said Kingo.

"What you got in mind, Dread?"

With a bright smile on his face, Kingo said, "Strippa club? Let's go to the strippa clubs and enjoy ourselves."

Steven, Kango, Brad, and Macho all smiled in agreement. "Girls will be girls, so the boys will be boys!" Macho said, and they all started laughing.

"So far, so good, Mr. Suarez. Everything has been moving pretty smoothly since the meeting the Jamaicans. We've begun to recoup some of the losses, and the money has started to flow again. Even the heat in our areas has subsided substantially," Castro said as he sat on the other side of Mr. Suarez's desk.

"This is good news. Now, we make sure everything continues to run smoothly. The Jamaicans will soon get relaxed, and when we feel the time is right, we'll strike them and bring an end to their pathetic existence. I've made a few discreet calls to some friends who also share in my dislike of the Jamaicans. Hopefully, I'll be able to gain the information needed for us so we can take the head out of the picture before we destroy the rest of the Jamaicans out here."

Castro smiled and said, "I cannot wait. I am truly going to enjoy taking the life of that cocky dread-headed bastard, Kingo. But what about Papio and his bitch?"

"I told you, when Papio gives us the money he owes us, he too, along with Special, will be at your disposal. There is no way I could ever let either of them remain alive after the disrespect they've shown me."

"What if they don't come up with the money by the time you gave them, sir?"

Mr. Suarez shrugged and said, "Do you really need an answer from me, Castro?"

"No sir, I don't. Do you think the Jamaicans will suspect anything from us?"

"I've run an extensive check on Kingo and his background. He's no dummy. As long as we continue to show patience and let things continue to progress on the streets peacefully, he will not be prepared for what we will bring to him."

"What about Papio? He knows us pretty well. You would think that he already knows that if he pays the money he owes, we will still come after him. That may make him want to try to make some aggressive moves of his own toward us."

Laughing, Mr. Suarez said, "Papio making an aggressive move toward me? Never. All Papio wants is the money to live good and remain in my good graces. He may think he has some strength on his side now, but when we bring down the Jamaicans, he will be trembling in fear. Most likely, he will try to run and hide. That's why I want you to catch him and Special right as we're making our move against the Jamaicans. I will not have the patience to let you go hunting for them. When we move, we will strike fast and precise, Castro. We will take Kingo out and already have Papio and Special in our grasp so we can punish them slowly for the betrayal and disrespect they've shown me. Until then, we wait. We patiently wait because *we're* the aggressors; *we're* the ones driving this car."

Castro nodded at his boss and smiled. "I cannot wait to see the expression on their faces once we have them. That will be a glorious day for me, sir. I have wanted to take that nigger scumbag piece o' shit's life for a very long time."

"I know, Castro. I know. Your wait will be over soon. Until then, business as always. Now that we've eased the tension with the Jamaicans, you can send some of these men back to their normal posts in the city. I don't care for this many men inside of my home like this."

"All of them, sir? I know that twenty extra men here was a tad too much, but I felt we had to have the extra security. I wouldn't feel right going back to the normal five men. May we at least keep ten of them? It will make me feel better knowing that we are secure in every way, just in case."

Admiring his man's dedication to his safety, Mr. Suarez said, "Sí, ten will be fine, even though you and I both know no one could ever penetrate our security measures. But one can never be too safe, eh?"

"Sí, sir. Ten should suffice. I know no one would be daring enough to attack us here, but I have been taught never to say never, and I intend always to be prepared for any surprises."

Laughing, Mr. Suarez asked, "And who taught you that lesson, Castro?"

Staring at his boss with a smile on his face, Castro stood and said, "A very wise man. A man wise enough to have gained all the riches in more than twenty-three of the fifty states in the U.S. A man that I would die protecting."

Mr. Suarez gave his right-hand man a nod in respect and said, "There won't be any dying for either of us any-time soon, my longtime friend. There's plenty more riches for us to obtain. You continue to keep us safe, and I'll continue to get us rich. Death to our enemies, and may they die painfully."

"You have never spoken truer words, sir. They will die by our hands, and we will live long and prosperous."

"Sí," Mr. Suarez said as he watched as Castro left his office. Neither of the Cubans realized that death was about to be knocking at their front door soon, and there was absolutely nothing they would be able to do about it. It was already written. Papio and Special would be the reason for their untimely death.

Chapter Thirty

Special was in the shower while Papio was in the bedroom on the phone giving Brandy an update on their situation. He seemed confident and calm, and that made Brandy feel as if everything was going to be okay after all. She had been a nervous wreck the last few days waiting to hear from Papio. To know that her idea about the device worked made her feel proud of herself for the contribution she put forth toward the demise of Papio and Special's enemies. Never in a million years would she have ever thought of being a part of such a notorious situation; yet, here she was deeply in love with two individuals, a man and a woman, and she didn't think anything was wrong with it at all.

Special came from the bathroom with a towel wrapped around her body and a smile on her face when she saw Papio sitting at the end of the bed. She dropped the towel and walked toward him. Once she was standing in front of him, she asked, "Now, who are you talking to, Clyde?"

Papio stared at her perfect body and pulled out his dick from the slit of his boxers and pointed toward it indicating that he wished to be serviced and said, "Brandy. Just putting her up on things."

"Did you ask her about the sex tape yet?" Special asked as she dropped to her knees in front of him and put her mouth on his dick and began moving her head rhythmically between his legs.

Papio moaned and put his hand on her head, entwined his fingers in her hair with his eyes closed, and said, "Nah, not yet."

"What sex tape, Daddy?" asked Brandy. Before he could answer her question, she asked another. "Are you two getting your freak on while we're on the dang phone, Daddy?"

"Mmmm, if you consider Special sucking the hell out of my dick right now, then, yeah, baby, we're getting our freak on."

"Ooooh, that's so unfair. I want some! I miss the taste of both of y'all," Brandy said as she eased her right hand inside of her panties and began manipulating her clitoris.

Papio heard her breathing change and instantly knew what she was doing, and this only caused his dick to feel as if it had become even harder than it already was from the ministrations from Special's mouth. "You're playing in that pussy, ain't you, Brandy?"

"Yes, Daddy. I'm playing in it, wishing I was there helping Special suck that big old dick," she whispered as her fingers moved faster and faster over her clit. "Tell me about this sex tape, Daddy."

"I want to make a sex tape of all of us fucking. But Special says no. She'll do it if you will, though, baby. Will you do that for Daddy?" he asked as he felt himself start to reach that point of no return.

Brandy was almost there as well, and the thought of her making a sex tape with both Papio and Special was too much for her, and she screamed out loud, "Oh! Yes! Yes! Yes, Daddy! I'll do whatever you want! I'm coming, Daddy! Come with me!"

As soon as Brandy started screaming that she was coming, Papio started to come as well, and they came together miles apart from each other in two different states. "I'm coming with you, baby!" Papio screamed as he sent salvo after salvo of his sperm inside of Special's mouth.

Special sucked him faster and faster and made sure she swallowed every last drop of his come and moaned. When she finished, she wiped her mouth, stood, and said, "Mmmm. Nothing like some midmorning protein from my Pussy Monster. Wish I had enough time to let you work this pussy over, but I'm running late already."

Papio lay flat on the bed trying to gather his senses before speaking. He then asked, "Where are you going?"

"I'm hooking up with Melkely, and we're doing brunch, then going to some more of her private spots out here to shop."

"You don't need to burn yourself out, you know. You need to be rested for tonight."

Special snatched the phone from his hands and said, "You don't have to worry about me. I'll be fine. You the one who needs some rest. I know you got wicked last night at the King of Diamonds with the boys." Before he could respond, she told Brandy, "Yeah, your daddy here went to the damn strip club yesterday afternoon; didn't come back to the condo until well past one in the morning."

"Humph. And you rewarded him for that? You should have made his ass jack off to get that morning nut off instead of giving him some great head." They both started laughing.

"Shit, nah, that was for me. I needed a good morning protein shake! So you want to make a sex tape with this creep?"

"I think it would be exciting. It's not like we're going to show it to anyone. It will be really wild to see myself making love to the two of you. Let's do it, 'K?"

Special smiled at Papio and said, "I guess I've grown to have a soft spot for your sexy ass. All right, when we finish up out here, we're going to fly you back west and make it happen."

"No way. You two will have to fly out here since I took back that time of leave request. There's no way I'll be able to take time off to come to California."

"Why don't you just quit that job and move to the west so we all can be together, Brandy? Shit, we can open up some kind of business for you to run out there. We don't need no fucking money, so you don't need no fucking job."

Brandy was floored by Special's offer and smiled as she whispered a question to Special. "You'd do that for me for us to be together, Special? I mean, you really feel that deeply for me?"

"Okay, you're like way too damn smart for this question, love. You are my boo-thang, and this fool is my Pussy Monster. We've formed a triangle now that will never be broken—never. You hear me?"

"Yes, I hear you."

"Good. So think about what I said, and I'll expect an answer from your ass in the morning. Let me go. I got a shopping date, and, girl, let me tell you when you see some of the fly shit I've bought out here, your mouth will water."

"Ooh, get me something, Special. I want some Red Bottoms and something real cute to wear with them."

"No, problem, baby," she said as she gave Papio the phone back and proceeded to get dressed.

"All right, you freaky, badass woman, you. Let me go. I need to get some rest."

"So, it's going down tonight?"

"Yeah."

"Make sure you call or send me a text when you're back safe at the condo, Daddy. I love you, Daddy."

"And Daddy loves you too, baby," he said and ended the call with a smile on his face.

Special was watching him as she slipped into a pair of Capri pants and shook her head and said, "You love this shit, don't you, pretty-ass nigga? You got the best of everything, and you love it, huh?"

Papio scooted up toward the pillows and got himself comfortable and said, "I love you and Brandy, and I love the life we got right now. But I won't be totally right until after tonight when those fucking Cubans are dead."

She could tell he was serious because he made that statement with the emotional coldness of a killer. Not the normal, happy, carefree Papio. It was almost game time, and she knew that no matter what, they couldn't afford to miss. She stepped to him and kissed him on the lips.

"After tonight is over, we live the rest of our lives together, totally happy, Clyde. Get some rest, you pretty-ass nigga." She squealed with laughter as he reached and tried to grab her for calling him pretty.

"I see I'm going to have to punish your ass to get you to stop that 'pretty nigga' shit."

"Yeah, yeah, promises, promises, you pretty nigga! Byeeee," she said as she grabbed her purse and left the room with a smile on her face.

Chapter Thirty-one

Kingo, Kango, Keily, Brad, Steven, and Macho arrived at the condo a little after one in the morning. They went over their plan of attack on the Suarez estate to make sure everyone knew their role. They were going to leave at exactly 2:00 a.m. to go meet up with Kingo's Rude Boys in Liberty City, then proceed from there to the Suarez estate.

Kingo smiled and said, "Everyting criss then, mon. We have the weapons all silenced and ready downstairs in the trucks. We let me Rude Boys rush the house after we use the device, and everyting is green. Once the first wave of me Rude Boys are inside, the next wave will come backing them up to secure the entire house. Then we come in, and you two can have the pleasure of ending Mr. Suarez."

"Hold up, Dread. How do you know your Rude Boys won't kill up everybody by the time we get inside of there?"

"Because they have strict orders not to kill Mr. Suarez or his number one man, Castro. No worry there, mon. You and Special will have that honor."

Papio nodded and said, "'K, that's what's up. Check it, though. Did you bring those pictures you had taken of Mr. Suarez's son, daughter-in-law, and grandkids?"

"Yeah, mon, I did. Please tell me why these photos are needed for what we're doing?"

Papio smiled, rubbed his palms together, and said, "There's no reason why we shouldn't make the most of this adventure, Dread. You know how I get down. Money stays on my mind. I know for a fact that that fuck has a whole bunch of money at his estate with him. I also know that he is a stubborn bastard that would rather die than give up the money."

Keily started laughing and said, "You are one smart American, Papio. By us bringing the photos of his family, this move will make Mr. Suarez give us all of his money because he knows he's going to die. He wouldn't want to take the risk of his son and his son's family dying because he didn't give up the loot."

With a satisfied smile on his face, Papio said, "Exactly."

"I love it. Papio, you are truly one of a kind, my brother," said Kango.

"Okay, that's the plan, then, mon. It's time now. Let move," Kingo ordered as everyone stood and followed him out of the condo. They were all dressed in the same black army fatigues they wore whenever they robbed banks or credit unions. Each also wore ear mikes inside of the ears. They would run mike checks once they met up with the Rude Boys in Liberty City to make sure everything was in operating order. It was finally time for this to go down, and Papio and Special were both so anxious for this to get started that they each had to take deep breaths to calm their nerves. Their lives and their futures depended on everything going right for them in the next hour or so, and each prayed that everything would go as planned.

After meeting up with Kingo's Rude Boys and making sure they understood the plan as well as checking all ear mikes, they all jumped inside of their SUVs and the six SUV convoy headed to the outskirts of Miami where the Suarez estate was located. Four of the SUVs had five of

Kingo's Rude Boys in each, while Kango, Brad, Steven, Keily, and Macho were in one, and Kingo, Special, and Papio were in the last SUV leading the convoy of killers. The time was here—now—and everyone inside of each SUV was ready to do whatever needed to be done in order to be back inside of those same SUVs headed home safely in a few hours.

At 3:00 a.m. exactly, the convoy drove past the Suarez estate. Kingo did this on purpose to make sure everything was kosher, and no one was seen roaming the grounds of the estate. Satisfied that everything was good, Kingo made a U-turn and turned off his lights as he headed back toward the Suarez estate. Once he was in front of the big wrought iron gate, he gave the order for his Rude Boys to get out of their SUVs and get the bolt cutters ready so they could cut through the big iron gates.

He then turned toward Special who was sitting in the backseat of the SUV and told her, "Time for that there device to work its magic, Special. Make it happen."

Special nodded and turned on the device and flipped the switch to make it operational. The light stayed on red for a full two minutes, much longer than it ever had, and Papio started to get nervous until he saw the light on the device switch from red to green. He sighed, and so did Special.

She looked at Kingo, nodded, and said, "It's good. Give your Rude Boys the go."

Kingo spoke one word into his ear mike. "Go!" An immediate response came from that one word. The lead Rude Boy and two more quickly began cutting the thick, iron gate. It took them less than a minute to have the gate opened. Then, ten of the Rude Boys with their silenced MP5 submachine guns at the ready began running as fast as they could toward the big house located fifty-some-odd yards from the front gate. The next ten Rude Boys who would be following the first ten were all standing within the gate waiting for the call from the first set of ten Rude Boys for them to come and join the fun. When the call came, they each took off running just as fast as the first group.

Kingo was sitting in the driver's seat of the SUV with a pair of night vision binoculars watching proudly as his Rude Boys moved and worked like the trained killers they were. Five minutes after the first group of Rude Boys had left the front, Kingo received a call from the top Rude Boy, Mikell, informing him that everything was secure and they could come and join them. The Suarez home was now under the control of Kingo and his Rude Boys. Kingo smiled as he turned in his seat and without a word said to his passengers, started the SUV and drove inside of the iron gates toward the Suarez home, followed by Kango and his group.

Papio was the first out of the SUV, followed closely by Special, both taking the four steps to the front door two by two. As soon as Papio entered the house, he saw dead bodies everywhere. Kingo's Rude Boys weren't to be played with he thought as he looked in awe at the dead Cuban guards lying sprawled out around the front of the house.

When his eyes locked with Mikell, he asked on his ear mike, "Where's the boss and his number one?"

Mikell gave him a nod to his right and led the way to where Papio knew was Mr. Suarez's office. When Mikell opened the door, he stepped to the side and said, "Here you go, mon, just as we planned it, eh?"

Papio smiled and slapped Mikell on his back and said, "You fucking right, baby!" He stepped into the office, and the shocked and angry expression on both Castro and Mr. Suarez's face was absolutely fucking priceless to Papio.

Special and Kingo entered the office next, followed by
Keily and the others of the crew. Two of Kingo's Rude
Boys had their machine guns aimed directly at Castro
and Mr. Suarez, just in case they tried to get stupid.

"Looks like the end has finally come, Mr. Suarez. Bet'cha
never thought it would end like this, huh?" asked Papio.

"I underestimated you, Papio; something I should have
known better."

"That's right, mon, you did. Never underestimate
someone with everything to lose. You do that, and you be
the one who lose. Now, get on with this business, Papio.
Tis no movie script here, mon. Handle the business so we
can go," Kingo said in a stern voice.

Papio nodded and said, "You know you're about to
die, Mr. Suarez, but before I take your life, I need all
the money you have stored here. Before you try to play
with my intelligence and waste my time, understand that
if you give me any bullshit, not only will you be dying
tonight, but your son Benito and his family will also have
a visit from some of these fine Jamaicans. So give it up,
and I give you my word your son and his family will not
be harmed. I know he has nothing to do with you or your
business. For that, I have no reason to feel any worry
from him trying to avenge your death. So give it up, fat
man."

When he heard Papio say his son's name, his heart
sank. Mr. Suarez was prepared to die, but there was no
way he would ever risk his son and his family. Papio had
won.

With a defeated look on his face, Mr. Suarez said,
"Downstairs in the basement there is over $65 million.
Take it. Take it all. Be a man of your word, Papio, and
don't harm my family. That I beg of you. I would never
beg for my life because I lost, and I accept that defeat,
and I wouldn't give you the privilege of hearing that, you

bitch. But I sincerely beg you for my son and his family's safety."

"You got that. But before you die, we have to make sure that what you've said is legit." Papio turned and told Kingo to send some of his men down to the basement to get the money. Kingo gave the order and gave Papio a nod. Papio turned toward Castro and said, "Look who gets the last laugh, you punk-ass flunky."

"Fuck you," Castro said as he tried to spit on Papio.

Papio stepped over toward Castro and pointed the barrel of his silenced MP5 and said, "No, Castro, fuck *you*." He then pulled the trigger and shot Castro at point-blank range in his face. "I always knew this day would come, and it feels way better than I ever dreamed it would be."

When Kingo received word from his Rude Boys who went to get the money from the basement that they were bringing several boxes of money up to the front, Kingo said, "Me men got the money, Papio. Finish this."

Papio smiled, turned, and said, "This is not for me to finish, Dread. You know that. Come here, Bonnie, and end this fat piece of shit."

The Rude Boy who had been standing next to Mr. Suarez stepped away from him as Special approached. He didn't pay attention or see as Mr. Suarez reached under his desk and pulled out a 9-mm pistol. Special was smiling as she walked toward Mr. Suarez, then in an instant, her smile turned to a frown when she screamed, "Clyde, watch the fuck out!"

Papio was turning around just as Mr. Suarez fired the 9 mm twice, striking Papio once in the chest which didn't do any damage because he had on a bulletproof vest. But the second shot hit him in the throat. He fell to the ground just as Special began unloading her MP5 into the fat frame of Mr. Suarez. She was screaming as she kept pulling the trigger until the entire clip emptied.

She then dropped the gun and knelt next to Papio, who was holding his hand over the wound on his neck. He knew he was dying. He could feel the life slowly leave his body. He tried to speak, but only a gurgling sound and death rattles came from his bloody lips. He let go of his neck and grabbed Special by her right hand and squeezed it. It was his way of saying goodbye, and she knew it. She squeezed his hand back and nodded as the tears streamed down her face.

She bent and gave him a tender kiss and said, "I love you, Clyde. I never loved a man in this world like I love you. You're my Pussy Monster forever, Clyde. I'm yours forever, you hear me? Forever!"

He gave her hand another squeeze as a single tear slid out of his eyes. He turned his head to the left and locked eyes with Kingo who was standing there with tears sliding down his face. He knew that his friend wasn't going to make it, and his heart was truly broken.

Papio reached out his left hand toward Kingo. Kingo came to his friend and took his left hand in his right, and they both gave each other a firm squeeze.

When Kingo saw Papio's eyes start to lose focus, he squeezed his hand harder and said, "Me love you, mon. Me will always be there for your seeds and mother, mon. Rest peacefully knowing that fact."

Papio closed his eyes and gave a nod of his head in understanding and breathed his last breath and died, holding both Special's and Kingo's hands. Special screamed so loud that it scared the mess out of everyone inside of the room. Kingo stood and grabbed her and led her out of the room while barking orders for his Rude Boys to come and grab Papio's body.

They left the bloody murder scene with a heavy heart because none of them thought this would be the outcome. Papio's luck had finally run its course. He lived the way he wanted and played the game the way he chose to. He didn't play fair; he played to win. Though he obtained all the riches he set out to get, his life still ended way too soon, and that was the saddest part about life: it rarely ends with a happy ending. When you live the life like Papio lived, odds were in favor of spending the rest of your life in jail or being buried way too soon. You get what you give in life. Karma's a bitch, no matter how you play the game, fair or not. It's a wicked way to live. Is it really worth it?

Chapter Thirty-two

The funeral of Preston "Papio" Ortiz was a small, private service held at St. Catherine's Catholic Church. The mass ceremony lasted a little over an hour, then the long drive to Inglewood Cemetery where Papio had said he wanted to be buried. He left strict instructions in his will that he had Q. make that he only wanted his loved ones to attend his funeral, and he didn't want his kids to see him inside of a casket. Mama Mia didn't agree with this, but since this was her son's last wishes, she reluctantly agreed. So, Li'l Pee and Bredeen stayed at Poppa Blue's home with Bernadine.

When Q. told Special and Brandy that they were left the bulk of Papio's estate, both were shocked and saddened even more because the love they had for Papio was so tremendous, neither of them could take what they were going through. It seemed as if the pains they were feeling got even more intense as the days went on. Papio left them in control of all of his finances and strict instructions to make sure that his mother remained comfortable and secure. He knew Mama Mia didn't care about money. It was him and his greedy nature that he inherited from his father that made him the way he was.

All his mother cared about was their safety and love for one another. Though she was grieving, she felt somewhat relieved that her son was resting peacefully now. No more stress or worry. He lived the life the way he wanted, and there was absolutely nothing she could ever have done to stop him. He was blessed in so many ways, and she prayed to God that He would have mercy on her one and only child's soul. Now, all she had left in this world is what her son left her. Two beautiful grandchildren and their mothers. Everything would be fine in time. Life goes on. Her son would live on with her through his children, and that helped ease the pain she felt as they drove toward the cemetery.

Kingo, his wife, along with Fay, Keily, Brad, Steven, Macho, and Kango, all attended the funeral and were equally saddened by the loss of their friend and crew member. Kingo especially felt cheated that he wasn't able to spend a lengthy amount of time with his longtime friend he had met in prison. He thought of the many, long conversations they had while in federal prison and smiled. He thought back to how Papio had thought he was manipulating him into assisting him when he got out. That made him smile because that made him respect Papio more and told him he was a man that would not be denied. He got what he wanted by any means necessary. Even in death, he still achieved what he set out to achieve, and that was Special's safety and even more money.

Kingo gave Special $40 million of the $65 million they took from the Suarez estate and then gave the rest to his Rude Boys to be split between them. That money was for them all, but Kingo didn't need or want any of it. He wanted it to go to Special so she could do the right thing for the kids. He felt good knowing that he had done something good for his friend. He would miss him dearly. Though not a religious man, Kingo still believed that there was a God in heaven, and he prayed silently for his friend's soul.

By the time they made it to the cemetery, everyone seemed too drained to go through the last ritual rites before Papio's body was laid to rest. Poppa Blue held on tightly to Special and Brandy as they cried and screamed for the loss of their man. Mama Mia stood over the grave of her son and let the tears flow freely from her eyes without making a sound. Quentin was shaken just as bad as everyone else. He still couldn't believe that his business partner, associate, and good friend was no longer here. After so many close calls, he really thought that Papio was invincible. To see his casket lowered into the ground broke him down, and he began to cry and sob loudly. This was the saddest day of his life.

After the casket was lowered and the cemetery's grave men started to cover the grave, everyone returned to their vehicles, and the small funeral procession left Inglewood Cemetery and headed toward the Westin Hotel, Papio's favorite hotel. Special decided to have dinner there for everyone after the funeral because that was the one hotel Papio loved the most. She rented a conference room and had some food catered from Mastro's, a mixture of good seafood and steaks. She knew how much Papio loved his steaks, so she thought that would be fitting.

After a couple of hours of eating and drinking and everyone sharing their "Papio Moments," Special saw that Mama Mia was looking haggard and decided to bring this sad day to an end. She would do whatever was best for Mama Mia as long as she had breath to breathe because she knew that would be what Papio wanted. She led Mama Mia outside to the limousine and told her to sit tight while she went and said goodbye to everyone. Mama Mia nodded at her but remained silent as she let her head rest back on the seat.

Special stepped up to Kingo and gave him a tight hug. "I love you, Dread. Thank you for coming."

"Me loves you too, girl. You know there was nothing that would have stopped me from being here today. Remember, you need anything, you make sure you call

Kingo. Me and me family will forever be there for you and the children, Special."

With tears sliding down her face, she nodded her head because she was too choked up to speak. She then hugged Melkely and said her goodbyes to the rest of the crew. She walked over toward Poppa Blue and told him that it was time for them to leave so they could get Mama Mia home. He hugged her and went and joined Mama Mia inside the limo.

When Special saw Brandy standing by the bar nursing a drink in her hand, she went straight to her, wiping her face as she approached her boo-thang. When she was standing directly in front of Brandy, she sighed and said, "Okay, baby, it's time for us to get Mama Mia home. We'll pick up the kids and take them out to the house in Riverside. That will keep Mama Mia busy and keep her mind off of everything."

"What's going to help us keep our mind off of things, Special? How are *we* going to move forward without him? I feel so damn lost right now. I finally get the man of my dreams, and everything is right in our lives, and now we lost him. This is not right; it's too fucked up," Brandy said as she downed her drink and motioned for the bartender to give her another.

Special shook her head no toward the bartender and pulled Brandy away from the bar and said, "Now, you listen to me, and you listen to me good. We're about to do what that pretty-ass nigga would want us to do. Live. And live damn good. We're going to raise his kids and take care of his mother and enjoy this crazy-ass life. Period. He died trying to make sure that the way of life he wanted for himself and us was preserved. This is how it is, and this is how it's going to be. We're going to do exactly what he expects us to do. Do you hear me, Brandy?"

Brandy stared directly into Special's brown eyes and sighed. "I hear you, Special. I just feel so-so lost."

"Dead that lost shit! Girl, you got everything you need in this fucking world right now. That man made sure that you and Bredeen are set for the rest of your lives. Money isn't everything in the world, but it meant the world to Papio. All he wanted was the best for his loved ones, and he made sure that we would have that. It's time for us to keep his dreams alive, Brandy. Me and you, baby. We're going to play the game our way now. No crime, no violence. We're going to be great moms to our children and live a normal life together."

"Together?"

"That's what I said. You're moving from Oklahoma City to L.A., and we're going to get us a monster crib. We will all stay together . . . me, you, the kids, and Mama Mia. That should keep that pretty nigga smiling down on us."

Smiling now, Brandy said, "You do know how much he hated for you to call him 'pretty'?"

Special smiled and said, "Yeah, I know. I did it to drive him nuts."

"I miss him so much, Special."

"I do too, baby. I do too."

"I have a question."

"What up?"

"Can you be all things to me, my alpha and omega, and everything in between? I don't want anyone else, Special. As long as I have you and the kids, I'll be able to move forward from this. But without you, I just don't know what I'll do."

"I ain't going nowhere, baby, and, yes, I will be all that you need me to be. Now, as for all that alpha and omega shit, I don't have a clue of what you're talking about!" They both started laughing. "Listen to me, we got to live our lives and do right by our kids. We also deserve happiness, and we will do whatever we want to have that happiness. We can satisfy each other just fine, but sooner or later, we're going to need dick. And believe me, I got a friend out in Aruba that I think we can call on whenever we need him."

Brandy's smile went from sheepish to sexy in the blink of an eye; coquettish one would say as she asked, "Are you sure? I mean, wouldn't that seem disrespectful to Daddy?"

"Are you nuts? Girl, that Pussy Monster is in heaven getting at every fine angel up there! He knows we got to live, and he knows we need some good dick now that he's no longer here for us. It's all about us now, Brandy. Me and you. We're playing this game now."

Brandy smiled brightly and said, "And . . . we don't play fair."

Special returned her smile and said, "You damn skippy!"

The End

Bonus Chapters

Alternative Ending

Kingo, Kango, Keily, Brad, Steven, and Macho arrived at the condo a little after one in the morning. They went over their plan of attack on the Suarez estate to make sure everyone knew their role. They were going to leave at exactly 2:00 a.m. to go meet up with Kingo's Rude Boys in Liberty City, then proceed from there to the Suarez estate. Kingo smiled and said, "Everyting criss then, mon. We have the weapons all silenced and ready downstairs in the trucks. We let me Rude Boys rush the house after we use the device, and everyting is green. Once the first wave of me Rude Boys are inside, the next wave will come backing them up to secure the entire house. Then we come in, and you two can have the pleasure of ending Mr. Suarez."

"Hold up, Dread. How do you know your Rude Boys won't kill up everybody by the time we get inside of there?"

"Because they have strict orders not to kill Mr. Suarez or his number one man, Castro. No worry there, mon. You and Special will have that honor."

Papio nodded and said, "'K, that's what's up. Check it, though. Did you bring those pictures you had taken of Mr. Suarez's son, daughter-in-law, and grandkids?"

"Yeah, mon, I did. Please tell me why these photos are needed for what we're doing?"

Papio smiled, rubbed his palms together, and said, "There's no reason why we shouldn't make the most of this adventure, Dread. You know how I get down. Money stays on my mind. I know for a fact that that fuck has a whole bunch of money at his estate with him. I also know that he is a stubborn bastard that would rather die than give up the money."

Keily started laughing and said, "You are one smart American, Papio. By us bringing the photos of his family, this move will make Mr. Suarez give us all of his money because he knows he's going to die. He wouldn't want to take the risk of his son and his son's family dying because he didn't give up the loot."

With a satisfied smile on his face, Papio said, "Exactly."

"I love it. Papio, you are truly one of a kind, my brother," said Kango.

"Okay, that's the plan, then, mon. It's time now. Let move," Kingo ordered as everyone stood and followed him out of the condo. They were all dressed in the same black army fatigues they wore whenever they robbed banks or credit unions. Each also wore ear mikes inside of the ears. They would run mike checks once they met up with the Rude Boys in Liberty City to make sure everything was in operating order. It was finally time for this to go down, and Papio and Special were both so anxious for this to get started that they each had to take deep breaths to calm their nerves. Their lives and their futures depended on everything going right for them in the next hour or so, and each prayed that everything would go as planned.

After meeting up with Kingo's Rude Boys and making sure they understood the plan as well as checking all ear mikes, they all jumped inside of their SUVs and the six

SUV convoy headed to the outskirts of Miami where the Suarez estate was located. Four of the SUVs had five of Kingo's Rude Boys in each, while Kango, Brad, Steven, Keily, and Macho were in one, and Kingo, Special, and Papio were in the last SUV leading the convoy of killers. The time was here—now—and everyone inside of each SUV was ready to do whatever needed to be done in order to be back inside of those same SUVs headed home safely in a few hours.

At 3:00 a.m. exactly, the convoy drove past the Suarez estate. Kingo did this on purpose to make sure everything was kosher, and no one was seen roaming the grounds of the estate. Satisfied that everything was good, Kingo made a U-turn and turned off his lights as he headed back toward the Suarez estate. Once he was in front of the big wrought iron gate, he gave the order for his Rude Boys to get out of their SUVs and get the bolt cutters ready so they could cut through the big iron gates. He then turned toward Special who was sitting in the backseat of the SUV and told her, "Time for that there device to work its magic, Special. Make it happen."

Special nodded and turned on the device and flipped the switch to make it operational. The light stayed on red for a full two minutes, much longer than it ever had, and Papio started to get nervous until he saw the light on the device switch from red to green. He sighed, and so did Special. She looked at Kingo, nodded, and said, "It's good. Give your Rude Boys the go."

Kingo spoke one word into his ear mike. "Go!" An immediate response came from that one word. The lead Rude Boy and two more quickly began cutting the thick, iron gate. It took them less than a minute to have the gate opened. Then, ten of the Rude Boys with their silenced MP5 submachine guns at the ready began running as fast as they could toward the big house located fifty-some-odd yards from the front gate. The next ten Rude Boys who would be following the first ten were all standing within the gate waiting for the call from the first set of ten Rude Boys for them to come and join the fun. When the call came, they each took off running just as fast as the first group.

Kingo was sitting in the driver's seat of the SUV with a pair of night vision binoculars watching proudly as his Rude Boys moved and worked like the trained killers they were. Five minutes after the first group of Rude Boys had left the front, Kingo received a call from the top Rude Boy, Mikell, informing him that everything was secure and they could come and join them. The Suarez home was now under the control of Kingo and his Rude Boys. Kingo smiled as he turned in his seat and without a word said to his passengers, started the SUV and drove inside of the iron gates toward the Suarez home, followed by Kango and his group.

Papio was the first out of the SUV, followed closely by Special, both taking the four steps to the front door two by two. As soon as Papio entered the house, he saw dead bodies everywhere. Kingo's Rude Boys weren't to be played with he thought as he looked in awe at the dead Cuban guards lying sprawled out around the front of the house.

When his eyes locked with Mikell, he asked on his ear mike, "Where's the boss and his number one?"

Mikell gave him a nod to his right and led the way to where Papio knew was Mr. Suarez's office. When Mikell opened the door, he stepped to the side and said, "Here you go, mon, just as we planned it, eh?"

Papio smiled and slapped Mikell on his back and said, "You fucking right, baby!" He stepped into the office, and the shocked and angry expression on both Castro and Mr. Suarez's face was absolutely fucking priceless to Papio.

Special and Kingo entered the office next, followed by Keily and the others of the crew. Two of Kingo's Rude Boys had their machine guns aimed directly at Castro and Mr. Suarez, just in case they tried to get stupid.

"Looks like the end has finally come, Mr. Suarez. Bet'cha never thought it would end like this, huh?" asked Papio.

"I underestimated you, Papio; something I should have known better."

"That's right, mon, you did. Never underestimate someone with everything to lose. You do that, and you be the one who lose. Now, get on with this business, Papio. Tis no movie script here, mon. Handle the business so we can go," Kingo said in a stern voice.

Papio nodded and said, "You know you're about to die, Mr. Suarez, but before I take your life, I need all the money you have stored here. Before you try to play with my intelligence and waste my time, understand that if you give me any bullshit, not only will you be dying tonight, but your son Benito and his family will also have a visit from some of these fine Jamaicans. So give it up, and I give you my word your son and his family will not be harmed. I know he has nothing to do with you or your business. For that, I have no reason to feel any worry from him trying to avenge your death. So give it up, fat man."

When he heard Papio say his son's name, his heart sank. Mr. Suarez was prepared to die, but there was no way he would ever risk his son and his family. Papio had won. With a defeated look on his face, Mr. Suarez said, "Downstairs in the basement there is over $65 million. Take it. Take it all. Be a man of your word, Papio, and don't harm my family. That I beg of you. I would never beg for my life because I lost, and I accept that defeat, and I wouldn't give you the privilege of hearing that, you bitch. But I sincerely beg you for my son and his family's safety."

"You got that. But before you die, we have to make sure that what you've said is legit." Papio turned and told Kingo to send some of his men down to the basement to get the money. Kingo gave the order and gave Papio a nod. Papio turned toward Castro and said, "Look who gets the last laugh, you punk-ass flunky."

"Fuck you," Castro said as he tried to spit on Papio.

Papio stepped over toward Castro and pointed the barrel of his silenced MP5 and said, "No, Castro, fuck *you*." He then pulled the trigger and shot Castro at point-blank range in his face. "I always knew this day would come, and it feels way better than I ever dreamed it would be."

When Kingo received word from his Rude Boys who went to get the money from the basement that they were bringing several boxes of money up to the front, Kingo said, "Me men got the money, Papio. Finish this."

Papio smiled, turned, and said, "This is not for me to finish, Dread. You know that. Come here, Bonnie, and end this fat piece of shit."

The Rude Boy who had been standing next to Mr. Suarez stepped away from him as Special approached. He didn't pay attention or see as Mr. Suarez reached under his desk and pulled out a 9-mm pistol. Special was smiling as she walked toward Mr. Suarez, then in an instant, her smile turned to a frown when she screamed, "Clyde, watch the fuck out!"

She dove toward Papio, shoving him out of Mr. Suarez's line of fire as he got off two shots, both striking Special, one in the chest that didn't do any damage because she was wearing a bulletproof vest. But the second shot hit Special in her throat. She fell to the ground as Papio began unloading his MP5 in the fat frame of Mr. Suarez. He was screaming as he kept pulling the trigger until the entire clipped emptied.

He then dropped the gun and knelt next to Special, who was holding her hand over the wound on her neck. She knew she was dying. She could feel the life slowly leaving her body. She tried to speak, but only a gurgling sound and death rattles came from her bloody lips. She let go of her neck and grabbed Papio by his right hand and squeezed. It was her way of saying goodbye, and he knew it. He quickly placed his free hand over her wound, trying uselessly to stop the heavy flow of blood gushing from her neck. He squeezed her hand back and nodded as the tears streamed down his face.

He bent and gave her a tender kiss and said, "I love you, Bonnie. I never loved a woman in this world like I love you. You're my Special, my Bonnie, forever. I'm yours forever, you hear me? Forever!"

She gave his hand another squeeze as a single tear slid out of her eyes. Special turned her head to the left and locked eyes with Kingo who was standing there with tears sliding down his face. He knew that she wasn't going to make it and that broke his heart because he'd grown very fond of Special. He hurt even more because he knew the pain his friend was going through was tearing him apart.

Special reached out her left hand toward Kingo, and he quickly came and knelt beside her and took her hand in his, and they both gave each other a firm squeeze. She then placed Kingo's hand on top of hers and Papio's. Kingo understood what she was trying to say. She wanted him to take care of her man for her. He nodded and squeezed her hand again and said, "Me understand you, Special. I will take care of your man with everyting me have inside of me. Me word. Me promise to you, girl." She squeezed both of their hands one final time as they saw the focus in her eyes slowly leave. The tears flowed freely from both men's eyes as they knelt there next to Special.

"Rest peacefully, Special. Know that I will do all I can for your mon and your son."

Special closed her eyes and gave a nod of her head in understanding and breathed her last breath and died holding both Papio's and Kingo's hands. Papio screamed so loudly that it scared the mess out of everyone inside of the room. Kingo stood and grabbed him and led him out of the room while barking orders for his Rude Boys to come and grab Special's body.

"No! Don't any of you fucking touch her!" Papio screamed as he broke away from Kingo's firm grip and went back to Special and picked her up and carried her out of the office. They left the bloody murder scene with a heavy heart because none of them thought this would be the outcome. Special was gone, and Papio's heart was broken. The pain he was feeling was indescribable. Special didn't deserve to die. If anyone deserved that fate, it was him, he thought. She played the game the way she was supposed to—to win. But in the end, she lost, and that was just not fair at all. Nothing is fair about life, though, especially when you break all the rules. You do dirt, you get dirt. Karma's a bitch. No matter how you play the game, fair or not, living wicked just ain't worth it in the end. Damn.

Alternative Ending

Final Chapter

The funeral of Special Williams was the saddest day of Papio's life. He could barely hold it together through the small, private service held in the chapel of Simpson Funeral Home. Kingo and the crew flew out for the funeral, and he was so grateful for that because not even Poppa Blue could control Papio when they started to close the casket for the final time on the woman of his dreams. Kingo had to physically restrain him as he tried his best to get them to stop the morticians from closing the casket.

"Special! No! God, why! Why did you do this?" Papio kept screaming over and over. Brandy was so shaken up that Mama Mia and Quentin had to hold her because she looked as if she would faint. After twenty minutes of turmoil inside of the small chapel, finally, Papio calmed down enough to let the crew members act as pallbearers and carry Special's casket to the hearse outside. Brad, Steven, Kango, Macho, Poppa Blue, and Quentin loaded the casket inside of the hearse and joined the rest of the small gathering.

Kingo knew it was going to be even worse when they arrived at the cemetery. Papio was hurting so much he was afraid his close friend would do something stupid. When he got inside of the limousine with Papio, he stared at his friend and never in his days had he ever seen such misery. His heart hurt just seeing his friend like that. He couldn't even begin to think of some soothing words to say to Papio. Once Bernadine and Poppa Blue were inside of the limousine with them, the driver eased out of the parking lot, and the funeral procession headed toward the Inglewood Cemetery.

Bernadine reached across and put her hand on top of Papio's and said, "I know you're hurting, Papio. We all are. But to lose a woman you loved so much is a terrible pain, a pain that I hope I never have to endure. You have a son and a daughter that needs you. Special is depending on you to do what's right and do the best you can for your children. Take this pain and let it hurt, but use prayer and the good thoughts and memories you have of Special and what you two shared and move forward with your life. You have no other choice, Papio. Do you hear me?"

He nodded his head numbly and said, "I hear you, Bernadine. I just don't know if I can do any of what you just said to me. For the first time in my life, I want to just give up. I feel as if I'm nothing without that beautiful woman. I got more money than I ever dreamed of having, but I would gladly give it all away to the homeless or some shit if it could bring my Bonnie back."

"I know, Papio. I know."

Kingo frowned and said, "Me know you hurt, mon, but don't you ever let me hear you talk that give up shit. Your son needs you. If you not tere for him, then Special frown down on you from the heavens, mon, and know that. You got a good woman in Brandy and a beautiful daughter to take care of with your son. Your mother, Bernadine, here, along with me and me family and Poppa Blue, we all here for you. But that's nothing if you not here for yourself. You got to shake this off you, mon. That wonderful woman lived the life she wanted to. She was the most courageous, gutsy, and classy woman I have ever had the pleasure to meet. She is surely in the heavens now watching over you. Use that to push you forward, mon."

"I hear you, Kingo, you too, Bernadine, but it's hard. It's so damn hard even to think straight. I should be the one getting ready to be lowered six feet, not my Bonnie."

"Stop it! You stop this shit right now! Dammit, Papio, it's not written that way. This has happened because this was how it was meant to be. I have run everything in my head from the beginning, and I mean the very beginning—way before you ever even knew Special. This is my fault for not being man enough to face my responsibility and raise that little girl the right way who had just lost her mother. Instead, I just spoiled her and gave her everything she ever wanted. But she didn't want things to be given to her; she wanted to get them on her own. She played this game flawlessly. I helped mold her into one of the best females to ever do it, and I should have known better! This game don't play fair, and sooner or later, we all lose at it. Yes, you lost the love of your life, but I lost my daughter. The daughter that I never had. The daughter I should have been a better father figure for. She's gone now, and it's my fault because I let her down. But I will not—I refuse to—I *won't* let you let her son down. You will be the man, the father, the best friend to Li'l Pee. You will do everything right for him because he deserves that. He deserves everything his mother didn't have. And you, Papio, are going to do that. If you don't, I swear to God on everything I love that I will kill you myself and you *will* be buried six feet deep, right next to where we're about to lay Special to rest. Do you fucking understand me?" screamed Poppa Blue.

Poppa Blue's rant made Papio snap out of it somewhat because he felt the old man's pain, felt the sincerity in his every word, and for the first time since Special's death, he felt like he would be able to move forward. He gave Poppa Blue a nod just as the limousine came to a stop inside the cemetery. They all got out of the limo and went and listened as the preacher gave the final rites sermon for Special.

After her casket was lowered into the ground, Papio stood over it and looked down on the all-white casket and cried. The tears flowed freely. He stood there for five minutes before speaking. "I'm going to be with Brandy, Bonnie. I'm going to move her out here, and we're going to raise Li'l Pee and Bredeen together. Your son is going to have the best of everything, but more important, he's going to have a father and a stepmother who love him the way he's supposed to be loved. No street life for him, Bonnie, I promise. Only the good life. College and all that stuff we should have done with our lives. I'm going to make sure Li'l Pee has all of that in his life. Rest assured, he will know who his mother is. He will know all about you, Special, I promise. Brandy will help me raise him, but only you will be known as his mother. I will speak about you every single day to him, okay, Bonnie?

"I didn't let him come because I didn't want him ever to have the memory of seeing you in a casket. I hope that was okay, baby. I want his memories of his mama to be happy ones and always remember that beautiful smile. Brandy has him at the house now, and she is making sure he is happy, okay? I'm about to go now, baby. But I'll be back to see you often. I love you so much, Bonnie. Thank you for coming into my crazy life. You gave me so much. You gave me more than I feel I was worthy of. I'll miss you forever, baby.

"The game is over now. I live for Li'l Pee and Bredeen. I live for your memory. I'll forever be your pretty nigga, even though you know how much I hated it when you called me that. I'd give anything right now to be able to hear you call me pretty one more time. I can't have that, but I do have your love and every good time we shared embedded in my heart. It took me losing you to realize that the life we were living wasn't even worth it. I got all the money I ever wanted, and sometimes it makes me sick thinking about spending any of it. I feel disgusted with myself in some ways. I lived all these years wrong, Special, and for the first time in my life, I'm going to live right. I'm going to be right for you, Li'l Pee, and most of all, for me. It took me losing you to realize that nothing in life is fair. Even when you do it your way, sooner or later, you got to face your wrongs. I'm scared to death of this Karma biting me in the ass. But if and when it's my time, I will face it head-on. I pray that I will be able to use the time I have left on this earth to do some good to try to make up for all of the bad things I've done, all in the name of the dollar. Your Clyde is about to square up, Special. You always told me I had the square-nigga qualities, and I guess you were right. Watch over me, baby; watch over me and Li'l Pee and keep us from slipping. I love you," he said as he turned and walked back toward the limousine where everyone was waiting for him.

When he made it to the limousine, Poppa Blue smiled at him sadly and said, "I'm sorry about that outburst, son."

"No need to apologize, OG. I needed that."

Kingo slapped him on his back and asked, "You good, mon?"

Shaking his head no he said, "Nah, Dread, I'm far from good, but I'm here. And I ain't going anywhere anytime soon. I got two kids to raise. And that's exactly what I intend on doing."

"Praise the Lord!" yelled Bernadine.

"Come on, y'all, take me home. I need to hold Li'l Pee, Bredeen, Brandy, and Mama Mia in my arms."

"Family. We're all family," said Poppa Blue.

"Yeah, you right, OG, and we all we got."

The End

Author's Note

All righty, then it's a wrap! The Play Fair series has ended. Did you get the message? Karma. You may get away doing wrong for a little while, but sooner or later, you will have to pay one way or the other. Karma comes in all shapes, sizes, and forms. Not just criminal stuff but the simple things, as well. You do wrong—any wrong—it can come back and bite you in the ass! Believe that. Live right and be right. Enjoy life and take nothing for granted. You can have everything you want in this world if you put your mind to it and strive to be the best you can be. Patience. That's all you need.

I hope you liked the alternative endings. I was undecided on which one to kill, Papio or Special. So I decided to do both with two different endings. This way, I can give fans of each character what they wanted. A lot of my partners in prison didn't want me to kill either one, but you have to understand, I was still writing these books while in federal prison, and my partners are inmates, and they love the criminal aspect of the story. Hopefully, the punch line hit them in the heart so they can wake up as I have woken up. We get what we put into lives. I know this now, even though my wonderful mother told me this many times. I hope after doing this fifteen-plus years in prison, I have faced all the negative Karma I will have to face. If not, then, so be it. But I intend to get out there and do some good with my life and bring some positive Karma in my life. I suggest you all do the same.

Peace and Love.

Spud